DIRTY BUTTER FOR SERVANTS

By the same Author

NO BONES ABOUT IT
MIDNIGHT HAG
NOTHING IS THE NUMBER WHEN YOU DIE
THE CHILL AND THE KILL
DEATH OF A SARDINE
WHEN I GROW RICH
IN THE RED
MISS BONES
MALICE MATRIMONIAL
MAIDEN'S PRAYER
YOU CAN'T BELIEVE YOUR EYES
A CUP OF COLD POISON
THE MAN FROM NOWHERE
A DAISY CHAIN FOR SATAN
YOUNG MAN, I THINK YOU'RE DYING
GRIM DEATH AND THE BARROW BOYS
SCREAMS FROM A PENNY DREADFUL

Dirty Butter for Servants

BY

JOAN FLEMING

'Dirty butter for servants . . . !'
—Old Dublin Street Cry

HAMISH HAMILTON
LONDON

First published in Great Britain 1972
by Hamish Hamilton Ltd
90 Great Russell Street London WC1

SBN 241 02261 4

Printed in Great Britain
by Ebenezer Baylis & Son Limited
The Trinity Press, Worcester, and London

Ten items of the NOTICE TO EMPLOYEES on pages 183–4 have been inserted in their actual wording by kind permission of the Managing Director of the firm from whose archives they have been borrowed and to whom my thanks are due.

AUTHOR

APOLOGIA

I FINISHED the story of my life in the Diplomatic Service, as Ambassador in three capitals and up to the time of my retirement. I much enjoyed writing it, standing at my desk, first in my house, then in the flat over the stable with Sheffield, our old groom, for companionship, and finally back in my own house: it has taken me two years.

When it was finished, I felt, for the moment, that I did not know how to fill my time; this was only temporary, of course, because I had always my books.

I strolled across the moors to Overscar, taking with me the black retriever I have purchased since the death of my second wife. In fact, I went to tell Mary Ann that my book was finished and that I proposed visiting my son-in-law Monsieur le Comte d'Houdenard, a semi-invalid, who at that time was on a long visit to Bath, hoping that the waters would benefit his health.

This dear woman was within a week or so of giving birth to what turned out to be her fine elder son. Owing to the fact that she was not young in years there had been some physical trouble which indicated caution and Mary Ann was lying upon a sofa, which necessity annoyed her considerably since she had never, in her life, she grumbled, had a period of 'doing nowt'.

She lay with a light rug over her and upon the rug was a penny exercise book and a pencil which she tried to thrust out of sight as I entered; but I saw it all right and asked her if she had been writing the story of *her* life.

Before leaving I persuaded her to allow me to read what she had written; and though at first she protested, at length she let me take it away saying she would not write another word of it, since some things in her life had been too sad to dwell upon; it was best to let them lie. She was so happy and contented, she said, she did not wish to stir up recent horrors.

So I took it away and read it; I could quite understand why she could not write any further than she did, but on my return from Bath I had the effrontery to continue it, as though still written by her, to the end; that is, to the end of how it all came about.

I have not told Mary Ann I have done this; the birth of her son occurred when I was away and since then she has been too busy and happy to recall her pregnant waiting period. But I myself have had much satisfaction in my task. I am leaving it to her, amongst my papers, and when I am gone Mary Ann may in her later years find time to read it, and to alter it to her satisfaction, particularly regarding the conversations which took place when I was not present. At the time she and I discussed everything at great length; I feel myself to be so versed in the affair that I have even had the effrontery to guess at the thoughts in the minds of others—but she may delete, as she wishes. Someday, posterity will gobble it up and, I must say, they should remember that all its imperfections are upon *my* head.

(H.H.)
Halliwell Hobshaw

ONE

MY LOVER was killed at Quatre-Bras; shot dead instantly through the neck, his horse bolted with him straight into the enemy lines and neither his body nor the horse was ever recovered; I think of him as lying in a common grave in Flanders' soil. Three days later our, or should I say, my, baby was born during the battle of Waterloo. She was born in the historic thunderstorm the sound of which obliterated the thud of guns to which the city dwellers of Brussels had been listening with apprehension, off and on, for three days. She arrived a week early and the Flemish midwife was so frightened by the storm, which she believed was the arrival of the Emperor Napoleon upon her doorstep, that she dare not venture out in answer to the call and my dear lady herself took my daughter in her hands and at once christened her Anne-Marie, my own name in French.

Napoleon left Elba on March 25, 1815 and advanced slowly towards Paris. My lady and her husband were friends of Queen Hortense of Holland who had an apartment in the Tuileries where they had often stayed. My lady said that we must see the Emperor and I must come with her, acting lady's maid, instead of the cook I was, and am. Since my dear lady achieved anything she wished to achieve I was pressed unobtrusively before her and thus occupied at the Queen's window, overlooking the court, an observation post such as should have been claimed by the mighty. Looking down upon the historic scene

I was elated to an unforgettable excitement and, I know not why, since I was a Yorkshire lass to my bone marrow, a kind of ecstasy.

In the distance we heard the cries of 'Vive l'Empereur' and as the procession approached, the sound swelled to a great roar when he entered the courtyard.

'Oh, Madame, Madame . . .' I could not help but reach for her hand and weep for this much abused tyrant who had caused so much misery. Yet she, my dear lady, was weeping too.

He rode upon a lean white horse, that world's wonder, and he wore his cocked hat straight across his brow, no feathers, only a cockade.

'Vive l'Empereur!' They lifted him from the saddle and carried him shoulder high into the palace where he kissed the eagles. When he disappeared from our view, my lady and I smiled at one another through our tears: 'Voici! Mary Ann, use that . . .' and she handed me her handkerchief; we were like sisters.

The next time we were in Paris the King passed me in a sober carriage as I hurried through the Place Vendome, wearing my long black Flemish cloak: King Louis XVIII of France. All the National Guard were wearing their white cockades and from the windows the ladies fluttered their white handkerchiefs and cried: 'Vive le Roi!' It was the King whom we English were thrusting down the French throats, the choice of Lord Castlereagh and not that of our beloved Duke of Wellington, so I hurried past unmoved.

My baby came unremarked into an exciting world; I considered myself yet another war casualty in a city full of *enceinte* girls, clutching their heavy cloaks around them to hide their condition as they hurried along the hot summer streets.

'Who is her father?' of course my lady asked and surprisingly she herself answered her own question: 'A fine handsome French soldier,' but I could not smile away the truth even before he was killed, and after I had to say: 'We were to marry on St John's Eve, a midsummer baby we were to have had. . . .' And after the birth, when my lady had wrapped the baby in the shawl I had made, and put her in the basket I had bought in the fish market, my lady said nothing more about the father, but stooping over me she put her arms round me and pressed me to her for a moment.

I wondered, then, if she knew the truth. She did.

It was a terrible time for us all, my lady lost her dearly loved brother at Quatre-Bras which took place three days before Waterloo, a prelude to it, and a bitter struggle in which neither side could be said to be the victor. At twenty-eight Giles Hobshaw was acting orderly to an English general when he was shot. He had fought with the now Iron Duke in Spain and after the Army's arrival in the Low Countries he had stayed with us in Brussels in the Hotel d'Houdenard in the Rue Gabain. He intended leaving the Army as soon as the fighting was done and taking up painting. I have heard him teasingly urge his sister to rent an apartment in Paris that he might share, rather than stay with friends on her frequent visits to that capital.

My lady was Madame la Comtesse d'Houdenard and her husband Monsieur le Comte d'Houdenard had also been with the Iron Duke in Spain but he had been brought home severely wounded in battle. In due course his injured leg had to be amputated and, to alleviate the considerable pain from which he still suffered, he had to spend much time at one or other of the new spas which were becoming popular on the continent. At these times my lady could not always accompany him because they had three boys at a French Academy in Brussels.

My lady was born Harriet Hobshaw of Underscar in the West Riding of Yorkshire. Her father was a diplomat and she, as a girl of eighteen living with her parents attached to our Embassy in Paris, had met the Flemish nobleman d'Houdenard and married him. My own father and mother were servants at Underscar, my mother the cook and my father the head groom; they were caretakers in a manner because the family were constantly abroad. But still some poor relations of the family resided at Underscar in their absence and my mother, queen of the catering, was allowed to keep me beside her and as soon as I was able to totter about the huge kitchen, she commenced to teach me the elements of cooking.

My lady was ten years older than me, she remembered my birth and when they were at home she would play with me as a tiny child. When she married I was twelve and she had a serious talk with my mother, causing her to promise that she would allow me to go with her as cook to my lady's own household in Brussels as soon as I was old enough.

It was a strange bi-lingual household, not only bi-lingual but bi-everything else. Monsieur le Comte was master of the household in deed but master of a Yorkshire household rather than a Flemish one. It was not that he had a weak character so much as his wife had a strong one, she was outspoken in a way that is not common on the continent; she was full of energy and enterprise and laughed very much at what she called the artificiality of certain French modes and manners. But she was never deliberately unkind and she adored her husband and once I heard her cry: 'How he came to marry me I cannot guess, but it is as well since I should have perished without him!'

She was at pains to impress upon her little boys that they were Flemish and made sure that regarding their religion, they were good Catholics. She, however, made no pretence of being sympathetic, frequently saying proudly that she belonged to 'Chapel folk' and often she would take me in her carriage across to the other side of the city to attend the Lutheran church.

I owe it firstly to my dear mother and secondly to my dear lady, that I am to a small degree educated; my mother and, indeed, my father too, taught me to read and write by the time I was seven and, together in our family life in the apartment above the stables at Underscar, they talked constantly of current affairs. At the time of writing this my father is still living in the stable flat but my mother died some years before as the result of a severe chill.

From time to time my lady's father, a widower, came to stay with us in Brussels and his presence delighted my heart. He would come into the kitchen, something which Monsieur le Comte never did, and sitting upon the edge of my great table would discourse at length to me upon the state of the world. And when my Anne-Marie was old enough to toddle about he would be vastly amused at the likeness between her and me, and my mother and myself as a small child twenty years ago in that Yorkshire kitchen I remembered so well.

Thinking it over now in retrospect I might have wondered why there was never any mention of his 'new' wife and 'new' children. Upon the occasion of his visit to Brussels after the death of his son Giles, he had aged almost beyond recognition. And later he wrote that he had retired from the foreign service and would take up his duties as Squire at Underscar. My lady thought it a pity, Underscar is isolated and lonely and often lost from sight in the moorland fogs.

And then, when Anne-Marie was around eight years, my lady heard suddenly, without warning, that her father had remarried.

When I visited my lady in her boudoir for the day's orders she was on the edge of tears: 'My poor, poor dear father. . . .'

'And you his only child now,' I ventured sympathetically.

'He has four new daughters now!' she returned, and from the pressing together of her pretty, full mouth I gathered that she had no liking whatever for her step-mother, daughter of a new-rich Manchester industrialist; she never again went to Underscar. I longed to hear news of that place where I was born and lived so happily but it was only the merest fragments which came my way. I seldom entered the dining-room and the breakfast-room where all the family conversation took place; my place was in the kitchen where I was mistress of three kitchen maids and the so-called scullion who kept the stove constantly stoked and went to market with me to wheel home behind me the truckload of purchases.

My lady had an old bachelor uncle on her mother's side who lived in Brussels, a short step away from the Hotel d'Houdenard, the uncle was English Professor in one of the Lycées until his retirement; he lived in the same small house for many years and eventually when my daughter was about nine, and, I am proud to say, able to read and write in both French and English, my lady unfolded her plan for Anne-Marie to me. The old Professor was lonely, she told me, he no longer had pupils visiting him, since they preferred a younger man. He also had difficulty in finding someone to attend to his daily needs and she suggested that we send one of my kitchen maids, and she mentioned which particular one, every day for a few hours to clean and wash and cook for him. And—this was a crux of her idea—Anne-Marie should go with her and, in short, get herself educated, seeing that the old man liked to teach more than anything else in the world.

'What are you smiling at, Mary Ann?' she asked sharply and I distinctly recall my answer: 'I am smiling so that I shall not cry; it is so like you, Madame . . .' and in the end I wept because I found something unbearably touching about my lady's constant attention to the needs of others.

They do not come like that now!

*

Let me say it out loud, Anne-Marie was and is a bastard and I use the good old English word deliberately. Twenty years after Waterloo, with Progress upon us and the English people becoming more refined, the word is not used in polite society and as polite society grows yearly the word has become permissible only in the context of Shakespeare.

People of my generation now divide their lives mentally into Before Waterloo and After Waterloo; to us the periods seem to belong to different worlds.

But as I was saying, Anne-Marie, as a bastard, has been unusually fortunate: the old Professor took her to his heart and made it his life-work to educate my daughter; not only in the elements of learning but in the reading of books. Anne-Marie was fortunate in that she enjoyed reading and read with great speed, eagerly absorbing what she read; at seventeen she was reading with apparent enjoyment the books of such writers as Victor Hugo and Jean-Jacques Rousseau. The now grown-up boys of my lady appeared to be enchanted by her; Pierre and Henri were already in the Army Academy and the youngest, Bruno, in his last year at the Lycée. When they were home they sought her out and took her riding in the parks, they invited her into their old nursery, now a study, and teased her with professorial questions, and upon several occasions they took her with them to routs which they attended in the town.

If it had not been that I am Yorkshire with more common sense than I feel I need, I could so easily have lost my head, imagining my daughter married to one of the Houdenard boys and a lady. As it was, I was pleased that they should be treating her as a younger sister so that she came to accept the presence of young men as normal and not, as so many young ladies, an occasion to underline their sex with idiotic and simpering coquetries.

And since I had not known them myself and had brought upon myself what at the time was a disaster, I took it upon me to instruct her, my hands sweating with nervousness, in what I hoped were sufficiently clear warnings regarding the sex act.

I told her that she was a child without a father in that I had not married and was a single-woman-mother and as such a person not wholly acceptable in society. I said that owing to the goodness of my lady she and I would not suffer, perhaps, as some might; my lady had decreed, after my baby was born, that I was to be known as Mistress Sheffield instead of plain Mary Ann Sheffield, the cook, and that the baby was to be Anne-Marie Sheffield whose father had been killed in battle. And as there were a great many Waterloo dilemmas similar to my own, my problems as an unmarried mother were considerably lightened.

'And remember, my dearest child,' I said severely, 'that a girl's best friend is her virginity . . .' and I tempered it, hating myself, by adding: 'That is . . . a very young girl!' (Unless . . . unless . . . at the sound of the beloved's voice your heart banged against your ribs, and the sight of his face sent you dizzy and you want never to be out of his presence again in life. But I did not say that.)

That is the only time I have ever spoken to her about such matters; I do not consider that I did my moral task well, as time has shown. I did it badly, inadequately, for who am I to guide her? The happiness I had can be counted only in months and I have lost for ever my dear love but I feel those golden months have fully paid for the emptiness of the rest of my life.

That talk occurred eighteen years after Waterloo and Anne-Marie was part pupil, part companion, part servant to the old Professor. My dear lady was approaching fifty and I was close on forty and I think both of us had privately started to wonder what was going to take place regarding Anne-Marie's future. Since she was bi-lingual I had hoped that she might join the staff of one of the educational establishments with which Brussels abounds, as English teacher, but this seemed to be so outrageously ambitious for the daughter of a servant that I did no more than think it.

And then there was the large bedroom we still shared beneath the eaves. I had been greatly favoured by a fine bedroom to myself when I first joined Madame's household and, in this room with the three dormer windows perched high in the

Mansard roof of the Brussels mansion, all my youthful happiness had taken place, coming to me, as it were, up the back stairs. But now it was time that Anne-Marie should have her own room and I failed to see how it could be, since the whole of the remainder of that attic floor was taken up by a dormitory for the rest of the servants; the successive stewards, as butlers are called in large households, living in some state in their own two rooms in the basement. I had been turning over in my mind the suggestion that Anne-Marie and myself should move out of the house to some tiny apartment of our own nearby for which I would be able to pay out of my savings.

But then my dear lady detained me in her boudoir after she had given the day's orders, bringing a letter out of her bureau drawer and handing it to me to read:

My darling girl,

I can no longer dissemble; Sheffield and I will perish if help cometh not. I doubt not that I have brought it all upon myself, misplaced loyalty and native qualities of endurance. Sheffield wants, nay must have, his daughter home and so must I. I can say no more, this letter may well be opened.

Father.

It was a cry for help, written in Mr Hobshaw's typical not wholly serious manner.

It was a dozen years or more since I had returned home for a week or so when my mother died of that neglected cold and I felt that it was but the other day. A great rush of remorse came over me that I had for the past ten years not considered going back home to see my poor father. I wrote to him three or four times a year. I had a sketch made of Anne-Marie which I sent one Christmas but I realised that I had considered my life as that of my dear lady's and had she gone back to her old home, I too, would have gone with her. Otherwise the idea had never entered my mind. All these thoughts rushed through me as I sat as though stunned, with the letter in my hand.

'Why . . . why . . . Madame . . . ?'

'I know what you are thinking, Mary Ann . . . why have I never been back to visit my home, in all these ten years?' She ran her finger over and over the ormolu pattern of the handles of her writing bureau, wondering what to say and what not to say. 'I escaped from Underscar the last time I was there. Mary Ann, I should prefer not to discuss my father's second wife with you; if you are to meet her it is better that you should consider her under your own judgement and not be prejudiced by me in advance . . . she could even be well-disposed to you. . . .'

But the shock of realising that I was to go and there was to be no question about it turned me momentarily dizzy.

My lady realised the acuteness of the shock I had received and bade me go away and 'think it over . . .'

Think it over! Unwilling though I was to admit it, I was going, I had to go and when the final 'thinking over' did come I realised that I had been slightly anxious about the relationship which I saw, as it were, strengthening between Anne-Marie and my lady's youngest son . . . Bruno.

Next morning I said I had thought it over and I would go; my lady and I looked for a long time at one another straight in the face and it was as though we exchanged thoughts which we could not put into words. I very much wanted to ask for how long I should be going. I could not decide whether it would be best to take Anne-Marie and this particular thought she knew of, because she said: 'I can keep the dear child here, Mary Ann, she can continue to go daily to the Professor as she has been doing. The old man will miss her intolerably if she goes. . . .'

'But when you are away with Monsieur le Comte . . . ?' and Anne-Marie alone occupying our room with its easy access from the courtyard. History might repeat itself.

'You are right,' she said soberly, 'when I am away with Monsieur le Comte . . . oh, my dearest Mary Ann, I fear he must die, he is so unwell, the visits to Spa no longer ease his constant pain. If he were to die, Mary Ann, you will return?'

'But am . . . am I,' I stammered, 'am I going *for good*?'

'If you mean for the good of our two fathers . . . you are but if you mean for always, let us pray not. It must depend, my dear, upon what you find, what conditions exist. Our fathers are two old men evidently in trouble. . . .'

'But what kind of trouble . . . ?' I had to burst out.

She leaned forward and pressed her hand upon mine. 'Dearest Mary Ann, may I allow you to discover this for yourself; I think it would help if you were to undertake the journey and arrive back home in our beloved Yorkshire dale unprejudiced by anything that I have to tell you. And for your own peace of mind, I think it would be better were you to take Anne-Marie. Alas, my poor uncle, I can hardly bear to contemplate his distress at losing his one constant pupil . . . be sure you go and say farewell. . . .'

I hated saying farewell to such friends as I had made and to the old man who had been so wonderfully kind to Anne-Marie. I found I had become attached to the old city, all my adult life had passed within the sound of the bells of St Gudule in my ears and three years ago, in 1830, we had lived through a small revolution: the Prince of Orange at Antwerp surprised everyone by declaring the Independence of Belgium; my dear lady and I were pleased and felt ourselves belonging to this brand new country in which we had lived happily for so long. I went round the market for the last time and sadly bade farewell to the old familiar faces of the peasants from whom I had purchased eggs, butter, cheese, fish, fowl and good red herrings for so long. My attempts at the Flemish dialect had always amused them and we parted with smiles, if somewhat marred by broken or missing teeth, rather than tears.

That parting in Brussels in 1833 was more than a simple leave-taking from all we had treasured; it was a small death in that it was the end, and I mean the end, of two familiar lives, mine and Anne-Marie's, and the start of two new ones. Nothing was ever the same again because we were changed in ourselves, we lost our confidence and possibly the sense of judgement that had been based upon security, and we had, perforce, to build up a new series of values.

*

Since I left England my country had changed kings twice, old George III was replaced by his son George IV, a thoroughly raffish fellow who died three years before our return, and his brother William IV inherited the throne, a milk-sop if ever there was one. The year previous to our return, the Reform Bill was passed under the Whigs in June and there was started a change which affected the whole country. I do well remember my lady telling me that the Czar of all the Russias had screamed that the King of England had thrown his Crown into the gutter.

We left Brussels in the diligence and travelled to Antwerp where we sailed in the steam packet early on a Sunday morning.

As we drove up the Great North Road, sitting high upon the outside seats in the Mail Coach to Grantham I was amazed at the changed appearance of the countryside, much of which was apportioned into what is now called fields. But when we gazed from the local coach which brought us to my native valley I could not but cry aloud at the changes that had taken place in the village: on either side of the turnpike and facing it were a row of bright red brick cottages in a close line with no space between them. I should have been glad that some of the tattered cottages of my youth had gone to make room for these small red brick palaces but as I used to say in those days, it is nobbut human nature to regret the passing of the childhood scenes.

As we approached Underscar my unsettled heart subsided for all was the same, the low stone house sitting squat and sturdy against the weather, under the scar, with its Scotch pines group and directly upon the ling and heather with not a scratch of a kitchen garden, where no fruit but bilberries would grow. Across the courtyard the stables looked shabby and tumbled-down and grass grew between the cobbles in a way I had never before seen. To my horror I saw my father as an old man coming down the outside stone staircase that led from the courtyard to the flat above the stables; just as I saw he was small and shabby so I realised how small and shabby was the whole messuage and that the iron handrail, to which we had clung when mounting the stone steps, had gone; but it had certainly been there and not a figment of my dreams because the iron stubs which held it into the stone were still to be seen, sticking up dangerously.

I wept a little, of course, as he greeted me and I wept more when, up in the living-room, I encountered my lady's father: with his hands so mis-shapen with arthritis that as I held them it was not possible to believe that they were, indeed, his hands. He was still a fine-looking man but now old.

I drew Anne-Marie forward and as I did so I had a curious experience; as she bob-curtsied she looked a picture in her pretty summer dress with the small travelling cape and the frilly pantaloons. I stared bewildered at her as though I had never seen her before. We were standing in our old living-room in the home in which I was born and had lived for eighteen years; there I was: Mary Ann Sheffield, a middle-aged woman, and I was staring at my daughter as though I had this instant encountered her for the first time. She was my pretty, loving, indeed devoted appendage of myself until this moment when I saw her as a young woman detached from me and alone. It was as though a young lady, clearly of the gentry, had been my fellow passenger.

'Do not trouble to bring up your baggage, dear child,' my father said to me, 'for you are to reside in the house, you and Anne-Marie. . . .'

I started to make friendly remonstrance. There were two

bedrooms in the flat but I realised that the old men wished to have a room apiece so I tried to argue no more and meekly accepted the ruling. But being the way I am, I could not leave it at that but turned from my father who was slightly breathless from his climb up the stairs in our wake, to Mr Hobshaw; 'Sir, do you not, yourself, reside in the house these days?'

'I find it more comfortable over here, Mary Ann,' and, catching my father's eye, I said nothing but raised my eyebrows.

Not looking at me, my father, who was pressing upon the handle of his gnarled old stick and fixing his look upon his shabby carpet slippers, told me that when the lady of the house had heard that we were coming she dismissed her servants, only this morning they had left the house and we were to replace them. She had often heard tell of the excellence of my cooking; it was now to be done by me and the food would be carried over by Anne-Marie. I opened my mouth to point out vigorously that I had come over for the express purpose of looking after both of them and happy though I may have been in the kitchen of Underscar as a child I had no wish to work there for a new mistress and one whom I had not even seen.

My father raised his head wearily and shaking it slowly he laid a finger upon his lips. There was a turf and log fire burning on the hearthstone even on this warm summer's day and now Mr Hobshaw, whose chair was on the opposite side of the hearth, stooped forward and replenished the fire with the comparatively light pieces of turf he picked out of the log basket. Head turned well away from me he told me that his wife was the person in authority here: 'I have retired to the peace and comfort around me up here. Good friend Sheffield will be pleased to give up cooking,' he smiled slightly, 'he will be the first to agree that under his ministration there has been no variety . . . he has other things to do. He is a great craftsman, Mary Ann, your father.'

'You will be kept busy in the kitchen, Mary Ann,' my father

said with a slight gleam of amusement clearly upon his face, 'You will be seven women in the house . . . and us two men over here.' What he actually said was, '. . . ovver yer,' I delighted in hearing his flat Yorkshire monotone, without any change of pitch. I determined to make no effort to keep up the refined English I had spoken for so long with my lady and her young family. I said in the dialect, something that Mother often said in a teasing manner: 'Art te barn ter lig i'bed wol soon melts thack off?' and we both laughed.

*

But it was no laughing matter and this I realised as I lay in bed, alone in a tiny attic room with Anne-Marie in a room of similar size next door. I stared up at the ceiling and wondered at the homing instinct that had caused me to leave the Houdenard household at my lady's suggestions with no more considered thought than I seemed to have given to my child. I did not pause a moment to wonder if I should find at Underscar the same easy conditions as I left behind me. And there I lay, staring up at the ceiling, wretched at my lack of care and already planning a return to Brussels, if not upon the instant, as soon as I could possibly arrange it without wounding anyone.

I had not yet met the mistress of the house who was 'too busy' to see me today. But I had met the plain daughters, I had cooked an evening meal, and I had sat and talked to the two old men until, even though it was still daylight, they were nodding in their chairs. Anne-Marie, in the meanwhile, was being shown about the house by one of the four sisters, daughters of the mistress of the house, so that she would carry out her household duties, which were very heavy, in the swiftest possible time.

I felt disgruntled regarding the evening meal; in the larder there had rested upon the slab a piece of carp which I cooked but regarding the sauce I could find nothing with which to make it: no sweet herbs, no anchovies, no horseradish, no shallots, no mace or Jamaica peppercorns . . . *no white wine*, but even as I write I am smiling, my frustration at this first meal seems to be ridiculous in view of what was to come . . .

The two old men were on excellent terms, my father treated Mr Hobshaw with the old deference but there was a contented *cameraderie* between them that it did me good to see. With a manner of patient endurance they told me facts which I should know but they gave no opinion on these facts, leaving them deliberately for me to discover for myself, much as my dear lady had done.

Did I remember the hut down the clough where the young fellow Silas Clopton, a Lancashire man from over Oldham way, had set up, in a shed by the stream that ran through the clough the business of making carpet slippers? Even before I left the country Silas Clopton had a dozen manual workers in his shed. In the years I was away he has achieved an unimaginable success; having set up a large handloom, he started to weave carpets and these have sold so fast with such an increasing demand that there had been further extension and there were three large looms and thirty-five workers even before Hobshaws took over.

Neither the one nor the other old man could start to tell me what I felt to be the crux of the whole affair but at last it was my father who brought it out: 'The mistress is virtually the mill owner; there is a business arrangement between her and Mr Silas Clopton whereby she provides the cash to buy the looms and he . . .'—there was a long pause as my father searched for the right word and Mr Hobshaw found it for him—'. . . works them.'

It was no surprise that I could not see the results of this enterprise on our arrival; it was not visible from Underscar, the clough being too deep to see from the vantage point of the house. I had failed to see the top of the chimneys on our journey here. The clough was the joint property of the

Underscar estate and the one further up: Overscar; a torrent of water rushes down this ravine and instead of the looms being turned by water, as they were in my young days, they are now powered by steam, the mill pond unused, and yet the mill wheels pound from dawn till dusk.

Young Clopton, now in his late forties, had finally bought the property of Overscar after the old owner died, torn the house down stone by stone. He had rebuilt in that curious brick that nobody had ever used before for a house but which they say was being made in quantity to be used on the railroads since the Manchester to Liverpool railroad was opened three years ago.

'It's purple,' my father grunted.

'More dark blue-grey . . .' Mr Hobshaw remarked.

'Purple,' my father repeated.

Much later I lay in the small attic which had been vacated only that morning and did not smell too fresh, the tiny lattice wide open and an intermittent streak of moonlight falling across my bed. I had so often visualised my return home and it was, in the event, so strange and unexpected; there had only been one really basic alteration in my life to date; excitement caused sleep to flee altogether, my mind in a bewildered and over-lively flutter. I rose and crept into the room assigned to Anne-Marie; I knew she was not asleep but I was distressed to find her hot and tearful; I tasted the salt tears upon her cheek as I stooped to kiss her.

'Never mind, my darling,' I whispered, 'it will not be for long; when I have been dutiful as our dear lady wished and for a reasonable length of time, we shall return . . .'—I was going to say 'home' but I had always called Underscar home—'. . . to Brussels.'

'But when? How long must we be here?' she whispered back urgently.

I couldn't answer and such was Anne-Marie's private distress that she must have thought I had left the room. I stood there irresolute, trying to think of a satisfactory answer to her anguished exclamations; as though she were hugging herself in pain, she rolled over from me with her face turned to the wall and I distinctly heard a sigh which was more of a moan and she shook with tears.

As I crept out, little did I think how far, how very far from realisation was my feeble promise to return, or should I say . . . retreat, as from an untenable situation.

But as I climbed back into my own uncomfortable bed I was racked with shock. I was recalling Bruno, the beloved youngest son of my master and mistress during so many happy years in a foreign country! For my daughter to be 'in love' with young Mr Bruno could be disastrous, if Anne-Marie were not the sensible girl I thought her to be. In mental agony I asked myself if my dear lady had any thoughts at all of this; I went back in time eighteen years to the fateful 1815 when I was near demented with worry in case my dear lady might guess who was responsible for my own plight at that time; nay, not plight for I had been as willing to surrender to him as any girl truly in love. There was so much between us, she and I, and yet there must have been very much that she could not discuss with me, so very much left unsaid during that time. My trouble had been wonderfully ironed out. Yet now prophetic and gloomy platitudes wrote themselves across the moonlit strip: one of them was, *a chip off the old block*, and another, *as the old cock crows the young 'un learns.*

And during this kind of *nuit blanche*, as the French phrase goes, the mud is stirred from the very foundation of the brain and I found myself thinking: 'Clop! Clop!' we called the vagrant youth who had begged at our door for 'summat to keep up his strength', many and time and oft. 'That lad walks off with summat every time he comes,' my father had grumbled, 'he'd steal the eyes out of a dead cock's severed head if there was nowt else to tek. . . .'

A vagrant, yes, he built himself a sack shanty up on the

common outside the village and, as residence on the common was forbidden by law, he was turned away over and over again, but each time he settled in somewhere else carrying his sack roof and walls with him under his arm, and stayed until someone discovered him and he was once again turned off. He was despised as a foreigner from over the border, recognised by his pronounced Lancashire accent and rough manners, and whenever he was mentioned folk would ask one another why the lad couldn't return to his *own* country, a few miles west. They were saying that, even when, in some way beyond the imagination of everyone in our valley, he had set up in a tumble-down and abandoned weaver's shed, making carpet slippers on a loom; they said, those who had seen it, that it was beyond belief cranky.

'Clop' belonged to my childhood and before I left for Belgium he was Silas Clopton and had a couple of hands to assist in the manufactory. But there was more to it than that because when I was about sixteen and out by myself, down the clough picking blackberries one mid-autumn, he had made certain alarming advances so that I had, in a panic, picked up my Sunday best skirts and fled back home to receive a scolding from my mother for tearing my petticoat upon the brambles. I said nothing to her about my unhappy encounter for very shame.

So my new mistress and Silas Clopton were now business partners . . . the fact seemed so grotesque that I could not lie still any longer. I rose from my bed and letting myself out into the fitful moonlight I made my direct way to a tiny dell some half mile from the house where there still grew, beside the same stream, St John's wort, *tutsan* we called it in my childhood, as hortening of the French name *tout sain* (I had once found some in a wood near Blankenberg). I picked some and held it tight against my breast under my cloak, thinking what a lot of water had flowed through that tiny beck since those far-off childhood days when I had rushed to pick the plant at the slightest sign of danger or misfortune, and I was surprised at the inherent instinct which caused me to seek it now in these enlightened times, for I must still have believed that it is a cure for all ills. I made myself a tisane and, after drinking it, I slept till dawn.

TWO

A WEEK passed and during that time I could scarce bring myself to look Anne-Marie directly in the eye. The way things were turning out was so shaming, indeed desperate, that I felt certain that my child must feel a grave resentment against her mother who had willingly torn her up by the roots and brought her to what she must feel to be a disastrous employment.

Of course my new Mistress Hobshaw was a miser, bent on the accruing of money, for only God or maybe Satan knew what exact purpose, but she also believed that I had been sent back from Brussels in flimsy disguise, as a spy, sent to discover for her husband's titled daughter what the exact situation at Underscar might be. The which, in bare honesty, was the case.

Since no married woman's money is her own in the eyes of the law, it behoved a wife to retain the affection and approval of her husband in all circumstances because the husband could, in fact, will away her money as he wished. Thus the relationship between Mr Hobshaw and his second wife hung precariously upon a knife edge and the fact that Mr Hobshaw had moved himself from *his* house, leaving her in charge, in order to share the stable flat with my father the ex-groom, was extremely singular not to say ominous. She so clearly did not wish this and wanted him under her eye. But knowing Mr Hobshaw as I did, in his heyday a fine man of strong personality and great wisdom, I could sense that even though he was living only across the yard, she felt great unease and dissatisfaction.

But how any normal man could have lived at all in that dear old house under the circumstances I found there was a question which had no answer. The four daughters which the second wife had brought to the establishment had matured to a sickening middle-age; though still referred to as 'the girls' or 'the young ladies', they were all between thirty and forty, and had become so in-grown and in-looking that they were, as far as I was concerned, incommunicable with. They would come as far as the kitchen door and stand there issuing petty orders and without waiting for an answer they would scurry back to their den where they would sit all day over their work, as I supposed, in an evil huddle, to my mind, plotting against us. They would take it in turn to emerge, rushing back to the rest with the news of my reaction to such and such an order. In a tiny way it was like a household poised upon the very edge of war, the enemy being two old men apparently contentedly living out their lives across the way with no ambition other than to be left in peace. Every day Mistress Hobshaw would sail across the yard and mount the steps after breakfast and stand irritably jangling her keys and waiting for any complaints or requests her husband might have.

I knew not how long this situation had existed but I guess that it was about a year, I also gathered that it had started with a formidable quarrel in which dear Mr Hobshaw had declared that he would not live under her roof one minute longer, and that since that moment when he had walked across the yard and taken shelter with my father, he had not returned to the house and the relationship with his wife had been that of armed hostility.

I can but wonder at the mentality of your true miser for they deny themselves as much, or perhaps more, than they deny others.

At first I was entertained by the miserliness of the mistress of Underscar; I could not understand and have never yet understood, for what purpose she accrued money; the whole household lived in what it is not an exaggeration to say was sheer penury. Apart from the master's own horse there were no carriage horses in the stables; only a cob and a pony and one knobbly-kneed nag which lived out winter and summer to avoid the providing of bought fodder for her and almost starved on a diet of bracken and heather. The elderly 'girls' were constantly mending, patching and turning and re-turning their dingy gowns. The youngest one, Miss Lavinia, who was the only one whose behaviour was not an exact copy of her mother, I overheard to ask her mother to buy herself a new bonnet: '. . . for it is indeed become an absurdity, Mother.' And her mother snapped that it would last out her lifetime and Lavinia said resentfully that she had had it ever since she, Lavinia, was born and that she would appreciate a change of headgear just once in her lifetime for her dear mother. Her answer was a kind of snake-like hiss: 'Psthss!'

I found this group of elderly girls so depressing that I could never bring myself to distinguish one from the other, with the exception of Lavinia, the one with a slight spark of life to her.

It was an insoluble enigma to me and one which I always fell to marvelling upon as I kneaded the bread or scrubbed the potatoes: Why, why, *why* did Mr Hobshaw marry her? or, equally mysterious and unbelievable, did she marry him, knowing as well as anyone that he would have complete control of her money?

If I ever spoke to anyone about the riddle, the answer was boringly the same, even from my father who had a mind of his own: 'There's nowt so queer as folk.' It was an answer which did not satisfy me because I have a deep interest in people and the longer I live the worse it gets. I find myself obsessed by it and I knew that one day I must relieve my tortured mind by the unheard-of impertinence of asking Mr Hobshaw straight out, I would say it in broad Yorkshire to underline the simpleton I am: 'Why, in the name of God, didst marry her, lad?' No, it would have to be . . . Sir.

But in my own kitchen, the kitchen in which my mother had reigned supreme for most of her life, I created chaos. I would have a kitchen maid or I would walk out. And there I had a good handle because she had sent the servants packing in the worst possible manner and one of the 'young ladies' had gone so far as to tell these departing servants never again to darken our doors. Their dismissal was done cleverly, starting some time in advance, when it was first known I was returning from Brussels; the family found constant fault with the servants, daily increasing the dose, as it were, timing our advent perfectly; the final burst of contumely fell upon the morning of our arrival and under the pretext of their having committed some final unforgivable act, they were expelled, staggering down the clough to seek some help with their tattered baggage, and with none of the payment owing to them.

'I can't feed a household of nine on nothing!' I screamed. 'Call yourselves gentry? You live like inmates of the Union! Bread and scrape! You're starving those two old men over the way . . . what if they're found dead from malnutrition one of these days? It wouldn't half be a scandal, and I'd be the first to show the gentlemen of the press round my larder!'

Yes, I have a very nasty streak in me when it is roused. But I knew I had the upper hand; I held myself in for the first week but after that I let go; she would not dare to sack me and if she did I would not go; she could hardly hire a platoon of the musketry to get us out. She could, of course, murder me, and her look told me to watch out but I reckoned she would never have the courage. Afterwards, however, I was bitterly ashamed that I should have carried on so with Anne-Marie within earshot.

And talking about murder is not so soft the way the world is going; those of us who read the papers, and my dear lady received the English *Times* every day, have had to think about it a good deal these last ten years, since the Cato Street trouble, and at this time the Central Criminal Court was a-building in

Old Bailey, London. There have been terribly troublous days since the battle of Waterloo . . . I don't know what we're coming to, to be sure, I don't. It is the spread of industry as has put into the minds of the people ideas about the importance of money which they never had before.

Well, amongst my troubles that first week was the fact that I never had the chance for a good long talk with my father alone and with Mr Hobshaw alone. All was rush and bother and I came to the opinion that it was deliberate, it was not intended that I should spend much time, indeed, any time at all, in the flat above the stables. I observed Anne-Marie with some surprise and a fair amount of admiration, I was amazed at her forbearance. Going daily to the old Professor, as she had done in Brussels for so long, had made a young lady of her in more than looks only. She had learned to talk with him at his own level; she read the newspapers to him and received instruction from the old man on daily affairs so that her mind was developed and unlike many a young lady of her age she raised her eyes upward and outward and saw the world round her with intelligence.

Here, at Underscar, upon the acid soil of her roots, she reverted effortlessly to the status of servant: on her knees she polished the stone flags in the downstairs rooms, cleaned the casements, carried in the huge logs to replenish the fire which smouldered constantly, even in June, in the hearth in the hall. There is no doubt that the second Mrs Hobshaw would have dispensed with this fire if it had been possible, but it was essential for keeping down the sweat which I remembered would appear on the walls in all weathers but the very hottest.

One would have thought that the 'girls' would have made their own beds and attended to their own washing arrangement, but no, everything was left to Anne-Marie.

'They don't want us here for ever, Mother,' she whispered one night during that first week, 'but since Madame and you wish it, I must play my part, but would to goodness it was over. . . .'

I should have been happier if I could have put a term to it, such as: 'Never mind, we shall be home by Christmas . . .'—by home meaning Brussels in the Hotel d'Houdenard.

I praised her and thanked her but nevertheless resolved to waste no time in making a proper assessment of the situation. I wondered much why there had been a feeling of urgency about our coming, in Brussels. Since Mr Hobshaw's move from the house into the yard took place, some time ago, I could see no urgency at all. I was watching but there was no doubt that I was being watched.

'Are they carriage-folk, Mother?' Anne-Marie asked in her thin little childish voice with its bewitching French accent.

'In my day they were carriage-folk, Anne-Marie,' I returned stoutly, 'but since they have no carriage now it is possible that they have met with misfortune.'

Not they! I thought, but did not say.

'She has not yet found you a kitchen maid,' Anne-Marie said.

'She's not trying, there are kitchen maids aplenty!' I returned.

'They must be poor now, Mother,' Anne-Marie mused, 'the ladies sit all day trying to make their dresses wearable. . . .'

'If they were *so* poor they would go out to posts as governesses,' I observed. 'But since I was young, Anne-Marie, the rich have become poor, some of them, and the poor . . . rich!' I thought of the house recently a-building of Silas Clopton, carpet manufacturer, from Overscar. 'In my young day the second Mrs Hobshaw's family had a large estate over towards Manchester.'

'They must have lost their money,' Anne-Marie suggested.

'They must,' I concurred though I could not for the life of me guess how. 'Though landowners are the last to lose their money unless they gambled it away. . . .' (*But those days, in the early thirties, there were not yet the huge quantity of railway shares on the purchase of which so many were beggared. H.H.*)

At the end of that first week my constant cry for a kitchen maid bore some fruit but very far from what I had expected. There was sent up, from what I can only refer to constantly in my own mind as the new mill, help of a kind, a young man tall of stature, with the face of one of those carved figures I have studied in the Tuileries Gardens in Paris, which my dear lady called an 'Apollo Belvedere'. His face, indeed, was a joy to look upon but his appearance as a whole was pitiful because he had a clumsy club foot and walked with a wickedly ugly lurch from side to side. He was 'odd job man' indeed, for in addition to going innumerable errands to and from the village for the mill he waited upon Mr Hobshaw every morning as I understood, sometimes taking away his soiled underwear for his mother to wash and repair, cleaning his shoes, bringing up the newspaper from the village shop.

I remembered his mother, a village girl of strikingly beautiful face, who had married a soldier called Delph and gone away. Shortly after I left home my mother had written to tell me she had returned to the village a widow, after her husband had been killed in the fighting under the future Duke of Wellington in Spain and had brought with her a baby son who was severely crippled. Her unmarried name was Esther Crump, but the name of the son was Isaak Delph. It was understood that his mornings were too full to permit of my having his help at the time I needed it most but he would come up after the midday meal and prepare vegetables for the following day. This afternoon lull in my work was the very time when I would have crossed the yard to the flat and sat with my two old men and I was considerably irritated by being unable to leave the kitchen until the supervision was done. It took him the best part of an hour to prepare the vegetables, of which we had an ample supply brought to the house daily; it was the meat and fish and poultry which were in short supply, and two hours was all I was allowed to keep him for; after the vegetables there was the kneading of the bread which had been rising during the morning and the pounding of anything I might need in the mortar; the picking over of any fruit that had been brought me for jam; this and the washing up of all the dishes from the midday meal and the washing of the stone floor in the scullery caused constant activity in the kitchen during the usually quiet time in the afternoon. And during this time Anne-Marie would be cleaning the pewter or ironing the 'girls' ' underwear, mending as best she could their threadbare bedlinen. The days simply were not long enough to do all there was to do and by sunset often we were both too exhausted to pay visits to the stable flat even to bid goodnight.

But visits there had to be, so once I had organised my new kitchen boy I told Anne-Marie to bring her work as far as possible into the kitchen and keep supervision over the Delph man to keep him from idleness. (In time I found him far from idle!)

*

'Father,' I said to him directly as soon as it was possible, 'what is the worst complaint you have about your situation here and how is my presence to benefit you and Mr Hobshaw? The Lord knows you have been long enough without my poor mother, and without me, and neither of you is exactly decrepit. What is really wrong?' My father was a peace-loving man, early in my life I realised that he would do anything rather than encourage any kind of dissent whatever.

He said there was no call to stir up trouble; he had wanted to see me, of course, his own dear daughter, but he had no wish to tear her from her happy position in Brussels. As far as he was concerned he was not gravely maltreated but he did admit there were folks that one could easily bear to be shut of . . . mentioning no names of course, there were some folk not fit to live. Yes, indeed, folk that made other folks' lives a misery were best got shut of! And he gave a long shuddering sigh which amused me since he would be the very last person to assist in the getting shut of any living soul.

He was a happy soul and he got much pleasure out of his constant occupation of carving away at horn spoons in his chair beside the constant fire. He made a small business of selling these, and at other times he would give them away to people who brought him suitable horn; there was some art in his handiwork; over the years he had developed quirky handles to his spoons, ranging from a twist to a soffit and on the wooden spoons he would carve the initials of the owner-to-be in elaborate untutored letters, folk art of the most pleasing kind.

And after a period of thought, with the long sigh still, as it were, hanging in the air between us, he said that it was as well I be come: the master was in an unhappy situation. I respected this close loyalty; my own folk of Yorkshire are not, as they say, forthcoming; there is nothing of the chatterbox about them but as I was summoned from my happy position with my lady in Brussels, for an unspecified length of time, I hoped, nay, expected to have the situation explained to me. Did they fear to tell me the real cause of their *malaise*?

I resolved to have a heart-to-heart talk with the master, and with this purpose in mind I left Anne-Marie cleaning the pewter and went across the yard full of grim purpose.

He was reading *The Times*. It was a pleasant evening and with my hand upon my father's shoulder I suggested to the master that he should come forth, out into the soft early summer evening with me.

The rough wandering path up from the yard through the heather, leading across to Overscar, a matter of two miles or so, was still there, just as it ever was.

'And now, sir . . . ?' We walked slowly, master and servant, and indeed the evening was breathtakingly beautiful. First he talked about Anne-Marie, in whom he has always had the greatest interest. My daughter was not strikingly beautiful: she was a little, thin, graceful creature, whom it was impossible to see without wishing to have her near you. Thinking about her now and my momentary bewilderment upon our arrival I realised what a most unselfish creature she was but one who had a well-formed idea of her own identity. It was this last quality about her which had been surprising. I saw that she was quite resolved to be somebody amongst her fellow creatures and as the daughter of a peasant woman and a man of different social status I later, upon thinking it over, marvelled at the processes of heredity. *Blood will out*, as the old saying goes.

What took my breath away on this airless, quiet evening was the knowledge at last that he knew, must always have known, that she was his grand-daughter. In all the happy years in Brussels, at the back of my mind had been the question and then, walking along the heather-bound pathway, I knew at last.

'I am proud of you, Mary Ann. You are my hope for the future of our country because I now see how it is possible that in the years to come there will be no more ignorant peasants. I see that education can and will come to what we now call "the working classes" rather than "the lower orders". And in your case that self-help, about which we hear frequent murmurs from the intellectuals, can and does come about. Regarding Anne-Marie she owes much of her education to Harriet's Uncle Peter in Brussels, but you, Mary Ann . . . you're a marvel . . . my girl.'

I smiled, thinking I was no more a marvel than I was a girl . . . however. I bided my time whilst he continued in this vein for some moments. Then he told me what a shock our reception at the house had been to him. My father and he, as soon as they knew we were coming, had planned to move into one bedroom in the stable flat and leave the larger one for Anne-Marie and myself but the whole idea had been taken from his shoulders upon his asking for a large bed for two, from the house. *She* had made her plans and as she must be obeyed, her plans had taken place and his had not. He had no idea at all until the morning of our arrival that the servants were to be dismissed and that Anne-Marie and I were to replace them. 'Since nothing is achieved by loss of temper, argument and violent friction, I cannot thank you both enough for falling in with the plans, it was the constructive behaviour which I might have expected of you, Mary Ann, but scarcely of the child Anne-Marie whose personal relation to others is not, *not* that of a skivvy!'

We strolled along in silence for a while and I wondered how long it would be before he reached the core of his discourse, whether he was turning over in his mind the advisability of telling me, now that it came to the point, why we were summoned to his help.

Throughout the week my various distresses and painful pressures were more than added to by the condition of the master, once a career diplomat of stature and importance, one of His Majesty's plenipotentiaries abroad and a fine figure, ripe, one would have thought, for a baronetcy at least. And thinking back it now seemed so clear that his gradual loss of ambition started with the death of his dearly loved wife, a very fine woman who, for me, had all the qualities necessary in the wife of a great man. I realised then that since that death from that all too common disease of consumption I had never seen him as the same person. And then his son Giles, killed at Waterloo, had caused his loss of heart to the extent of his early retirement.

It seemed almost as though he had understood the train of my thought when he murmured: 'In my heyday I was not an inconsiderable figure, Mary Ann; but I am now ground down . . .' and he stamped his stick into the pathway; 'I am ground to a shadow of my former self, I have no initiative any longer, I am reduced to the mentality of a vassal and a vassal who has nothing left but tenacity, that is, the fast failing ability to hold on to my feudal tenure of this estate to the last gasp.'

It took me some moments to grasp all this and he waited until I had thought his words over.

'I have three Belgian grandsons, Mary Ann, whom you know better than I myself am acquainted with them. The lads I am proud of but they are rich foreigners. I have thought it over and I have talked it over with my dear, dear Harriet and she is absolutely at one with me . . . I wish to make over my property, the house, some of the land that goes with it, aside from the moors there are a few acres of grazing and arable, as you know, at present let to a farmer; as I was saying, I wish to make over legally and in a watertight manner her share, to my granddaughter. The ancient squirearchy is at the present time, under the Reform Bill, being abolished. But the major part of the estate must remain in the boys' name, even though it be d'Houdenard. Anne-Marie will have to change her name legally to Hobshaw and I shall make it certain legally that when she marries her husband, whoever he may be, he add Hobshaw to his own name.'

I gasped and could have fallen faint upon the heath.

The unmentionable had been, at last, after nearly twenty years, at long, long last . . . mentioned.

My mouth went dry and my lips quivered so visibly that I could not turn to him or answer for some moments; when I finally did so he was looking at me in the most tender manner, smiling.

I burst into tears and fell down upon the heath, and he sat down beside me and poked his stick constantly into the ground until I had pulled myself together.

'Does . . . does my lady know?' I stammered at last.

'Of course!'

It was as though I was looking at my life through the wrong end of a telescope, a great distance away.

'She has known from the first . . . ?'

'Of course! Did you know how beautiful you were, Mary Ann? Indeed, still are. There is a wholesomeness about you that could act as a positively fearsome attraction for some men. In a day and age when women are fashionably artificial, when a man cannot decide whether women are being themselves or fanciful artificial devices of themselves, you stand out, my dear, good and clear and to be trusted and relied upon till the Day of Resurrection and beyond. And at his sister's house, Mary Ann, Giles saw you, I need hardly ask if you remember. You and the other upper servants sat at the foot of Monsieur le Comte's table, eh? Do you remember Giles carrying his plate down the table and sitting beside you? Eh? No need to ask.' I was in tears.

'His sister remonstrated, much later, when he knew you better. "Don't do that, Giles, it will upset the other servants . . ." but Giles explained: he would like her for a wife, he had never seen a girl yet, in twenty-seven years, that he *wanted* to marry. He said he had known girls aplenty but never one about whom he felt as he felt for you.' He paused for a long period whilst I once more dried my eyes and listened:

'To her everlasting regret my Harriet wrung her hands and asked him to wait, to wait till he was quite sure. Oh, he was quite sure. But Mary Ann had an admirer, Harriet told him, a young French soldier who was paying her court, she had already been spooning (the new expression!) with him. "All the more reason why we should marry!" Harriet says now that she felt them too young and inexperienced even though Giles was nearly thirty, to make a quick wise decision. The only remark she could find as an assent to Giles's wishes was to murmur that the Sheffields were Chapel folk, like the Hobshaws, and which absurdity Giles dismissed with a curt, "Then she shouldn't be spooning with a Catholic!" '

I was certainly hysterical there amongst the heather because I heard myself laughing and God knew there was nothing to laugh about. But I could *hear* Giles saying that.

'My daughter's love and regard for you, Mary Ann, might have spoilt you were you not of the calibre you are. I quite understood, and understand now; we were in the midst of war, in Brussels the war was very near you, it must have been all too easy, indeed, imperative with Giles's young life likely to end at any moment, to anticipate your marriage. Forgivable, dearest Mary Ann, in a case of true, true love.'

'It was true, true love indeed, sir. But I could not forget, and I still cannot forget, that though "educated" as you have just said, I was and am still a servant and it did not seem to me right and proper that Mr Giles Hobshaw should marry a servant and that was why I constantly refused, as he begged, to "go and get ourselves wed". It didn't seem to me right and proper then, though I know better now!'

'Meaning?'

'Meaning that Giles and I were meant for one another. Not so much similarity as the ability to live together, to suffer together and to love together . . . instinct, not careful consideration, drew us together and, may I say so, sir, would have kept us together in love, for the rest of our lives. It was instinct that drove us together then, now I am old and have had time to think over these years, I know that we were one. I know that I have never been able to take the overtures of any other man seriously, nor shall I ever . . . I have known perfect happiness and it has been worth a lifetime of lonely spinsterhood.'

We were almost lying, and almost side-by-side in a dreamy communion: the sun was hurrying down a now clear sky. We were half-way to Overscar and Underscar was out of sight. Down beneath us the trees were crowded together in the clough and there was a loud commotion of the rooks making preparation for bed. The path beside which we reclined made a division in the sour soil between the heather upon which we lay and the lusty young bracken now tall enough to hide a prostrate fugitive if necessary. Away over to the left was that same clump of Scotch pines which grew above Underscar and acted as a landmark for that birthplace of mine. Remembering, over the years, my mind had always seen the pines before it saw the house; perhaps it was the thing seen by my new-born eyes when they first opened.

'And so, Mary Ann,' my master went on at last, 'things being as they are in my house and I having vacated the position of master of the house as being untenable, we shall have to choose with care the moment when I shall convey you and Anne-Marie to the solicitor in town. Anne-Marie being not yet of age you will have to act as her trustee. I have talked to your father about changing both your names by deed poll to Hobshaw. The dear man prefers not to speak of this since he was deeply grieved that you had a child whilst still unmarried, even though secretly a mite proud that the father was a Hobshaw, but I think he has no strong objection.'

I could not bother to worry about this, I had heard too much to take in for the time being, I wanted to be alone to think over the marvel. However, Mr Hobshaw was loyalty itself to the present mistress of Underscar who, incredibly enough, was his present wife. Now, if ever, I should be able to ask him why he ever married her. But yet I could not.

We watched the sun set, in a companionable silence, then he stood up, grunting slightly and saying that he had just reached sixty-eight years.

It was impossible for me to say what I should have wished, that he was a sprightly young marvel for that great age, it would have been untrue. I looked sadly at his hands and, with consummate impertinence, took his arm and together we walked slowly back. I knew he liked me to have done so and he seemed for the moment to be happy and contented.

Then, as we approached the house, looking down at the roofs covered with those huge roofing slabs of stone which grew lichen and went a luminous green in the winter with the damp, he hurriedly dropped my arm.

'It may be,' he strangely said, 'that I have trained myself to look an older man even than I am. Were I too sprightly I might die by accident; as it is, the older I look the more likely I am to die quietly and peacefully of old age. Though of course if I take too long about it... I shall have to be helped into eternity.'

I was not sure if I had heard correctly. I thought over his words as we started the steep descent to the stable yard. 'I ask your pardon,' I murmured finally, 'but I did not understand your last words.' We were now standing at the foot of the stone steps up to his rooms: 'She wants to be without me but she is too afraid to assist me into eternity.' He looked carefully at me to see if I had understood and, oddly enough, I had. He kept his voice low and went on 'She wants me to die before I have had time to will away my property.'

'Since when has this been the case?' I almost whispered. I was irritated that this vital exchange should have been kept for the duration of our peaceful walk together until we returned home and only spoken out of the side of his mouth, casually, as we were in full view of the kitchen premises.

'Only recently, since I believe every halfpenny of her own fortune has gone into the new mill; she now realises that money can beget money and she has become voracious; I have had to send my wife's jewels . . . I mean of course my first wife, the second is no wife to me . . . send them to Harriet for safe keeping. I have nothing left to sell but my property and I live upon the income from it . . . we all do. Whilst I live, my property is mine, if I die it becomes hers. . . .' He turned away and started to go up the steps slowly, 'I am such stuff as *fools* are made on. . . .'

This was the moment when I could have asked him the question, why did he marry her, in full view of the peering eyes, the pricked ears . . . and it was torture not to be able to do so.

THREE

I SENSED upon arrival that she had no wish to see me, that is, to interview me and to discuss family affairs. She put me firmly in my place at an early date, summoning me to the closet which was now called her office, which used to be a small library for the use of the master of the house and only to be entered in his presence, so carefully did he guard his precious books. Many of the books were still there leaving space upon the shelves for files and loose untidy piles of printed matter and other papers. Upon the occasions when I had been interviewed, twice in that first week, she had made it perfectly clear that I was a servant and to be treated as such, thus I was given my orders with particular emphasis upon the segregation of the lives of Anne-Marie and myself from the rest of the household. The rooms relegated to my daughter and myself were to be kept spotlessly clean, she informed me; the tin bath hanging behind the door might be carried down to the kitchen on Saturday nights when the rest of the household had retired, and Anne-Marie and myself could take our baths before the kitchen stove; this, it was pointed out, was not for our comfort but to avoid unnecessary splashing and knocking of the woodwork which would be involved when carting water up to the attic floor bedrooms we occupied.

Anne-Marie and myself could have one whole Sunday off a month on condition that the larder was left fully stocked with the eatables for two major meals for five in the house and the two old men 'across the yard'. The used dishes would be stacked in the scullery and the washing up done on our return.

In the larder (and she would ask her daughter Miss Lavinia to supervise) there would be a space set aside for the servants' food; upon no account was any food eaten by the household to be shared with the servants, i.e. Anne-Marie and myself. Miss Lavinia would count out our rations every Saturday morning, our sugar, special butter and flour for our bread; modified corned beef would be sent up from the butcher with the family meat every time there was a delivery. As for vegetables, an old man from the village came every day with these; we would be able to eat as much cabbage and potatoes as we wanted, she added graciously.

My outburst regarding the kitchen requirements, which had been endured by Miss Lavinia, was ignored but the air hung heavy with disapproval; the inference was that my behaviour was too unheard-of to be mentionable, a lapse which was neither forgiven nor forgotten.

Bold as brass outwards, I was astonished at myself inwardly to hear myself say that I was sorry to see the condition of life at Underscar had fallen so low, and she, no doubt as shocked as my inward self, stared at me with the disgust she might show had I handed her an asp from the bosom of the white apron I was caused to wear.

She said: 'Please to remember what century you are living in, my woman; if you will cast your mind back to your eighteenth-century early youth you will perhaps admit it was a different world; progress has taken place and with progress has come an advance in wages . . .'—I cleared my throat meaningfully, my wages were exactly the same as those of my mother, back in the dark ages of the last century—'and with the industrial benefits that are being showered upon us, the cost of every day life, eating and drinking and travelling, has increased proportionately.'

'Therefore there is every need to increase wages,' I snapped but added 'ma'am' hurriedly.

'Mary Ann, you have acquired a number of ideas above your station and these do not become a woman of the lower orders, peasant born. I will have none of it here. . . .'

'Peasant!' I cried, 'Progress and peasants do not walk hand-in-hand. . . .'

'Be quiet, I pray, you are becoming insufferable. I am well aware that my step-daughter-in-law . . .' (and for a moment I did not realise that she was referring to my dear lady) 'has sent you over here for the express purpose of reporting back to her intimate details of our daily lives, particularly with regard to her father . . . ;' and she added with unpleasant emphasis, '. . . *my husband*. I am watching you carefully because I think you are a trouble-maker. You have my step-daughter-in-law's ear, I am told, and rule the roost over there in Brussels. I will have none of that here. Any trouble from you, Mary Ann, and you will be turned out . . .'—she was lashing herself into a climax, her voice became shriller as she goaded herself along—'and you and your bastard child will be cast out. Oh, I have no hesitation . . . I will not have the tranquillity of *my* house interfered with by a termagant like you.'

'So now we know where we are,' I returned, my arms tucked into the bib of my apron and my feet four square upon her carpet. Bastard child? The words did not concern me. I have never found they hurt me, but did she know *whose* bastard child?

'Progress,' I said clearly and distinctly, 'has made the position easier for the "bastard child" and more especially since her father died a hero's death at Waterloo.' My lady, so long ago, had created the imaginary father when she first saw my baby: '. . . a fine French soldier!' she had told me and so it was; in my mind I could describe him accurately and, if I could draw, I should be able to draw lovingly, this imaginary character of a *fine French soldier*. So I stood staring at her and she stared at me across her table with a look of such loathing that I would have cringed had I not been confident and stout of heart, knowing that my dear lady, though far away, was staunchly behind me.

And now that I stood close to her I could see that this second Mrs Hobshaw was not an ill-favoured woman. She had a well-shaped head and a fine beaky nose; the skin of her face had the firm texture of an egg-shell and the cheeks were now a blazing pink with her ill-concealed anger. But she was unfeminine and wore her keys at her waist in the manner of a jailer, it looked as though she would swing the chain and strike me with them at any moment. One of them was of such a size I wonder she was not bowed down by the weight. I stood firm and said:

'I have nothing to be afraid of. You have far more to fear me, than I to fear you. I will have you know . . .' (yes, my tone was insufferable, I could watch the colour in her face increasing) '. . . that I am not totally destitute, in fact, far from it. I have my savings of twenty years safely secured, and not in my *bas de laine*. If the position here becomes intolerable my Anne-Marie will be sent back to Brussels and I shall fight you here alone.'

'Get out!' she shouted.

Why did I say *fight*?

But it came over me with a rush of remorse as I left the room: why did I bring Anne-Marie? Why did I leave as my lady wished without careful consideration for my dependent and beloved child? Why was it not in either my mind or apparently in my lady's, that Anne-Marie should stay in Brussels and I should come alone?

*

A day or two later I was out early in the morning in the messuage, searching for wormwood with which I intended making a tisane with a tablespoon of honey for my Anne-Marie who said she had a pain. I tramped about among the weeds, remembering the position of the plant in my youth in the same way that I had remembered the *tout sain* soon after my arrival.

The spot I was searching had once been my mother's fine herb garden of which some few hardy plants still remained. There had been an abundance of rosemary in my day and I chuckled at the thought that the rosemary had gone, true to the old legend that rosemary never flourishes when the woman is the master. Looking up I saw the second Mrs Hobshaw standing watching me. She was wearing a shawl and her night-gown was visible round her feet. She must have seen me from her bedroom window, awake with the daylight.

I called across to her a good morning, as though there were nothing between us.

'What are you looking for, Mary Ann?'

'Wormwood; my mother's herb garden was just here; there is nothing left save the hardy plants and the rosemary is gone altogether,' I leered slightly.

'What do you want it for?' she snapped.

'For my little daughter, her courses. . . .'

'It is a mistake to cosset a girl at such a time; my girls. . . .' I turned my back upon her and walked away but could feel the hatred, almost a pain between my shoulders from those gimlet eyes of hers.

*

The speed of my life in Brussels had been as that of one of the new railway engines in comparison with the tenor of our existence at Underscar. As the bells rang out nine o'clock I would have done my shopping, bringing home a basket of freshly baked bread for the household (as opposed to the brioches I made for the dining-room). The marketing would have been over and done with, my purchases having been wheeled home in his truck by the scullion.

As I stood beside the kitchen table under which I had played in safety for hours as a child, I was aware of a depression enveloping me like a chill North Sea fog. Once again I asked myself for how long had we come to this now alien house? Had any term been put to our visit? I tried hard to think whether in the excitement of our preparations my lady and I had discussed when we were to return to the house I soon discovered was much more my home than where we now found ourselves. As I kneaded my bread I watched Anne-Marie stagger across the kitchen with two laden buckets of sea-coal for the young ladies' parlour and I wondered at myself that I should thoughtlessly bring her with me on this mission of mercy.

'Why do you not leave that for Isaak?' I murmured.

She gave me a reproachful look: poor Isaak with his club foot! And yet Isaak was as strong and sturdy as any young countryman.

Anne-Marie and I, in order to keep up with the advance of our day, would rush about like mad things, trying to get everything done; by contrast, all but Mr Hobshaw of those around us were as inert as invalids. I had my one long talk with my master but I now understood that he had sometimes to take to his bed with what my father called 'stomach upsets' and I would send Anne-Marie across the yard with gruel or bread-and-milk of which she would often bring back the congealed and almost untouched remains.

I resolved to write a long letter to my lady; up to now I felt I had not been at Underscar long enough to understand the situation and I still felt this but I could see that I might be here years before I could penetrate the inert surface of the household as it was and I had not yet been into the village or looked round the neighbourhood of my girlhood. So come the next Sunday I resolved to take the whole day off, leaving the Sunday dinner to be heated up by Anne-Marie with the assistance of Isaak and with these two resolutions in mind I went across the yard and up the stone steps and stood before my father. 'What is the matter with Mr Hobshaw?'

My father put down his work in deference to my urgency: 'Mary Ann, my child, I do not know, I know nowt about it. . . .'

It was a right pity I scolded him but then there were many things about that time which I did and which I now feel were a right pity. 'Is he going to die?' My father looked shocked, he put his fingers to his lips and looked round furtively 'Ss . . . sh, Mary Ann!' But I had seen Mr Hobshaw walking up the moorland path a few minutes before. 'If he is going to die he should be with my lady, I should take him back to Brussels; this is no home in which to die. . . .'

In an emergency I could ask my lady to come but who could know whether or not it was an illness which would turn to emergency? And how could my lady return to her old home in the present circumstances? Unthinkable. I saw only too clearly why I had been sent.

'I feel my lady would wish him to consult a physician of the first order.'

'Where would we find one of them?' my father grunted.

Harrogate spa, I thought, but being unsure I said nothing, I merely resolved. 'I am going to the village, Father, to look up some of Mother's old friends, to greet them and see how they fare.'

'Tha'll find a big change, lass, and in all that foreign finery I reckon they won't know thee!'

'I'll see they do. . . .'

And I did! But woe, woe! What a strange condition I found in my native village: Sunday morning and the whole female population coming out from Church or Chapel accompanied in the main by their menfolk. But what a change! They were all, or all that I saw, dressed decently, the children in proper footwear and the little girls in bonnets and the little boys in caps, and I was welcomed with a reserve which I never met before. A foreigner now, they greeted me coolly and asked how I did, as though by leaving the village for so many years I had somehow or other become a stranger. I realise now that

I looked less like a servant at Underscar than a foreign lady, my clothes were over-smart and townish. Though made by a poor dressmaker living in an attic in the Rue Flamande, she had both skill and taste and thus I stood out, that Sunday morning, in a manner which I would have done much to avoid had I realised it in advance (though I had, in fact, taken the trouble to leave my gloves behind).

My mother's best friend, now a widow, shared her dinner with me but I felt uncomfortable because she treated me like a refined stranger. She also made constant references to heaven, to the wickedness of the world and to her longing for a haven of peace beside her Saviour which she knew, with a startling degree of certainty, to be reserved for her in Paradise. In fact, I finally said a trifle tartly that she was fortunate, I personally had no such certainty in my mind though I might continue to hope for the best. I thanked her kindly for the meal but hurried away as soon as I was able.

It being a fine and agreeable afternoon, I resolved to take an exploratory walk and my first big surprise was, as I mounted the slope from the village, to see the tops of any number of tall black chimneys rising from the valley in which the town was hidden. There were a dozen or more and some of them, even on a Sunday morning, were pouring out thick black smoke. There were now two tall thin black exclamation marks above our Underscar mills. I looked down as I passed above them, keeping to the path which would lead me to Overscar because I wished to see what they were doing to the old house and a Sunday morning seemed an excellent time to explore.

Alas, no architect I, but there was no doubt in my mind that the mass of brick which I soon came across did nothing to improve the delightful surroundings of this once admired house. I hurried forward, trying to discover if the original house had been entirely demolished or whether it had simply been added to. And as I walked round I discovered the remains of the old stone building round the back; the front was entirely rebuilt of new purplish railway brick such as had been pointed out to me in Brussels along the new railway embankment then building. The outside was evidently almost complete, the casements were large windows with great plain sheets of shining glass so that the rooms inside seemed to be filled with glaring light. I went up more closely and standing on tiptoe I put both hands to my face and tried to see inside.

'Good-day, Madam, can I help you?' I jumped almost out of my skin with fright and turning round I saw I was face to face with Silas Clopton, the old alarm of my youth: Clop. But how changed! At first sight he looked like a gentleman; he was wearing a suit of local tweed but with the tight trousers and long tails of the city gent and he wore a beaver hat such as the Duke of Wellington sported to the admiration of all, and he swung a fine cane with a silver knob. It was clear that he had no idea who I was so I said straightaway that I had known the house in its better days, a challenging remark at best and I could see him stiffen.

'It will be a very fine house indeed,' he said reproachfully and I said that maybe but not here, atop this particular rising ground above the scar; it would be visible for miles around and less able to resist the wild winds than the humbler stone house, low-built against the draughts.

'They knew what they were doing, the older builders of homes,' I said, 'they built more for comfort than for grandeur.' And I turned away; I would have pulled up my gloves in the way my lady did when she was departing gracefully, but I had no gloves with me. I got part of the way down what was once the path from the house but what was now almost a turnpike road which I have no doubt they would dub 'the drive' when he caught me up, recovering from his surprise and saying in full warm tones: 'You don't hoax me, Mary Ann Sheffield . . .!'

'Nor do you hoax me, Silas Clopton,' I snapped back.

'Who do you think you are, Mary Ann, not the widow of Giles Hobshaw, surely?'

It pays to be slow to anger, dear God how it pays! I would not have felt anger then if he had slapped me across the face; I felt simply intensely interested. Curiosity always quenches anger with me as sure as water dowses a fire. 'As a matter of fact, not,' says I, 'but his widow in everything else *but* fact.'

'That is utter nonsense!'

What was the point, after all these years and we were middle-aged, to have a quarrel? I looked him pointedly up and down and said that I perceived he had gone up in the world and he retaliated by saying that I, too, had gone up in the world. At which I argued that, far from that, I had recently come down in the world since I was at present servant, and general servant, not simply cook like my mother, at Underscar. He fell back, overdoing the appearance of being astonished.

'But you're every inch a lady, Mary Ann, a version of Madame la Comtesse d'Houdenard, born Harriet Hobshaw, in your speech and manner . . . to the life.'

'I can't help that,' I snapped, 'since I have lived longer with her, seeing her daily, than I lived at Underscar. I have certainly not "gone up in the world" but I understand, Silas Clopton, that you have. You have "made good" and are now the mill owner and look it, every inch of a gentleman. It's the hat that does it.'

In his excitement he ignored this slight insult. He was anxious for me to know that he was no mill *owner*, not he! But in time he might well be. He wanted to know how I was 'getting on with' the present Mrs Hobshaw, mistress of Underscar, and I said coolly that there was no question of 'getting on' with her, she was the mistress of Underscar and since she had dismissed her servants shortly before our arrival, my daughter and I were now the present servants, and I had had little to do with her, other than take orders.

'You're a cunning girl, Mary Ann,' he said, looking at me with narrowed eyes, 'you've always been too clever by half. It is quite clear to everybody that Madame la Comtesse has sent you over to spy out the land.'

'In what way "spy out the land"?' I asked sweetly. He tried to take my arm, and to stroll friendly down the drive, but though I commenced to walk slowly I dodged his arm gracefully.

He said: 'Since you must play the idiot I must play it too and "explain". The squire is getting no younger, that is clear and the question of the inheritance is in everybody's mind, everybody's including his. And the fact that his present wife is extremely, I should say *gravely*, rich does not indicate that she has *enough* money, really rich people never have, did you not know? She would like to own all this land,' he waved an arm graphically, 'all the land we see now and a lot more besides.'

'But not land of much value, or in the least productive except to sheep, to the larks perhaps and to me!'

He quite clearly jumped slightly: 'To you!'

'Yes, to me,' I paused, 'because I love it, it is my native heath.'

He blew out his cheeks scornfully and I turned away laughing. He had certainly grown into a fine figure of a man, not so much good-looking as distinguished.

'Are you married, Mr Clopton, sir?' I asked with a change of mood, lightly.

'Not yet, Mary Ann. I have been far too busy forging my way ahead.'

'There are four excellent opportunities for it. . . .'

He thought this over and finally saw what I meant; for a few moments he was quite aghast: 'You turn me sick at the thought,' he mumbled.

'Mr Hobshaw's step-daughters, all eminently marriageable. . . .'

'Really, Mary Ann, your language; it might be Madame la Comtesse herself speaking!' There was a long pause as we strolled on.

Then he said with real bitter truth from the heart, as to an old friend: 'There is not one of them I can stand and I have given attention to each one from the eldest to the youngest, they are quite intolerable, motivated entirely by their mother, they are like tiny children clustering round her skirts. The money tempts me, of course. Much as I need it there would not be enough to compensate for the terrible burden I would take on as one of them for a wife.'

Curiously enough I found myself, as I listened to him, liking him. There was a friendliness towards me which was unexpected after my morning's experiences, an acceptance of me as an old acquaintance which was by no means repulsive. I felt he was in fact lonely and had no one to whom he could talk as he was now talking to me; it might be that everyone in the district knew him too well and I was, indeed, a passing receptacle for his pent-up feelings.

I cannot remember the whole conversation, we talked for an hour or more, but I remember clearly the outstanding things he said and one of them was that I was a clever girl, cleverer, probably, than he and I had not his grave handicaps. My life had been based on love and security; I knew my parents for one thing, and that was a good base for a good life. And then it came out that he never knew his parents or, indeed, if he had had any at all. Some folk, he thought, were conceived as casually as the thistledown, parentless. He first became aware of being himself in an orphanage and had been named after the warden. This warden showed no interest in him whatever and one day when, he reckoned, he was about seven years old, he just walked away, unnoticed and, he had no doubt, unmourned.

'What then?' I could not help but ask. I knew but I wanted to hear what he had to say. He shrugged his shoulders.

'It would fill a book but an unremarkable one. I went for the gentry, you may be sure, and I learned how to speak and write and read and sponge on other people so I don't know what I have inherited in the way of talents or wickedness or any other thing. But I know what had been thrust upon me,

Mary Ann, and that is the determination to rise up in the world and have the things some other people have. One thing I know I have inherited and that is great physical health and strength, and I was literally starving many, many times. And when you're starving and thankfully snatch at crusts fallen in the gutter . . . something inborn within a man . . . he never forgets . . . and he is never satisfied, he must have more and more and more because always, not far at the back of his mind, but up near him, right in the front of his mind, is the determination never to fall again to the state when you reach for the discarded crust. It eats into a man, Mary Ann, so that he is nothing *but* aspiration and will let nothing stand in the way of his ardent desire for distinction.' And then after a while, he said, 'It may be that my new house is vulgar but it is well-built and strong and it is a roof over my head of which no one will ever deprive me . . . a good strong roof and not a mere packing case. It looks the house of a somebody and not the home of a skinny, filthy lad crawling after a fallen apple between the feet of the passers-by in the streets of Manchester.'

In the end he had walked with me right back to Underscar. He stopped on the path from the moor, looking down at the house. I looked, too and thought of the great stone flags with which the roof was constructed, at least more sturdy than the slates on the roof of the new Overscar. He said dreamily, as though thinking of something else, 'A clever girl like you would marry your old master and give her right name to her bastard, even at this late date.'

I snapped back that I was neither clever nor a girl and 'my old master' by which he meant Mr Hobshaw, was well and truly married. And he said that was so but that if the present Mrs Hobshaw fell off her horse and broke her neck. . . .

*

As I closed the yard gate behind me I turned and saw him walking up the slope to the moorland path: a fine figure of a man, there was no doubt; at least he looked as much a gentleman as he declared I looked a lady. We shall all be ladies and gentlemen if education is carried out as they plan. I thought of my round-faced placid Flemish peasants, sitting patiently behind their wares in the markets of Brussels and I wondered.

Before going into the house I mounted the stone stairs to the flat. The fire smouldered in the grate this early summer's evening and my father sat in his chair beside it, chipping, chipping away. The master stood at his high desk which he had had brought over from the house, he was writing with an old-fashioned quill pen and he had several others standing like a vase of flowers in a heavy pewter mug beside him.

'And how did you find your native village, Mary Ann?'

'Very greatly changed indeed, sir. Much new building which alters the face of the old place, and what I found pleasing was, there was less dirt and signs of poverty. The new dissenting chapel seemed to have as many worshippers coming out as the church itself and the folk much better dressed than of yore.' I told them about my dinner with my mother's old friend and my words with those who remembered me and said that I could not but notice that they were much more afraid of hell than they had wont to be, their talk constantly turned on the wrath of God and the Life to Come and I reckoned I did not take to it. 'And in their leg o'mutton sleeves and their big collars and huge bonnets, they were a smart lot, I can tell you; when I left home our clothes were of the simplest style and I still retain my wadded coat which you gave me, sir, to this day.'

I told them how I had walked down the village along an enclosed turnpike, dull and shadowed by plantations on either side instead of those open spaces and commons of yore. And the little mere opposite the Fighting Cock inn, covered with green weed, is now a muddy pond. And in places the cottages have disappeared to make way for gentlemen's parks.

Mr Hobshaw said they were no longer gentlemen who made the parks but successful manufacturers aping the gentry.

'Ill fares the land, to hastening ills and prey,
Where wealth accumulates and men decay. . . .'

Goldsmith

the master quoted.

And my father surprisingly put in his word: 'You'd have to have one eye shut and the other eye not open to see what way things are going; Mistress Hobshaw and her servile underlings; they'll have mills with half-a-dozen mill chimneys filling the clough and they'll have solid blocks of workmen's cottages right across the moors to the Lancashire border afore they're done. Progress they call it . . .' and in the ensuing silence my good father, in a manner which I so clearly remembered from the past and which would greatly amuse my mother, chose to add sagely: 'And what's the use of pockets lined wi' brass to a miser if they never spend a penny?'

I could see that a lot more remained to be said and that the old men spent much time criticising the events in the house, to their own comfort. And since for the present I must not appear to take sides because to do so would mean that I would learn less, I changed the subject by asking if my daughter had waited upon them satisfactorily and what further food in the way of supper I could supply.

And as I walked across the yard to the kitchen door I had a stab of anxiety: what man could fail to look twice at my flower-like daughter? How would Silas Clopton feel about her when he was to set eyes upon her on what must be one of his frequent visits to the house to talk business with the mistress? But what young girl will be warned against a man? To tell her that Clopton was a fine figure of a man but as untrustworthy as the weather would merely be to rouse her interest. Upon entering the kitchen, however, I heard laughter and the sound of dish-washing from the scullery where Isaak had come up to help my girl with the washing of the supper dishes. She is but a child, I thought happily, and was comforted.

FOUR

My very dear lady,

This is the first moment I have had time to write even to tell you that we are safely here. I have now had my first day out and as the sun sets I can sit down to give you our impressions. First, the master has left the house, moving across the yard to live with my father . . . all of which you had wind of. I find my own father in perfect content and health, not active in body but as active as ever he was in mind, which is not very active. He has a small market for his horn spoons and once or twice a week he takes his wares down to the village in a basket where he meets a middle-man from the town who pays him at least enough to satisfy the old man.

The dear master is not so happily placed. He has all his books piled up around him and the desk at which he used to stand for hours has been brought across too and he writes constantly, what or to whom I know not.

The old house appears somewhat the same; the oak dresser with the old pewter dishes not kept as clean as they were; the stone flags, scrubbed by she who has done it so many times before (myself). I have no serious complaints regarding the manner in which Underscar is kept.

But the atmosphere of the house is foul and tainted and that is not to put it too strongly. There is an evil spirit abroad in the rooms and in the living-room and up and down the stairs. The top attic which you will remember as one big dormitory for the maids, has been divided into small partitioned chambers with room barely for a bed and a row of hooks on the back of the door; the mistress of the house does not encourage social gatherings between the servants under the roof. Indeed, when night comes we are too exhausted to do anything but fall into bed and because we are separated we cannot talk over our problems. And she knows this.

Madame, I cannot describe the mistress exactly to you yet; she is thin like a reed and her mouth but a thread; she creeps about the house wrapped in a long cloak, holding it together with her hands across her chest. Not a happy woman, it would seem she has no social life nor any friends.

And the 'girls'! Maybe those daughters are folk like the rest of us but they never let on they are. They carry refinement to ridiculous lengths; I cannot believe they were born in the West Riding of Yorkshire but I have no means of finding out. They believe that servants should be kept in their place and as they now have no other servants than Anne-Marie and myself there is no time to clamber out of our place. A rack of bells has been fixed up so that if they wish for anything, they pull a handle fixed against the walls in whatever room they are and the corresponding bell clangs in agitation in the kitchen.

I bear in mind constantly your wishes, my dear lady, and I trust you will not be disappointed with the meagre contents of this letter in regard to the intents of either the master or the mistress. I must add that the return home to Underscar (for whatever length of time is decided) has not been the pleasure that has been anticipated. There hangs so strongly in the air one breathes the feeling that all are waiting for something; ominous is perhaps the right word, a constant air of ill omen.

Now the light is failing and no candles are provided for the servants so I must end.

With my ever-loving respect, dear Madame,

Your faithful servant

Mary Ann Sheffield.

If your ladyship would kindly send a phial of those excellent liver pills we have used from time to time, I will administer them to the master who suffers intermittently from liver upsets and looks rather poorly. In the meantime I am dosing him according to my Culpeper Herbal.

*

By the time I had reached my signature it was almost too dark to see. In the morning I would ask Isaak to take my letter to the post. It was a black night but for me who had slept soundly for the fourteen nights we had been at Underscar it was as the first; I lay until daylight with wide-open eyes. My 'day off' had done me a power of good in that my brain, jammed with new and unexpected experiences, had adjusted itself and had time to work things out in an organised manner.

As I now saw it we were involved in an affair quite typical of the district, concerning property, trade and inheritance but not concerned with any question of love; it was every man, or woman for him- or herself. 'Here's to me and my wife's husband, not forgetting meself,' as the Yorkshire toast goes.

Ten years ago, when my lady's father had taken this second wife, I now remembered discussing it with my lady. 'I only know the woman by repute but she is a horror,' my lady had said. 'She has been left a rich widow and I cannot but suppose that my poor father has married her for that reason and that reason only.'

I could understand, now, that this was so. For hundreds of years the Hobshaws had lived on their wool but since the Americans' freedom they had been building such quick handy clippers that there was a weekly delivery of wool from New York to Liverpool, taking only twenty-three days on the eastern journey. And with this new development of steam, goodness knows where it will end. I can see now that the early attempts of the Hobshaws to get the weavers all under one roof were feeble and this is quite understandable since there is not a business man amongst them nor has there ever been.

Mr Hobshaw, with his only son killed in battle and his three half-Flemish grandsons who would inherit, was tempted by the rich Yorkshire widow with notorious business acumen . . . and fell; a literary man, a dreamer, miscast in a society suddenly rendered greedy and grasping, like the gold-diggers who all at once become insensible to anything but the anxiety to find gold in their pans however much discomfort there might be in the search. I had no doubt whatever that Mr Hobshaw adored his daughter and her sons, and detested his wife and his step-daughters. But did he have any feeling at all for his land? Did he care in the least that the rash of workmen's houses would before long spread slowly, or even quickly, up and over those brown hills of his native heath so that soon he would be living in the most up-and-down town in the country. Unless he died. And if he died, the three young men in Belgium would be the absentee landlords . . . unless. . . .

My lady once quoted some big nob, I don't know who but I remember distinctly my lady saying, years ago when her father had just married that woman: '. . . the chastity of women is of the utmost importance since all property is dependent upon them. . . .' And yet, I don't think that, even if Mr Hobshaw died soon, the second Mrs Hobshaw could will his property away from his family, which is what my lady fears. I must find a solicitor for myself in town as soon as I can find time, I remember deciding at last; I am an ignorant woman knowing nothing of the law, but I shall find out.

Then, since no waves of sleep began to overwhelm me, I took to thinking about my Anne-Marie. She has the innocent sweet face of a kitten, that girl of mine, but she acts and speaks like an educated lady; she has brains and I believe common sense; she also has the sweetest nature in that she is slow to anger and quite without pangs of envy but with all this she is extremely reserved. Why do I say . . . *but*? Surely I should be pleased that she is reserved? Yes, I am. But nevertheless, as her mother, it renders me impotent to influence her in any way. But further . . . I should not want to influence her, if I really believe she has common sense and probably more than I.

Thus it has turned out that as mother and daughter Anne-Marie and I are not 'close', we are two separate individuals. I was grieved and worried that I brought Anne-Marie back with me to my old home, seeing the way things have turned out. My lovely girl, who had hours of discussions on every topic with the old Professor in Brussels, was thrown back to what might have been her status, if fortune and my lady had not been wonderfully kind to me and mine. It was wrong that the regular servants at Underscar should have been dismissed on the very day of our arrival. It was understandable: the present lady of the house had started as she meant to go on, we were servants from Belgium and servants from Belgium we would remain. And Anne-Marie said not one word of complaint to me after that first night.

Perhaps she was waiting for me to make the complaints?

I heard the old clock on the stairs strike three and there are those who believe that thoughts thought at these small hours of the coming day are totally unrealistic. Unless you lie in a bed of illness, I believe that thoughts thought at three a.m. can be the truth and nothing but the truth; at three o'clock in the morning on this late April day I knew only too well why my dearest lady had included Anne-Marie in my return to my old home seeking information; I knew why she had quietly assumed, right from the starting discussions on our movements, that Anne-Marie would go with me.

She wanted Anne-Marie out of the house because in the

evenings, when the day's work was done for both young people, she and Bruno would spend the late hours together. They would talk and laugh and look at books of the wonderful Flemish painters and read to each other in turn. They were becoming too fond of one another: too soon? Or too unsuitably? Which? Or both?

I at once started an imaginary letter to my lady:

> '. . . the predicament in which we find ourselves could be avoided for Anne-Marie if she might return to Brussels and take up residence in the old Professor's house. . . .'

or even in lodging with one or other of my many women friends in that dear town?

And then I took to wondering what I wanted for my girl? Was I ambitious for her, did I want her to make a fine marriage? If so I was no better than the rest of us 'gold diggers'. If I really wanted a rich future for her there was this fine (if elderly) eligible bachelor about to occupy a grand new house two miles from here. This was an extraordinary change of outlook since, only a few hours ago, I had a transient dread, as we approached Underscar after our walk together, that he might set eyes upon my girl and in due course ruin her.

In my strange tour of the village not twenty-four hours previously, I had never heard people talking about God with such familiarity as made me feel that they had all been adopted by Him; Chosen Folk; I had had God rammed down my throat even as much as the Devil; God could well have been a rich new landlord come to the district in my absence and about Whom, of course, I would not have heard.

'God helps those who help themselves,' I had croaked several times, but nobody had either listened or heard. It had all put me off saying my prayers this night and that was probably why I could not sleep.

I got up and went downstairs to start the bread-making.

*

I was still turning over in my mind the next letter I was determined to write to my lady about returning Anne-Marie to Brussels when Isaak came at dinner-time handing me a letter from that city. In return I gave him the one I had written before dark to my dear lady, and the necessary shilling for postage with one sixpence extra for the post abroad and one sixpence for himself. As he left to carry out my message he turned back to tell me that Mr Clopton was making his way across the yard. Involuntarily, in the manner of someone trying to avoid an accident, I hurriedly sent my meek child upstairs, thrusting in her hand a wash-leather with which to clean the bedroom casements.

'Good morning, Mrs Sheffield,' he laid his beaver hat upon the table and I looked at it as though at a dead rat he had placed in my territory.

'I have lain awake all night. . . .'

'Oh, I am sorry, sir. . . .'

'Oh, not ill, not ill. Marvelling, Mary Ann, marvelling.'

I would not give him the opportunity of telling me. I picked up the large bowl in which was the rising bread and edging him on one side as I staggered with it into the scullery I murmured: 'Out of my way, please, sir, it is dinner time or near, and I have much to do.'

He followed me into the scullery. 'But, Mary Ann, the miracle! The daughter of the groom and the cook is become a fine lady.'

Yesterday I had worn a gingham dress in blue checks, beautifully made with tiny pearl buttons down the front and a little frilled cape of the same stuff. It had cost me all of what amounts to five shillings. Today I was wearing a large starched white apron over one of my grey working dresses, but that too was exquisitely made by that clever Flemish dressmaker, it had a high neck with stand-up collar and straight cuffs and a skirt without flounces. 'All of five shillings,' I grunted.

'But it is not your clothes, Mary Ann, it is your speech and manner.'

I rattled out something in such broad Yorkshire that nobody other than a Yorkshireman could have understood. It was vulgar and uncomplimentary.

He laughed. He returned the insult and, annoyed though I was, I could not help, well, not laughing but smiling.

'Eeeh, Mary Ann! You're a right lass!' he returned enthusiastically and for an unexpected moment we stood face to face, smiling at one another.

'The young ladies are awaiting you, sir, in their . . . in their parlour.'

Hour after hour, day after day they sat there, stitching away, one supposed, at their work. They had a piano in there and sometimes a tinkle would reach my ears, miserably inept. There was also some kind of pipe or simple flute with a chilling note.

'Ask them to play for you . . . gipsy.' I couldn't resist it but I instantly skipped out of his reach and back into the kitchen where I buried the top half of myself in one of the deep cupboards. I felt ashamed because I had started what might well develop into a game of tig. I felt my temper rising more at my own indiscretion than anything else. I straightened up and waved him away: 'Go on, get thee out of my kitchen afoe I sling summat at thee!' I begged, the manners of the past twenty years falling about me like broken china.

He went and I breathed relief but I knew it was only momentary. Silas Clopton was going to prove himself a problem and I had enough problems on my mind. Above all I wished to be alone to read my lady's letter. He left the kitchen and I heard his step along the stone passage to the hall. I picked up the beaver hat which still lay upon the kitchen table and stealing after him down the passage I threw the hat into the hall and ran back into the kitchen. I can never be my age, that is one of my many troubles.

*

My dearest Mary Ann,

I should have heard if you had not arrived. I have had the shortest note from my Papa starting '*Bless you for sending her*' so that should be your first reward for what I realise is a sacrifice. Nothing but good can come of it, so if you have reservations and doubts about the wisdom of your action take heed and be assured that all will be well.

There has been another outbreak of cholera in the Chaussée d'Ixelles area, this time a mild one, thank God. But Monsieur le Comte has suggested that I send Bruno to him in Spa for a few weeks where he can continue his studies alone. He wishes me to go too and I hope to do so when I have arrangements made to replace you. Alas, it is not easy, you have made such a place for yourself in this home that it can never be the same without you. God send you back safely when your task is done.

I remain your loving friend,
Harriet d'Houdenard

THE END OF THE BEGINNING WRITTEN BY MARY ANN SHEFFIELD

FIVE

THE CONTINUATION WRITTEN BY HALLIWELL HOBSHAW

'NOTHING but good can come of it. . . .' Oh, Madame d'Houdenard, what a temptation to providence to use those words! Four middle-aged women virtually captive, and their gaoler a woman who has brought conservation to such a pitch that many would consider her quite out of her mind. For what was she saving her daughters, or for whom? For what was she saving her money? Was it for security for her four daughters? There had been, at the time of her second marriage, more than enough for a fine dowry in the form of a Trust for each and every one of the four; it was not possible that whilst spending on building new mills she felt she was betraying her off-spring.

Mary Ann timed her visits to the old men's flat carefully so that they would not coincide with the very rare visits of the mistress. Soon after Silas Clopton had closeted himself with the mistress, she fled across the yard with her first letter from Brussels to read it aloud to the old men.

'Oh, what a rush of a woman!' Mr Sheffield complained as he carefully chose a fresh piece of horn from the basket beside his chair. 'The master is not yet about, I have took him a cup of tea, he looks not so well this morning, Mary Ann. The mistress has called and after she had looked at him she said she would get Dr Lack from Harrogate to call "next time he is in the district". That may be months but she'll not pay him for the special visit, be the master half dead!'

The master did indeed look poorly and Mary Ann, after straightening his bedclothes, promised to bring him a tisane of a curative nature. But as she went back across the yard she felt sure suddenly that she had left her old Culpeper in Brussels, being amongst the possessions they had accumulated over the years and were unable to bring with them. She mentioned it to Anne-Marie who smiled secretly, as it were, and said that she had picked it out from the things they had left behind to be stored in an attic awaiting their return. 'I couldn't see you without your Culpeper for more than a few weeks, Mother!'

Mary Ann loved that old book; she and her lover Giles, strolling round the city of Brussels, had found it in the market at a stall which carried a large basket of old books.

N. CULPEPER'S
COMPLETE HERBAL
Consisting
of
A COMPREHENSIVE DESCRIPTION
of nearly all
BRITISH AND FOREIGN HERBS
with their
Medicinal Properties
and
DIRECTIONS FOR COMPOUNDING THE MEDICINES
extracted from them

There were directions for making and keeping distilled waters, syrups, juleps, decoctions, oils, electuaries, conserves, preserves, lohocks, ointments, plaisters, poultices, troches, pills and the way of fitting medicines to compound diseases, of all in this order. And when Anne-Marie handed it to her, Mary Ann put her arms round the neck of her daughter and kissed her warmly.

'What a strange little silent thing,' Mary Ann said, 'why did you say nothing about it?'

But it had been so ever since Anne-Marie was a tiny child. Secretive was a word which Mary Ann avoided mentally about her child but even at the age of three the child would wrap up small gifts, like a beautiful dead butterfly, and keep it for days before she would bring it out for her mother as a 'surprise'. To be secretive was to be 'needlessly reserved' according to Madame's English Dictionary, but to be 'reserved' meant to 'postpone use or enjoyment of . . .' which was a different matter and the word which Mary Ann preferred to use regarding her daughter.

During their fragmentary midday meal Mary Ann fingered through the herbal; nearly all the plants mentioned came 'under the dominion' of heavenly bodies. '*Mars owns the herb*', it said of Flax-weed, also called Toad-flax. Of Money-wort, called also Herb Twopence, it stated: '*Venus owns it*', and it is good for 'driving forth the dead child and after-birth'.

Mary Ann would chuckle with delighted laughter; she would declare that she consulted the book only 'for the laugh' and she now read out over the meal: 'Spignel (Broad Leaves, also called Baldmoney), *under the dominion of Mercury in Cancer* and an excellent plant in disorders of the stomach from phlegm, raw crude humours, wind and relaxations, ruchtations, loathings, colic, gripes, retention of the urine and the menses . . .' Mary Ann laughed so unrestrainedly, her apron thrown over her face, that her daughter smiled in sympathy. 'I reckon that's what I need,' Mary Ann cried, 'since it's good for "loathings".'

But the recipe for which she was looking was one she had used to great effect once when Madame d'Houdenard had bilious attacks. As every other herb, it would seem, was good for the liver, she took time and care over the search. The basis of the potion she had in mind was wormwood, a herb of Mars and, as Mary Ann said, laughingly, very commonly found in churchyards. The tops, used fresh-gathered, were excellent for the liver and had the capital side-effects of killing worms.

'The agony of drinking it . . . aside from other things, takes the patient's mind off their troubles; do you remember I gave it you once, little one, and you screamed the place down, very near, and wouldn't touch it after the first sip?'

Anne-Marie did remember, very well, and found nothing to smile about.

'But there was something else I mixed it with when I gave it to Madame . . .' Mary Ann flipped through the pages and finally found what she was seeking: 'Here we are, no wonder I couldn't ever remember, it has ten names: Crowfoot, Frog's foot, Goldknobs, Gold-cups, King's Knobs, Baffiners, Troil Flowers, Polts, Locket-gouleons and Butter-flowers, and it was praised greatly by Socrates. It blisters the tongue so it's worse than wormwood but it's also under the same dominion of Mars. . . .'

'Oh, Mother! Take care . . . you might do the old man some harm. . . .'

'Perhaps you're right, love, but it flowers *now*. . . .' She turned over the pages. She was taken by the description of Cuckoo-pint or Wake-Robin, that too belonging to Mars and about which N. Culpeper said authors had left large commendations, but for his part 'I have neither spoken with Dr Reason nor Dr Experience about it', and it happened to be one remedy not mentioned for liver troubles.

'Snakeweed and many other names but as common up in the North as heather. Your Grandma often used it and it flowers in May. I'll be off and get some now, I know where it grows, the narrow-leafed sort. And it's tasteless, I remember your Grandma often used to make your Grandad hold a leaf between his teeth when he had toothache.'

Mary Ann threw a shawl round her head and rushed away on her errand of mercy; Isaak was coming across the yard as she left: 'Go and help Anne-Marie with the washing up, there's a good lad,' Mary Ann cried.

*

What did the witches of Endor talk about as they sat day after day huddled together upon their blasted heath?

What did the four witch-like step-daughters of Mr Hobshaw talk about as they sat, day after day, week after week, year after year in their small room with permanently closed casements, stitching, playing their tinny piano, sipping frequent cups of tea which they made with their own silver kettle and inlaid tea caddy with the two locks?

At a guess, they talked about their ailments: their shortage of breath (because they rarely took exercise); the cat they did not have; the servants; Mr Clopton; the vicar; the curate; their indigestion; the trouble they had with their hair; the dog that had died of old age a long time ago, called Trusty; the geese they had which had to be disposed of because they ate too much; the imaginary cat's kittens; Isaak, the servants . . . and now (oh glory! they had the new servants), Mary Ann and Anne-Marie. So there was a constant sound of voices and all day long they talked, and they talked even after the sun had set because there were two bedrooms between them and two in each bedroom. They fell asleep early and slept the clock round, almost, worn out with talking. There was not time during the daylight hours to say all that they had to say about the new servants. The concensus was that these new servants were extravagant, not to be trusted because they were not good Yorkshire characters but folk with strange continental ways. Mary Ann was an absurd creature for her age, flying about like a girl of twenty-five with her slim waist and not bothering to cover her head often when she went out. But Anne-Marie, after the first few criticisms, was faultless, a young angel, a saint heavily burdened with the weight of responsibility for her frivolous and absurd mother.

After the first fortnight Anne-Marie could do no wrong, even though she played and laughed with Isaak in the afternoons. But nevertheless, it was important that Anne-Marie should be disciplined and kept in her place, even though she bore this fearful burden of her mother. Like mother, like daughter; she might well turn out a bad lot were she not kept under very strict supervision and, in due course, warranted a session in mental and moral discipline.

At the present moment they were carrying on an argument with their mother about the advisability of taking Anne-Marie to church on Sundays with them, for rain, hail or snow they set out every Sabbath wrapped to the eyes in their long tweed cloaks and tramped the mile there and the mile back.

Though nowhere near the flamboyant looks of her mother, Anne-Marie was of the sweetest turn of face, of soft fair hair, of tiny breasts (though they did not actually mention these in so many words), of child-like charm. And educated well above her station with the merest of foreign accents.

They had to bear in mind, of course, that Anne-Marie was a bastard and though there were more bastards in the village now than ever there were (Lavinia had made a black list and there were on it no less than nine children born blatantly out of wedlock!) it was only Christian charity to recognise them; if not like others are, still, it must be admitted, human beings. The vicar said so.

With their poor mother slaving and toiling, trying to make money to keep a roof over their heads, they must consider themselves lucky that they had not to perform the cooking and the household chores. What fortunate young women they must be, waited upon hand and foot, and they so near, so perilously near starvation. Mother said so.

One afternoon shortly after dinner, they watched Mary Ann flying out with a shawl round her head and shoulders. There was a front and a side window to their sitting-room so they could observe all the comings and goings other than those actually through the yard. She went running off towards the village and Anne-Marie must have been left alone to do the washing-up for the whole household. After discussing this for several minutes the eldest of the four ugly sisters went into the kitchen premises to sympathise with Anne-Marie, ostensibly, but in fact to find out where Mary Ann had gone.

She came staggering back into the sitting-room, clutching her breast as though suffering from a sudden heart attack. It was several seconds before she could regain her breath to recount what horrors she had witnessed. Anne-Marie and Isaak had been wrapped in each other's arms. After half an hour's excited questioning and discussion it turned out disappointingly that Isaak had had his arm across Anne-Marie's shoulders and together they were leaning over one of the stone slabs and prodding, with the end of a wooden spoon, an awakening butterfly, captive in its chrysalis for months, spreading its wings to welcome the warm sunshine which had crept round to the dairy window.

The verdict was returned that this had *gone too far*. Anne-Marie must be saved from herself; that child-like elf must not be ravished by the club-footed fetcher-of-the-milk and Mother must be called in to regularize the situation.

Mother was only too ready to 'regularize the situation': she issued a command that Isaak was not to come to the house at all. She did this with such pleasure and anticipation that her mouth actually watered and Mary Ann, standing before her to receive her orders on the next Monday morning, in fact saw a small trickle of fluid flowing from the side of her mouth.

'We have to remember, my good woman, that Anne-Marie had an unfortunate birth; she was misconceived, mistimed and she should have miscarried. . . .'

Mary Ann stepped forward and Mrs Hobshaw thought she was going to strike her but she simply allowed her fist to hit the table.

'Anne-Marie was conceived in great love,' she cried, 'by a

soldier who lost his life for his country within forty-eight hours. Give over, will you, give over such nasty talk, I'll not stand for it.' Unconsciously she spoke in her broadest Yorkshire as though making sure the mistress understood.

She at once answered: 'Talk to me like that again, and you'll walk straight out of this house and your baggage will be thrown after you from the back door. I'll have you begging in the streets of Leeds before I'll put up with it, Mary Ann.'

Mary Ann folded her arms and looked maddeningly complacent; she knew that, upon the death of the master, Anne-Marie would be in a position to throw the second wife and her gaggle of daughters out of Underscar even as completely as the mistress threatened for them both.

Perhaps the second Mrs Hobshaw's intolerable manner arose from the fear that Mr Hobshaw intended, or had actually carried out, generous endowments to his grand-daughter, born out of wedlock. Her hatred of Mary Ann now took on dimensions quite out of porportion to her status as servant. It was evident that her husband's intentions regarding what was to happen to his property upon his death had been used as an instrument for keeping the second Mrs Hobshaw in some sort of hold over her, otherwise neither Anne-Marie nor her mother would ever have been allowed to cross the threshold of Underscar.

Thus when Isaak arrived with the post and the milk the second Mrs Hobshaw marched out into the kitchen, forewarned of the arrival by one of the daughters, and ordered him to go back to the mill and continue his duties there; in future Anne-Marie would fetch the milk and the post, and she stood there in the kitchen waiting for him to depart upon the instant.

Anne-Marie happened to be at the top of the house dusting the bedrooms and knew nothing of this but when she did she set her lips tightly, a frown appeared between her brows and she became even more silent than usual.

And from then on, for someone with less stamina than Mary Ann, life became intolerable.

'We must hold out, my love,' Mary Ann told her daughter.

'Why?'

'Why indeed?'

But sitting upon the edge of her daughter's bed at a little while before midnight, the thoughts which Mary Ann had kept in a pent-up jumble for three or more weeks came pouring out.

'For many reasons, Anne-Marie, we must stay yet awhile. We have the upper hand, you must remember that!'

'How do you come to that idea?' Anne-Marie's whisper became louder.

'Ssh! She may well be listening at the door.' Mary Ann got up and opened wide the door to the landing. From there she had a full view in the dark, lightened by a skylight, of the wide shallow staircase up which the bales of wool used to be carried for winter storage. She sat down again at the top end of the bed, her arm round Anne-Marie; there being no pillows provided for the servants on the assumption that they would encourage lice, she leaned back against the iron bedstead.

'Our mistress in Brussels sent us to ease a difficult situation for her father, not to make things worse for him, and it is he only we must bear in mind, his welfare . . . not, in fact quite *only* because my father's welfare is also important, but his comfort and happiness are not at stake. Mr Hobshaw's are. Your grandfather is unimportant to the second wife's plans but Mr Hobshaw's life and, when it comes, death are very important indeed. And as you must have observed, dearest Anne-Marie, Mr Hobshaw is a man of peace, of *laissez-faire*; his books and his writing at his old desk are his happiness; there are many English gentlemen like him. A dear, dear soul but impractical, you understand? There is the question of the future of this place and the land which goes with it which has belonged to the Hobshaws since Adam was a boy. And there is the problem of new laws and new manner of life under the Reform Bill. Feudal systems disappearing, enclosures being enforced, and this means many small farmers dispossessed by so-called Commissions which means gentlemen sent by the Government to say who is to have what, distributing the Common Land in a manner which displeases as many as it pleases. . . .'

Mary Ann cleared her throat. Anne-Marie was cleverer than her, she reminded herself, and what the mother was actually thinking uncomfortably was: 'I reckon I'm teaching my grandmother to suck eggs!'

But from her absolute stillness she knew she had her daughter's attention. It was more than likely that Anne-Marie had heard all about the Reform Bill from the old Professor in Brussels, however she said nothing and let her mother stumble on.

And finally Mary Ann said that their troubles might soon be over. Mr Hobshaw had told her that he had plans in hand for his property and soon she and Anne-Marie and Mr Hobshaw were to go into the town and consult a solicitor about these plans which were to be made firm and legal and would cut out any question of that rich woman, now his wife, inheriting his property.

Once this was settled Mary Ann intended to persuade Mr Hobshaw to go back with them to Brussels with no time-limit. This was not going to be easy as the old man had a fierce independence but she would manage it somehow, with her dear lady behind her.

As for her fine old father . . . he was as occupied as one could hope for an old man in his position, wifeless and almost daughterless. He was as content and happy as anyone could wish and she had every intention of going through the village carefully and weeding out some nice woman, someone who had known him for a long time, to come up and clean and cook for him daily.

'So you see, love,' and Mary Ann put her arm round her daughter and gave her an encouraging squeeze, 'we just have to put up with and endure everything for the time being and soon, God willing, you will see . . . all will be well!'

But Anne-Marie's brow did not clear or her mouth turn up.

SIX

HOWEVER, for the moment all was very far indeed from well. It was as though their sentence had been intensified from hard work to Hard Labour. Firstly, the pantry door was now kept locked and each morning Mrs Hobshaw herself would come into the kitchen and picking up a basket she would go into the pantry and bring out the food rations for the day and she weighed out on the great scale a minute amount of sugar, butter, beans, flour, dried peas, and so on, consistent with her idea of the basic amount of food needed for continued existence. The rations for the dining-room were pushed together and a small group of the requirements for the kitchen would be separated with: 'And this is for you and Anne-Marie; you will be able to work much better upon an empty stomach.'

'Have you found out, then, how much we need to keep alive?' Mary Ann demanded.

And now two of the daughters in turn, two or three times a week, would traipse down to the village, carrying the large basket between them to do the shopping from a van which brought supplies of meat and the occasional fowl in a cart from the slaughter-house in the town.

It was assumed that the meat left over from the midday meal would serve, cold and congealed, for the servants. Very often there was none at all. Mary Ann could make a tasty something out of nothing and this she would do, charging

Anne-Marie to bring up in her pocket anything she could find in the village to supplement or replace what they were apparently 'allowed to have', on her way back with the post and *The Times* for Mr Hobshaw. Had it been winter-time the situation would have been well-nigh impossible. As it was, the cuckoo was constantly heard from down the clough and up on the moors the larks sang with all their strength, seeming never to pause to take a breath, and the sun occasionally shone warm and comforting so that they could sit out in the yard to clean the pewter and the morning washing-down at the pump in the stable was less agonizing than when they had first arrived.

Meanwhile Mary Ann waited for Mr Silas Clopton to fall in love with Anne-Marie and this she was sure would happen, with a sickening certainty. Furthermore, she could not foresee how they were to have a weekday off to take the journey into the town to see the lawyer with Mr Hobshaw, as he had promised.

Mr Silas Clopton had taken the habit of approaching the house across the moors and coming down the path to the yard and thus entering the house through the kitchen. Unwillingly Mary Ann set herself to be civil to him; the two old men across the yard would seem such a long way off, and isolated in the house she felt friendless. She was no longer permitted to take the meals across to them; the young ladies took it in turn and at every meal one of them would come into the kitchen and stand without speaking beside the table waiting for the laden tray. And later on the same one would go across the yard for the empty dishes and bang them down upon the side of the sink on her return.

Defying the mistress, she allowed Mr Silas Clopton's manner to grow more familiar and confidential; telling him nothing but allowing him to tell her anything that occurred to him, and she learned a great deal more than would have been approved by Mrs Hobshaw.

Small details at first emerged; he was hoping to buy wool from America and told her his reason for this in some detail. He hoped that he would find a market soon for their wares in the new United States. He would like to go himself because he was sure he would have a fine harvest, the Americans were aping European ways of life now that their journey was made easier by the fine new clippers; if he could go over there himself there was no limit to the orders he might bring back. But alas . . . he spread his hands to show how impossible this would be and when Mary Ann looked intelligently interested he explained that he could neither be in two places at once nor trust anyone with such an important mission. Besides, he had to keep an eye on the finishing touches to his new house. The carpets to be put down there were made in the mills, some of them, the newest, made in the Brussels style, that in the best rooms having a green background scattered with red roses—beautiful!

She told him about the fine carpets in the d'Houdenard ménage and how Madame took such pride in them and how they had to be brushed with the utmost care and how they were hand-made and she described the factory to which Madame had once taken her and all the brilliant piles of coloured wool. . . .

And this gave him to talk about the trouble connected with dyeing and the great vats he hoped before long to be able to buy.

But this pleasant state was not to last.

'What is going on between Mary Ann and Silas Clopton?' one of the sisters said at dinner in front of their mother.

'Nothing, I hope,' their mother replied but one of the girls knew better: 'Mary Ann and Silas Clopton knew one another when they were children.'

'How do you know?'

'I heard her telling Anne-Marie that he had been nothing more than a beggar.'

'You heard them talking together about him, indeed? What else was said?'

Flattered to have gained her mother's attention she went on: 'She told Anne-Marie that he begged from door to door and that in the winter the farmers would allow him to sleep in their barns in exchange for hay-making in the summer. And that he educated himself, there now!' She looked round triumphantly at her sisters, daring them to say this was impossible, since she was the only one who was still making an attempt to do just that: i.e. educate herself.

'We shall certainly have to put a stop to that!'

'He's after Anne-Marie . . .' one of them put in slyly.

'Nothing of the sort!' her mother cried. 'I'll have none of that talk.'

But Silas Clopton was now commanded not to come to the house through the stable yard but to rap on the front door and enter 'like a gentleman'.

*

'Christ,' Mr Hobshaw said cheerfully, 'they say, was given wormwood as a draught as He was dying upon the Cross, so I am in good company,' and bravely put the cup to his lips and valiantly swallowed the hot drink that Mary Ann had prepared for him, in one draught but with much spluttering and coughing.

'Give over,' Mary Ann laughed, 'it's not that bad!'

He brought out a large bandana handkerchief and mopped his damp face. I'll never get used to it.'

'It's cured you, this time, there's no need for another dose. You're looking fine! You have not been looking after yourself, that's the trouble. The mistress can send one of the young ladies over with your food if she so wishes, that'll not stop me coming over. It's tisanes you need, plenty of fluid; kidneys I would say was your trouble; you need a deal of fluid and I'll see you get it.'

'What a comfort you are to me! "My strength is as the strength of ten" when you are here, I can stand up to Her. Your dear father lets everything flow over his head, Sheffield fears not, neither does he hate; a fortunate man and a good man, he is happy in his old age.'

'He always has been, he's one of the lucky ones, sir. Contentment is a great blessing to any man or woman.'

'Sit down a minute, Mary Ann. I want to talk to you about my grand-daughter. We cannot leave things like this, you know. You have been here a month now . . . quite aside from the affairs about which I talked with you out on the moors the other day, Mary Ann . . . Anne-Marie cannot remain, to put it plainly, a "skivvy" for much longer. It is not good for a girl of her calibre.'

Mary Ann felt a great relief flooding over her. She had upon occasion spoken to Madame d'Houdenard about her hopes and aspirations for Anne-Marie. Indeed, she had talked about the kind of girl Anne-Marie was turning out to be. As a baby she had enchanted everybody . . . and this enchantment seemed to have held good over the years so that everyone in the d'Houdenard household accepted her as they had always known her.

Mr Hobshaw said that in his opinion it was a great pity Anne-Marie had left the household of Madame's Uncle Peter, the Professor, and went on for some little time regarding opportunities for Anne-Marie to meet young people of similar intelligence and so on.

Mary Ann knew now that the time had come to keep back nothing; she realised that the opportunity to speak her mind might never occur again in this world and if there was an opportunity in the next world it would certainly be too late. In her nervous anxiety to get it out before she changed her mind she started to speak in French: '*Monsieur, il me faut . . .*' then apologised and changed to English. It was quite clear that she was nervous and abashed by what she intended to say and she had several new starts. It was about Bruno . . . Bruno who was a very fine young man indeed both to look at and in his character. He was the son of a nobleman and it would be folly for him to become attached to Anne-Marie.

But sometimes very young men needed to marry . . . Mary Ann stammered on, and 'Anne-Marie has always been there, in a manner of speaking, they have grown up together'. And now Bruno was at the Université it was, to say the least of it, an undesirable distraction to have Anne-Marie before his eyes every evening when he should be at work in his room. It was not unknown for young men, very young men, to marry the girl *who was there* and later on in life, when they had matured, they would, as it were, 'grow out of' the girl they had so much loved when they were nineteen.

Mr Hobshaw nodded, giving his attention to his pipe; he looked solemn and contemplative and finally he said that he agreed with Mary Ann, the word she sought was 'propinquity', he said, 'meaning nearness, and even meaning "kinship".'

Encouraged by his kind sympathy Mary Ann went further than she would ever have dared and said: 'So you deliberately recall . . . they are cousins!'

Mr Hobshaw said the marriage of cousins was no serious disadvantage, it was a matter of what qualities were inherited, if there be a bad quality and chance make it that this bad quality be inherent in both marriage partners, there might be trouble in the children of the marriage but in the main . . . there are many happily married cousins.

Then after a long pause Mr Hobshaw said it might be as well that she be removed from Bruno's actual gaze every day of his life but that if Bruno were to feel she was the girl for his life, maybe he would seek her out when he was older.

'But what is seriously worrying me, Mary Ann, is the quality of life here, up on our lonely and sometimes savage moorland. We love it, you and I, we were born here and when I look back and remember the foreign places in which I have lived in His Majesty's service, I remember distinctly how, in my heart of hearts, wherever that may be, I have wished to be back here in Underscar.' He looked questioningly at Mary Ann.

'It is not so with me though I was happy here as a child, I find the place has gone sour on me.'

'I know why that is, and so do you! You are sensitive to atmosphere, Mary Ann. For centuries the house has been occupied by simple, yes, simple, contented folk, you could feel it in the air; it has never changed occupants and the folk living here were satisfied and asked for nothing more than the constant rising of the sun and the setting of the moon to be maintained. Now, everything is changing, you can feel it in the very air. The condition of the poor is wonderfully altered and thank God for it; less and less folk, we hope, will starve in the streets once this terrible Irish famine is over. But a middle class is being created; the yeoman is becoming a manufacturer and progress means more and more . . . and more. They are not satisfied with enough, they want a lot more than enough. Eeh dear! Where will it all end? And this all brings me to the feet of an idea, Mary Ann. Not a good idea, I admit. But an idea. What can a girl, and I could even call Anne-Marie an educated girl as educated girls go (which they hardly do!) . . . what can a girl, as I ask myself, employ herself with beyond her needlework and the helping of the mistress of the house with gentle pursuits such as making preserves? She can do something, about which you know as well as I.'

'Governess?'

'Quite so. Bi-lingual she would be a godsend to any well-to-do parents with young children they wish to educate, both boys and girls, because the boys who do not go away to school are so often taught by the parson of the district and what parson is bi-lingual? One or two, perhaps, but they are the exception.'

Yes, but . . . Mary Ann thought . . . this would mean we were here for ever.

'What are you thinking, Mary Ann?' he asked, reading her thoughts. 'That this would mean you stayed here for ever?'

She nodded.

Very gently and kindly he said: 'Well then, my dear, it hurts me very much to have to say this, but we cannot have it both ways. If, amongst my friends, I could find a family who would readily take Anne-Marie as a governess, and I feel sure I could, you, as a good mother, would feel you must stay in the same part of the world as your young daughter, then . . .' he held his hands wide apart as though they were empty and he desolate.

Mary Ann could not answer, she stared down at her own hands nervously clasping and unclasping themselves upon her white-aproned lap.

'The trouble is. . . .'

'Go on, my dear.'

'The trouble is that I no longer understand my daughter. Or should I say, since we left home, I mean Brussels, I find, perhaps, that I have never had the opportunity or even the need to understand her. She was there . . . and the apple of my eyes. Under different, very different circumstances, I find her suddenly a stranger.'

'An unknown quantity?'

'I cannot understand a number of things. Why has she set to work without much complaint to do what in Brussels the scullion and kitchen maids did, and a lot more besides? A young girl of the very finest would grumble at the work she has to do and the exact amount of food that is doled out to us. I cannot help but wonder. . . .'

'Wonder what?'

'Now I become fanciful but in trying to . . . to understand her, I am become imaginative . . . perhaps. But I wonder whether she . . . whether she has made a pact with young Bruno. Whether, perhaps, she has promised herself to him and he to her. "Wait for me, wait until I am through the

Université, I will come for you, Anne-Marie." There's imagination for you!'

Mr Hobshaw knocked out his pipe in the hearth and for a long time scratched the edge of his hairy ear contemplatively. Then he said that she would have to observe carefully; with Anne-Marie all day long, she was the one who could best be relied upon to make discoveries. With him Anne-Marie was simply the pleasant young girl talking to an old, old man. 'I bore her.'

Mary Ann protested but she knew he was right. She also felt a leaden despair. Were they to continue this despicable life indefinitely? She did not know how long she would be able to hold out and then, suddenly, the big head of steam which she was trying so faithfully to keep under control would burst out of its bounds and she would shriek and shout and throw things about and nothing but hurting somebody in the process would quieten her. She could stick anything, she told herself, any ill-treatment whatever, so long as she saw an end to it.

But now she could not.

*

'Where are you going, Anne-Marie?'

'I am going down to the village to see Isaak!'

Mary Ann felt, quite literally, her heart shrivel.' *Ca commence*,' was what she said, what they all said, when the sound of the guns from Waterloo made everybody's hearts shrivel.

She had cleared away and washed up the supper things; there was no need to bank up the stove for the night, the evening was warm, the sky pearly-pink and the blackbird orchestra tuning up.

'But . . . you will not walk back in the dark?'

'Not alone!'

Mary Ann wrung her hands, then held them tightly together in an effort to behave in a proper manner. 'Anne-Marie, my little love . . . you know, you know that should not be.'

She returned snappishly in French: 'Then you do not trust me?'

Mary Ann could not answer, words crowded into her mind but would not come out of her mouth. It was as though she were choking. Anne-Marie's face relaxed, she relented. 'You object to my walking back with poor Isaak, then?'

Relieved, Mary Ann said she did not object, if it were poor Isaak who would bring her home. She felt this to be a big concession and congratulated herself as she made it.

'He lives in that pleasant thatched cottage next to the church with his mother, we will walk round the graveyard and sit upon the seat planted between those two yew trees.'

'And what will you talk about, Anne-Marie?' she asked in real surprise.

'I am educating him, poor boy.'

'In what?'

'History. That is what Bruno was teaching me.'

'*Vraiment!*'

'*Oui, vraiment, Maman!*'

'Then take a shawl with you,' Mary Ann said, quite defeated.

*

It was as though Mary Ann and the second Mrs Hobshaw were two female cats stalking round and round each other stiff-legged, each having a deep mistrust for the other, each seeing in the other a woman of much more than the average brains and neither believing the other someone of goodwill. It would be difficult indeed to imagine that the second Mrs Hobshaw had goodwill towards anybody, alternatively, there were those who might have guessed her to be not nearly as unpleasant as she appeared to be. To an outsider her four daughters gave the appearance of being, at least, civil and obedient and up to a point intent upon their mother's welfare.

'But nothing will come of nothing,' Mary Ann actually told herself aloud and in the small hours, as she threw herself about on her miserable straw mattress, she brought out into the open, for inspection, trenchant thoughts which might or might not 'have nothing to do with the price of meat'.

She had been spoilt, was a favourite penetrating thought, she had been more lucky than most women with the wonderfully friendly countrywoman who was her mistress in Belgium. A woman of great common sense and sensibility, married into European nobility whose only close friend was a girl from her Yorkshire home; Mary Ann had been treated like a sister, travelling to and from Paris and to the spas of Europe at a time when things were happening that would mark out the shape of things to come for a long time ahead.

Brussels for many years after the Napoleonic Wars was a town filled with English people who went to live there to have their children educated at less cost than in Britain; 'everybody who was anybody', as they say, found themselves in Brussels or Paris in those years after Waterloo. There were great and famous people to be seen and for the time being that part of Western Europe seemed to be the centre of the world. For a woman who had '. . . a daughter for her cradle 'ere she had a husband for her bed', Mary Ann was amongst the most fortunate. She was loved a great deal more by her mistress and family, it would seem, for this reason, added to the fact that she was a happy, lustrous being: cheerful, content and passionately devoted to the family with whom she lived.

But how changed was her life and how suddenly!

Had the time come to count the cost? Mary Ann asked herself. She had returned to her old home where, as a child, she had been so happy, to find it as though it were a different place. Not only the household itself but the villages and, looking at the larger picture, the whole of England.

No longer an agricultural society, as when she had left home at eighteen, the very village in which she was born had altered out of knowledge. This morbid and fantastic worship of the good God with whom Mary Ann had thought herself upon reasonable terms, seemed now to be mixed up with a weird sadism; there were small children in the village who wished to die, in order to be at Eternal Bliss with their Lord.

It seemed all to have started with a preacher to the people in the last century called John Wesley, but now this man's preaching had outlived him and grown out of all proportion to a point when Mary Ann declared to herself: 'It makes me retch.'

These 'methodical' people had succeeded in stamping out the joy of living to an extraordinary extent, Mary Ann had discovered, and furthermore they had engendered a vile loathing, a hatred they rejoiced in, waving it in her face like a flag of which they were proud. 'You are a Catholic!' and therefore foul, 'hanging would be far too good for you'.

Mary Ann was not, in fact, a Catholic but Anne-Marie was. From some deep-seated Yorkshire stubbornness, Mary Ann had refused to become one. But she was willingly persuaded to have Anne-Marie baptised into the Catholic Church and on Sundays in Brussels she sent Anne-Marie to the Catholic Church with the whole d'Houdenard family whilst she, 'chapel' though she was, stumped off independently to the Chapel Royal where the English Protestant services were then held.

Mary Ann, like everybody else who was literate, had read the first two parts of a book called *The Fairchild Family*, which she had borrowed from the English library in Brussels. The three English children about whom she had hoped to read to Anne-Marie, Emily, Lucy and Henry, had been taken to see the corpse of a murderer, hanging on a gibbet at a cross-roads, in chains, and this was supposed to be a warning against their occasional quarrelling. The reading to Anne-Marie of this book had been anticipated as a treat but Mary Ann had been so shocked and grieved that she had returned the book to the library and had hoped that Anne-Marie would not soon discover it for herself.

Thus Mary Ann, in these still small hours, would chide herself for having harboured suspicious thoughts about Isaak Delph who was, no doubt, a young man a great deal 'holier' than Anne-Marie. She might well sit placidly upon a seat between the two yew trees outside the church but the young man she was with might well have his mind's eye fixed upon hell fire and other miserable ends, since his mother was burning 'chapel'.

*

Nevertheless, refined 'European' though she might well be, Mary Ann fundamentally was a Yorkshire-born woman of great common sense and one who spoke her mind with the utmost readiness. Nothing could wipe that off the inborn pattern in which she was moulded. Her parents were not among those who 'catch' a religious trend as though it were the measles. But she had an uneasy suspicion that the second Mrs Hobshaw, every particle as Northern as herself, had a great number of inherited qualities which were even less desirable than those which she had just recognised in her countrymen and women. Her folk were steadfast, they were outspoken, they were reasonably brave, but they could be meaner than anyone else on earth. And they could appear to be without love to a terrifying extent; they lacked gentleness and, she had reluctantly to admit, there were many who lacked kindness, the ordinary milk of human kindness.

Mary Ann had known kindness to an unusual degree in her Mistress d'Houdenard, and in her parents, but she knew, nevertheless, that the lack of it was in the air, this unkindness, and she recognised it in her new mistress to a frightening degree.

When opportunity arose she declared: 'I shall not stay here any longer if more consideration is not shown to my daughter and myself. In the matter of a few weeks, we have been treated as never before in our lives.'

'Mary Ann, I am afraid you have been badly spoiled by my

husband's daughter, Harriet; she has made far too much fuss of you over the years. You must bear in mind that people like this Harriet are simple in mind. . . .'

'Not at all!'

'Are simple to the point of imbecility.'

'You will take that back . . . !' Mary Ann screamed.

'Oh, Mary Ann, how wild and fierce you are! I declare, your dear mother, who was cook here for so long, would be ashamed of you. . . .'

Mary Ann flung herself about, making as though to leave the office, but returning, pushing back her hair distractedly. 'You've no right, no right at all to speak so of my dear mother. . . .'

'And Sheffield, your father, Mary Ann. He may not be now, but in the past he was ashamed of you, bitterly ashamed. It is only recently, in his old age, that he has not borne hard thoughts towards you, thoughts arising from the hard words I have myself heard him utter when I came here as a bride.'

BRIDE! A curious description of the second Mrs Hobshaw!

'You would talk the hind leg off a donkey,' she cried, 'you think you can get the better of me . . . but you will see that you cannot. . . .'

'And as the old cock crows, the young one larns,' the mistress went on implacably, 'your little Anne-Marie is off down the village, wrapped in her summer shawl, as soon as she has, or even has not, completed her work!'

Mary Ann had as much to say to her in return as she received but was so angry that the last thing she could remember saying to her mistress at that time was: 'You do not deserve to be alive in this world where there are still things to enjoy and make for happiness. . . .'

After this angry exchange the family departed for Church upon a Sabbath morning. The next day Silas Clopton must have been consulted about the servants. He came into the kitchen from the office as Mary Ann was preparing the dinner and he came, evidently, as a mediator. 'I would fain understand, Mary Ann, how a woman of your sensibility can lose your temper so rapidly with a . . . well, I must say, a woman over whom you have such great advantages.'

Mary Ann snorted, she could see no advantages that she had over the mistress. Apart from any such 'advantages he might have in mind' there was the little matter of food. The young ladies sat in a stuffy room all the day round whilst she and Anne-Marie were expected to do the work of half a dozen; these same young ladies ate ravenously and had ample food but the rations allowed to Mary Ann and Anne-Marie were parsimonious to a degree. 'Never a cup of tea nor a mug of small beer; both are kept locked away and there is so little milk it has to be watered down. And the butter . . . we have "special" butter and it is uneatable.'

'You don't understand, Mary Ann. . . .'

'I do not!'

'You take it for granted that the mills are grinding out gold whereas we have had a great deal of trouble. We are now going through a period when every penny we make has to be ploughed back; we have to do bold actions and not all of them are successful. Some innovations which have cost much money succeed from the start . . . others take time to get established . . . other things are a loss from the start, it is a testing time . . . so you see, my lady has to go canny and to keep a reserve of capital to avoid sudden bankruptcy. . . .'

'Now, now, Silas Clopton! And you building that brick mansion up yonder, do not try to pull wool over my eyes! You are what the villagers call "booming" down there at the mills.'

'Well, if you will not believe me I cannot help it. But you must remember, Mary Ann, the pauper I was, the beggar at the gate. Of course you do! If you pretend not to recall it you might in the least grant that I can never forget it for a day, nor for an hour. And withal I have educated myself up to a point. And, Mary Ann, I did not receive much charity, upon my word, I did not! But I stayed here in this district because I had no money to go anywhere else and now that I have taken root here, I shall show them, indeed I will!'

And then for a while he walked up and down the kitchen, thoughtful. It was as though he were deciding whether or not he should say more. Finally he came up to the table where she was grating cheese and asked her straight why, if things were so wretched for them, did they stay?

'We must stay, Silas Clopton, though God knows we do not wish to. My mistress has asked me to do so because she is unhappy about her father and well might she be so. That the old man has found his own home so uncomfortable, to say the least of it, that he has removed himself to a room over the stables is proof.'

'Proof of what?'

'Of the desire for him to . . . to leave the house, to be unhappy, and if I must say it, the wish to have him out of the way by death at best and by ill-treatment if death fails. There you are, Silas Clopton, do not accuse me of mincing my words, will you? You've got it straight and you can tell who you like. We thought he might be persuaded to go to Brussels and live in the d'Houdenard household but no amount of persuasion has caused him to do so. But I'll tell you what, Silas Clopton, I don't reckon much on your progress ideas, there's ever such a nasty air around here, very different from when I was a child here. I was taught to love God and I reckon I did but now they're taught to fear Him and there's some nasty things told the children about the way they'll burn in Hell if they don't do this and that. Love one another, we've been brought up to think, but there's no love lost over folk that believe different from other folk, like the Catholics. They believe Catholics regular downright wicked . . . eeh! I don't know . . .' and now Mary Ann had talked herself into such a state that she threw her apron over her head and wept.

'You'll get used to it,' Silas Clopton said in a clumsy attempt to cheer her up. 'It's only you've lived so long away from home . . . you've lost touch. There has been changes but they're not as bad as all that!'

Since you can't go on crying for long when it's dinner time Mary Ann had to dry her tears and, when he felt she was in a condition to listen, Silas Clopton said he had his ideas for her and one was, that she should get herself wed, at long last.

'Who to?' she asked, astonished.

'To me!'

'Give over!' she begged.

Silas said that far from giving over, he had not started yet.

And Mary Ann suggested he keep his big mouth shut because marry him would be the last thing she would do.

'When will that be, then?' he queried.

It was a way of saying *never*, had he not heard it?

He said that talking about never, he had never yet asked a woman to marry him and Mary Ann, now having left her ladyhood a long way behind and still steaming with indignation, gave it as her opinion that he was a dirty young lecher. But having embarked upon what had evidently become a burning subject he ignored it but went on to assure her that it would be the best thing that could happen to her, marrying him. He did not go in for love or any of that but there would be many advantages in the marriage, aside from the question of a husband for her bed. There would be no house like it in the whole West Riding. Whereas Mrs Hobshaw had to scrape and save for improvement in the business, he had saved, all these years, he had saved for the one thing he had always wanted, not a roof over his head so much as a damned fine roof over his head. 'We'll be gentry afore we'm done!' His Yorkshire accent increased in proportion to his eagerness.

It would be a house, when finished, that any woman would be proud to be mistress of, he expatiated upon the glories for some time and finally, in an irrisistible outburst, he said: 'But what mistress of my house can I have, if it's not you? I've got to have a mistress to match, eh? Don't you agree? You've got the looks, Mary Ann, by God you have. You've got the figure, you look a lady even if you don't sound one, not when you're talking to me, anyway. And you've a lot of good native nowse. So you make up your mind and marry me, luv, you'll never regret it.'

'But you'd need a son to inherit and it 'ud be a miracle if I gave you one. What about our Anne-Marie?' Mary Ann shocked herself, so recently she had dreaded Silas Clopton as the dangerous Raper of her youth but now she, upon the moment, changed her mind and saw the possibility of a fine marriage for her daughter. She felt herself an opportunist, but told herself folk in her position had to be.

He turned away with a grimace: 'She's not my type. I don't understand her.'

Nor do I, Mary Ann thought but did not say, and at this moment Anne-Marie came in carrying broom and dust-pan. She put them down and started pulling down her sleeves.

'It's dinner time, Mother.' She pointed to the clock.

Silas Clopton became noisy and verging upon the rowdy, he asked Anne-Marie: 'How's the little one today?' and, 'You look after your mother, girl, she's a gem.'

Anne-Marie did not answer but looked annoyed whilst Silas Clopton picked up his cane and made much of putting on his hat before the fly-blown fragment of looking-glass propped up against the plates upon the dresser. He went out backwards into the yard, waving his stick at Mary Ann and saying: 'Think on, girl, now think on what I've said. You just think on, there's a lot to be said for it, think on now. . . .'

Anne-Marie slowly and carefully took off her soiled household apron and reached for the starched one she used when serving meals. She gathered her long straight hair into her hands and took the ribbon with which she tied it out of her pocket, and wrenching her hair back in the most unbecoming manner possible, she tied it tightly behind.

'Miss Lavinia is not well, she has retired to her bed and has asked me for one of your tizanes.'

'What is wrong with her?'

'She is not hungry: she looks ill and she has vomited.'

'Liver,' Mary Ann said promptly. 'Apple cider vinegar and honey, a small quantity but that is cold and,' she remembered, 'the honey is locked up.'

This reminded her that she had not carried out into the sun the vinegar she had just made to be used in two years' time. 'Help me out of the way with this. . . .' They carried the huge earthenware vessel into the yard where it would be in the warmth of the sun all summer, and put a tile over the bung-hole. 'I know what she must have . . . wormwood,' and Mary Ann smiled to herself.

'She'll never drink it!' Anne-Marie exclaimed.

Mary Ann put the shredded herb into a tumbler and poured on it hot water from the kettle on the hob.

'Tek her that,' she said shortly.

SEVEN

THERE was something going on in the stable yard. Mary Ann stood at the kitchen door and, shading her eyes with her hands from the bright morning sun, she cried: 'What's to do, Father?'

'The master. He's riding the cob into town, it's Quarter Sessions. Drat this harness.'

Mary Ann slipped on her clogs because although it had stopped raining there were puddles between the cobbles, and went across the yard to help him with the harness. 'It's too old, I reckon,' Sheffield said disgustedly, 'but if he was to buy a new one there'd be such a screaming and a screeching as ud be heard down in t'village from her who casts up the sums; that's all she's any good for, casting up sums!'

'I thought he'd retired from the bench.'

'Oh aye, he's retired from Chief Magistrate but he keeps on at the bench. Gives him summat to do, like.'

'You don't reckon you should go with him, Father?'

'Go with him? There's nowt I can ride; the pony is as old as Methuselah; oh, I'd go with him with pleasure but it's not possible when you're living on the smell of an oily rag. I do go with him when he takes the gig, in livery too but it's rare that happens these days.'

And when Mr Hobshaw came down the worn stone steps, without the handrail, Mary Ann was proud of him. He stood erect in his best suit and his hat worn slightly to one side in imitation of the Duke and a good pair of gloves on his gnarled hands.

He came straight up to Mary Ann who, from sheer force of habit, curtsied very slightly as she had been taught as a child. 'That little matter we spoke about . . . the governess idea. I intend . . . I shall be dining at the Beauchamp Arms with some of my fellow magistrates and I will make inquiries. I may hear of something for our girl . . .' he nodded conspiratorially and leaped into the saddle before Sheffield could give him any assistance.

Today he looked a fit and well old man, a fine specimen for his age and something of the kind must have been in his mind when he looked down at Mary Ann and said pleasantly that the draughts she had been giving him had done him a world of good, acting not only as a cure for liver trouble but as a fine tonic. And as he spoke he looked beyond Mary Ann and, with crop in hand, touched his hat. As he rode out of the yard Mary Ann looked behind her and saw the dark spectre-like figure of her mistress standing in the kitchen doorway, watching the departure. Sheffield turned and went back into the stable with his typical self-contained walk, as though his boots were full of bunions.

Mary Ann was, as it were, caught. She mumbled a 'good-morning' and made as though to push past the mistress.

The sight of the woman aroused such curiosity in Mary Ann that no sooner did she see her than she fell a-wondering, as she called it to herself.

She fell a-wondering as to whether she was a real woman and not something that had no existence other than in the mind; withal capable of causing infinite unhappiness. She walked towards her seeing herself taking hold of the neck of her terrible cloak which she always held clutched tightly as though she were cold, and tearing it from her crying: 'Let's look at you and see if you're a real woman and not a ghoul!'

She stared silently at Mary Ann and Mary Ann had perforce to stare silently back at her because she did not move aside to let her pass.

Mary Ann took a deep breath and said that the master was indeed a different man; she would have pleasure in telling her mistress so when she next wrote. And then out of her mouth came words which Mary Ann had had no intention of uttering, they fell from her lips involuntarily because she could not simply stand there, her entry so firmly and intentionally blocked, without saying anything and since it befell that she must be the one to speak, she spoke pleasant words because, though quick-tempered, it was not in her nature to quarrel, she preferred to be on a good footing with everybody.

'What a pity,' she remarked, 'that the master does not return to his own comfortable home; he fares not too badly in the loft up there but it grieves me very much that I do not see him in his own place. . . .'

'It grieves you, Mary Ann! Is that so? Well, it grieves me a great deal more, I can tell you. It is his own choice to live up there with your father and he has persisted in this absurdity for months now. He chooses to live with the old groom rather than with his wife.'

Mary Ann stood but half-a-dozen feet from her and simply looked now, without a word, since she was keeping words firmly behind her teeth, and these words were: There must be some reason for his actions. Since you are not newly married . . . he has resided with you, how long, ten years? Why, after all this time?

As though she had read the unspoken words, the mistress astonishingly answered the unspoken question with: 'He begged me to marry him, upon his knees.'

Mary Ann threw out her hands as though pushing away from her such extravagant assertions. 'He adored his first wife,' she went on bitterly, 'and after her death he could not even continue with his career, he was a man . . . bereft and out of his senses. He was desperate and . . . he made wrong decisions as so often happens after a bereavement; people make wrong decisions. I was a wrong decision. Quite simple . . .' and she at last took her black eyes, shrunk into their dark caves, off Mary Ann and said: 'That cuckoo drives me mad. All day long . . . all day long!' and screwing and unscrewing her clenched hands she passed Mary Ann and went towards the stables where she was going to annoy Mr Sheffield, Mary Ann knew.

And back in her own domain Mary Ann picked up the remnants of a once full sack and threw the potatoes into the sink, then poured a bucket of cold water from the pump over them and started furiously to peel them for dinner. There were the remains of another sack, the potatoes mushy with age, which Mary Ann had been instructed were for the two servants but these she had taken out and thrown upon the midden last week. Perhaps the mistress had found them, in her slow peregrinations round the messuage; and perhaps, Mary Ann thought, she had respected that sight of the rejected potatoes. It could even be that the mistress liked to have someone to stand up to her and disobey her, since everybody else in the house dreaded her. It could be that Mr Hobshaw, the mildest of men, could no more live happily with her than Mary Ann could make an eatable sauce of chalk and cheese.

Up to now the mistress had been an unpleasant object of one dimension, that is, she simply displaced air, something that Mary Ann found unbearable. But now Mary Ann decided, as she peeled potatoes at a remarkable speed, there were distinct possibilities that she could be a woman of sorts. But what sort?

If Mary Ann had thought those few moments at the back door in the morning sun and the sound of the cuckoo had been the start of a break-up of the ice, she was wrong. It was as though the mistress was trying to compensate for having spoken to Mary Ann on a level; she made the rest of the day a hell for everybody. Even the daughters, as the sun shone and the birds sang and the cuckoo joked, were commanded to turn out the linen room, a marathon task which it would seem had never been attended to from the time of the first Mrs Hobshaw. It had been one of the smaller retiring rooms which the Jacobeans had used for lavatories, of which there were several in the house; apart from the linen press it was now used for hanging clothes from nails on the walls. This closet was grey with grime and Anne-Marie was first told to scrub it from top to bottom. When it was quite obvious that it was not a good plan, the plaster being in such bad condition, she was told to fetch bucket and brush from the stable and mix whitewash and get on with it. Thus Anne-Marie spent the whole day, until the light failed, covering the walls, the floor and herself, with whitewash. Mary Ann had finally to hold her under the pump and work the handle with one hand, until her hair was clean.

At sundown the kitchen range was stacked up, very much against the rules at that time of night, in order to dry Anne-Marie's hair and whilst it dried Anne-Marie wept quietly from the sheer misery of her tiredness.

'We cannot go on like this, Anne-Marie. Either I shall send you back to Brussels post-haste or you must take work more suited to you physically. We may be servants but we have never been used to work like this; it does not matter so much for me since I am the child of working-class parents and have a strong physique . . . but you . . . I declare, I shall lose you if you go on like this.'

And then she brought up the subject she had discussed with Mr Hobshaw and asked Anne-Marie if she would like to take a temporary post teaching; Mr Hobshaw had himself suggested it and had this day dined in the town with friends of his on the bench. There might soon be news of a possible position. Failing that, they could perhaps advertise for an engagement in a school.

But Anne-Marie seemed unable to stop weeping and Mary Ann became considerably concerned because though she often cried she did not cry with the despair of the present. It was not consonant with the great pluck and physical energy she had shown at Underscar in the past weeks since their arrival and which Mary Ann had wordlessly admired so much.

She achieved no break-through into her daughter's unhappiness; both went to bed quite exhausted and Mary Ann fell asleep in the near dark whilst the blackbird sang its last song.

*

All the ancient yellow bedlinen was now stacked in wobbling mounds against the walls on the landing and the young ladies suffered from attacks of the 'vapours' owing to undue physical exertion. One of them lay on the horse-hair sofa in the morning-room after breakfast, another of them sat moaning in the rocking-chair, a third stayed in bed and made no appearance all day, and Miss Lavinia came constantly into the kitchen to revive herself with draughts of vinegar and water, taking the tumblers into the morning-room after having carefully unlocked the store cupboard where the honey was kept adding a spoonful of this to her beverage and quickly putting the honey away, lest the servants should even set an eye upon it. Mary Ann knew how much of a reviver this was and would dearly have liked to ask for some for her exhausted daughter but refrained from doing so because of the good terms she had been on with the mistress for that few minutes; the request would so annoy the second Mrs Hobshaw that Mary Ann felt it might wipe out any regard for her that the second Mrs Hobshaw might possibly have felt. It was essential, Mary Ann knew, that in order to find out what the state of affairs truly was, she must tread with the utmost care, otherwise their return to Brussels would be delayed unendurably.

Mary Ann was fully aware of exactly what Madame d'Houdenard wanted of her, as she always was, and she would not return until her task was done and she could give a complete story of the events at her old home, to Madame.

In the meantime, Mary Ann was angry and her temper was such that she could not keep it to herself but had to let it escape, like a big head of steam which it is preferable to release to avoid an explosion. She set Anne-Marie to the milder tasks whilst she took over Anne-Marie's rough work and she was vigorously rubbing the hall hearth with whitestone, which had to be done every day though nobody ever stepped upon it, when Silas Clopton came obediently to the front door. As it was a fine spring morning again, he stepped inside, doffing his hat and putting his stick carefully down beside it on a hall chair.

He came over to Mary Ann and stood watching her, which infuriated her to the point of making her look over her shoulder and shout, 'Have you nothing better to do than watch your betters working, yer great gowk!'

Gone, gone alas! was the elegant lady from Brussels. She stood up and indignantly waved the scrubbing brush in his face. There were five snooping women about the house (though he was not to know that one was confined to her bed) and though he had spent ten years of subservience to them and deference to their virginity, he now threw their great regard for him to the winds. He seized Mary Ann, knocking the pail out of her hand so that it spilt as it fell with a great clatter, then with a big shout of laughter he swung her into the desired position and kissed her enthusiastically and with great enjoyment and Mary Ann kissed him back, watched from the door of the sitting-room by Miss Lavinia who, with glass in hand, was sipping the last of her vinegar and honey.

'E . . . E . . . H!' Mary Ann exclaimed when she had stopped first kissing and then laughing, 'E . . . E . . . H!' She brushed herself down, straightening her cap, and joining again in Silas Clopton's laughter she gave him a playful slap. 'Just as well,' she spluttered, 'I wasn't a bit older when that happened last . . .' Silas Clopton knew to what she referred and joined in their unsuitable laughter.

'That's my Mary Ann,' Silas Clopton wiped his mouth with the back of his hand as though he had just enjoyed a good meal. 'I knew all the time you wasn't a lady underneath and thank God for it.'

Miss Lavinia sniffed loudly to make her presence known but Silas Clopton merely glanced at her as he stooped, snatching the floor cloth from Mary Ann, and ineffectively mopped up the major amount of water upon the stone flags.

He handed the bucket to Mary Ann and as she turned away he gave her a friendly slap upon the behind.

'Now, Miss Lavinia, tell your mother that and I'll wring your bloody neck.'

Later, when his business of the day was over he came with his hat and stick through the kitchen, contrary to the new regulations.

'The trouble is,' Mary Ann said, 'we must endure. I have to get to the truth of all this afore I get usselves off back to Brussels. I owe it to my lady.'

'But, Mary Ann, what further "truth" do you seek?'

'Not one single "truth" but a whole. Twenty years ago there was no more revered name in the West Riding than Hobshaw of Underscar and there was no family more proud to serve them than the Sheffields. What are they now come to? My lady believes that her father is being drained to the last halfpenny and not only drained of his worldly possessions but of all dignity and prestige. Though I've had the sight of the old dignity as the master went off to the Quarter Sessions. But, for example, what a miserable cob he rode!'

'Why does your mistress in Brussels, the legendary Harriet, not come and find out for herself?'

'Think, Silas Clopton, think!' Mary Ann cried. 'She has her own troubles with an invalid husband and three sons! And besides, she would be entering her father's house now in the hands of another woman and four other useless hags. . . .'

'Your language, Mary Ann . . .' but he said it teasingly.

'She cannot abide the mistress here,' Mary Ann murmured in a low voice but sourly.

Silas Clopton came closer to Mary Ann. He almost whispered: 'Do not make a fool of yourself, Mary Ann.'

She stopped chopping up onion and bent her ear towards him. 'You mean?'

'There is a danger of it. Twenty years is a long time and that is the length of time you have been away; there has never been such change in the world's history than has taken place during this period. You think you know your birthplace like you know your own hands. Well, you do not. Taken as a whole they are a different people from those you left in your youth. A new class is climbing up, I am one. I shall be a rich millowner before I am done. And then, respectability has come to us; we have the squalid poorer than poor, like I was myself, but we have those who have climbed out of the gutter and are become respectable.'

'God save me from respectability,' Mary Ann begged.

'God Himself is respectable now, so you have no hope of that!'

Mary Ann banged a pan down on the table. 'What has this to do with me and my lady's wishes?'

'Everything, my girl. Everything!'

'You're talking too generally, Silas Clopton; I could thole living in this house if we was treated like human beings, I'm not afraid of work and it's a miracle the way Anne-Marie sits down under it all; she was companion to my lady's old uncle in Brussels and now she's maid of all work. But the food that is thrown to us, just to keep us alive, would make my mother wild; in the past we were servants here, all of us, mother, father and me, but we were treated with respect. Now our food is doled out every morning; they even keep an eye on the butter we use and it's got sawdust in it . . . off the floor it is and used up on the servants!'

'Economy! When you're getting rich, it's a matter of getting richer; look after the pennies and the pounds will look after themselves. But look after the pounds too!'

'Yes, and what then? There's no pockets in a shroud, as the Bible says. . . .'

'Find that quotation for me in the Bible and I'll give you a shilling!'

'It's all very well, Silas Clopton, this high-falutin' chat about change and class and so on. What I want is for to take back home to my lady a clear and truthful account of her old home and her father. That's all; once we've got that clear and everything sorted out with Mr Hobshaw . . .' (and she deliberately refrained from any mention of Mr Hobshaw's plans regarding his will) . . . we'll be off. So the sooner you get rid of the idea that I'm taken with you enough to marry you . . . the better. Now get out of my road and I'll say a thank you for, well, trying to help.'

His good humour of half-an-hour ago left him; his face darkened.

'Don't fool about, Mary Ann. Use your head, you've plenty of brains if you've a mind to use them!'

Mary Ann swept her pan off the table and put it on the stove, appearing to have no further interest in him.

'Things are not always what they seem, remember that,' he added darkly.

'Then if you were as friendly as you make out,' she retorted without turning round, 'you'd let me in on it all. But now, all you're thinking about is what *you* will get out of this appearance of Mary Ann Sheffield and her daughter.'

'Now, gods, stand up for bastards! You should watch that girl, Mary Ann.'

Something was annoying Silas Clopton, he was waxing vicious. She turned round and stared at him indignantly.

'Larking about with that young larrikin . . . Isaak Delph!' he grumbled.

'You mind what you're saying: Anne-Marie is a good girl, not like her mother. She knows what she's about!'

He flung back his head and actually laughed scornfully and Mary Ann, badly stung, said she could warn him, too, over the question of choosing a wife for his new mansion. 'He's a mad yeoman that sees his son a gentleman!'

'Yeoman! Whose talking about yeomen! It's the rich manufacturer I'm talking about, no need to turn your mouth down like that, Mary Ann; you don't know when to do yourself a good turn and that's for sure!'

There were elements of enjoyment for Mary Ann in this passage, she delighted in a discussion with someone with a lively turn of mind and with a nasty streak in him as well: she found their talk stimulating. She felt almost refreshed. 'You'll be old afore you're wise, Silas Clopton. You don't know me; if you take as little care and thought over choosing a wife for this mansion of yours as you seem to be doing, you'll come to grief and pain.'

'I've known you since you were a girl!'

'You have not, you've known *of* me and there's a big difference. You don't know me.' And after a moment she added: 'No more than I know myself.'

But it had gone on too long. The kitchen door was opened and the spectre of the mistress of Underscar was revealed standing there like a Gothic caricature of Death, wearing a cap from which the wings dangled, lace edged on either side, elongating her grey face almost to absurdity. She enunciated rather than spoke, that is she barely moved her lips, saying 'No doubt you and Sheffield have much to say to one another, Mr Clopton, after all these years, but we await our dinner, if you please!'

This effectively relegated both of them to the status of serfs and Silas Clopton could not allow that. With grave dignity he picked up his hat and stick, he said that he had been acquainting Mary Ann with all the many changes that had taken and were taking place upon her native heath.

'Another time perhaps, Mr Clopton,' the lady of the house suggested.

*

Mary Ann was amazed at the ease with which Anne-Marie went off upon her evening jaunt. Ignoring all rules and regulations, disregarding authority itself, she skipped out into the warm spring evening as though she were slave to no one.

Instead of going over to see the old men that evening, as was her wont, Mary Ann put on her second-best bonnet, the one she used for the morning expeditions to the market in Brussels, and went down to the village too. *Followed Anne-Marie* might be the more honest expression and, though wearing a deliberate expression of mild enjoyment of her evening walk upon her features, Mary Ann was considerably worried not to appear to be interested in the whereabouts of her daughter. *There she goes, spying upon her by-blow*, she fancied she could hear the respectables observe, as they peered through their coarse lace curtains. There were many more lace curtains in the village now than ever there had been; if the house inside was barely furnished the lace curtains and white-stoned step denied this.

Lace curtains from Nottingham and carpets from the West Riding; the curtains might be coarse, the carpets thin and of quality far removed from the Savonneries of Brussels mansions, but they represented a progressive people, all prepared for the advent of the railway for which, at that moment, they were choosing a site for the station. Quite soon the worthy folk of the hamlet would troop down to their new station to be carried, clutching their bonnets and beavers, at the astonishing speed of ten miles an hour to the town five miles away, to do their shopping.

The abject poor, that is, the beggars, were too poor to be bothered by the appearance of Mary Ann; they had a lot to worry about, such as looking for the scraps which some of the more charitable threw out for them.

But the respectables were alert: 'Was you looking for your girl?' one, unable to contain herself, rushed from her hut to help. 'Well, no. I am enjoying a stroll through the village on this fine evening,' Mary Ann answered pleasantly.

She remembered the parents of Isaak Delph's mother, Esther Crump: they had lived in the large cottage beside the church and the father had had a loom in the living-room at which the whole family worked. Mary Ann looked at the cottage with some interest and found it greatly improved in appearance. There were the lace curtains and the whitened doorstep and there were also flowers planted next to the cabbages, yellow and brown wallflowers, and as she admired them Mary Ann saw the mother of Isaak herself sitting upon a pig-bench under an apple tree by the road making a sovereign-purse of silken thread.

'Good evening,' she called and received a good evening in return. She was a good-looking woman with a soft round face, a trifle given to fat, but she had nothing whatever to say to Mary Ann and thus, Mary Ann felt, she had nothing to say to her. For some reason or other Mary Ann felt herself going scarlet and blustering about her evening stroll.

'You'll find your little one in the churchyard,' the woman remarked coldly.

Churchyard! Mary Ann nodded and smiled and strolled on without making her progress one whit faster. Should she turn into the churchyard? Or not? The choice was agonizing until with thankfulness she saw her daughter sitting beside Isaak Delph meek upon a bench made, surely purposely, for innocent young people to sit upon of a spring evening, between two yew trees which, growing together in an arch, formed a screen between them and the graves.

Mary Ann appeared to give a start of surprise.

Unlike his own mother Isaak Delph had no shyness or diffidence; first he waved and as she approached he called: 'What can they expect? They won't let me up to the house so we reckon us can do as we like out ut sight!' a clumsy remark likely to incite ill-feeling against the speaker. 'I got a fishing rod and the trout is rising,' Isaak went on, 'Anne-Marie says she won't come on down alone to the river with me and watch me bring out a monster. Do you come, Mrs Sheffield, and us'll be all right.'

So Mary Ann went down with them to the tiny river's edge and watched the undoubted skill of Isaak Delph the fisherman.

The uncertain situation, upon this one occasion, was certainly saved.

But the problem remained.

EIGHT

Wednesday

Dearest Mary Ann,

Your letter gave me great pleasure and it maddens me that mine cannot give you any. My dear Monsieur le Comte is causing me great sadness on account of the constant pain which no doctor so far seems able to treat successfully. So often our hopes have run high upon hearing of someone who has treated so-and-so with great success; and time after time we have been aware of his feeling of hopelessness after treating M. le Comte for a time. As you will understand, dear Mary Ann, I have to spend much time with him in Spa. I know from what my friends tell me that Spa itself is no worse than other European watering places regarding the raffish lives of drink and gambling led by so many so-called invalids held there by their ailments. I have, indeed, turned over in my mind the question of taking him to Bath. I hear there is opened a new medical establishment where teaching of medicine is actually done at the bedside and there is an excellent man in attendance.

This, however, is out of the question for the moment since I am back home for a sad reason which I know will distress you and, more, Anne-Marie, for my dear Uncle Peter was found dead in bed three days ago. He was eighty-seven years and died a wonderful death, his candle being burnt out so the doctor is sure he fell asleep for ever whilst reading his book which lay upon his chest and his spectacles upon his nose.

Nevertheless, in spite of his age, this news has shocked many people who knew him; his mind was so alert and his wit so constant that his age seemed neither here nor there. So yesterday he was buried in the English cemetery and I had two hundred or more in to drink his favourite Rhenish wine to his memory, in our drawing-room. The house was closed, all the furniture covered up, as you will understand, since I was in Spa, and I myself did a hurried preparation, Nicky being very shocked when he found how busy I had been! He had to be much more than a footman for the day, bringing in three friends of his to help him serve the wine.

But this is not all my sad news, Mary Ann, your little dressmaker friend in the Rue Flamande who lived with her mother has died from cholera. It is too sad, she was so clever and her clients must be distraught, certainly her poor mother is. It is strange the way this cholera is not so much a scourge, like the plague, but can pick out one or two from a family. It is somehow more shocking because it is unexpected.

Well, dearest Mary Ann, I am alone in the house except for Nicky in the pantry and as soon as things are settled with the lawyers about Uncle Peter's property (by the way he has left all his possessions and his small house to Bruno who does not yet know!). . . . The boys, of course, were home for the funeral and have now returned to their garrison and Bruno to his really hard studies.

I feel I should make no comment at the present moment upon your, should I call it progress? Naturally I am anxious to hear anything you can tell me but I do not wish to ask for news which you are not ready to give me.

With my love to you, dear Mary Ann
Harriet d'Houdenard.

P.S. Having plenty of time in the empty house today, I have

written an equally long letter to Papa; he will be sad about Uncle Peter, his wife's uncle only, but a good friend to us all.

His letter from Brussels was awaiting Mr Hobshaw when he returned from his outing in the early evening and one of the young ladies took their supper tray over to the stable flat. Mary Ann made no attempt to make herself pleasant to the young ladies and did not even look at them unless it was strictly necessary: she did not, as she said, know 't'other from which'. She would leave the butler's tray with the food ready on a stand near the kitchen door and make no comment when they passed through the kitchen to deliver it. Mary Ann would have been surprised to hear that they were frightened of her. Her outburst of temper regarding the servants' rations upon her arrival had convinced them that she was a martinet and to be avoided.

She assured herself that it would be better not to go over to the flat that evening; it might give the impression that she could barely wait to hear whether any of Mr Hobshaw's fellow magistrates had shown an interest in employing Anne-Marie as a governess. Nevertheless Mary Ann's heart ached when she looked closely at her daughter. Her face was almost drawn, her lovely cheekbones even more prominent but not naturally. In a moment which was perhaps ill-advised, at the end of the day when both were quite worn out and under-nourished, Mary Ann spoke her mind, as she was wont to do from time to time.

'What's to do, lovey?'

Anne-Marie gave a sad little twisted smile: '*Je ne suis que fatiguée*, Mother. Are you not tired, too? Sometimes you look very tired.'

'Well, let us not fret, I feel sure help is coming.'

'How so?'

'Mr Hobshaw is another who is worried regarding you,

Anne-Marie. He has proposed that he try around the country-side amongst some of his friends with families and large houses, to see if he can find one who would welcome a French governess . . .;' at the sight of Anne-Marie's expression she hurriedly added: 'Temporary, of course, for the time being only. This terrible physical labour is not for you, my love, excellent though you have been. And aside from that, you are not receiving the nourishment needed for a young girl working so strenuously.'

She scanned anxiously her daughter's face but there was no joy therein.

'Well, think you not it a fine idea?'

'*Mais non!*' Anne-Marie returned emphatically.

'Why not?' Mary Ann demanded categorically, both hands on her hips, ready for an argument.

'Because I will not leave here and leave you behind, that's why.'

'As I have told you before, lovey, I am different physically; I come from hard working-class stock and there is only half of that in you. Surely you understand?'

'I understand what you are telling me but it does not change my mind. You are old and I am young. And if I go away and leave you, you will have twice the work to do that you do now, you will have all my work too. It will kill you, Mother. I will not leave you to do it. I do not want to be here at all, I do not fully understand why we had to leave our home but since I am your child, I have had to do as you wish. But I shall not leave you to kill yourself whilst I live in a mild and gentle job such as governess.'

And crossly Anne-Marie crammed the candle she was taking out of the packet into the chamber candlestick so carelessly that she was knocking off pieces, which would greatly grieve the Mistress as being wasteful.

'Well now, Anne-Marie, let us keep our heads and me my temper. Let us just consider carefully. . . .'

Anne-Marie laid out the candles upon the old decorated tin tray and carried them out into the hall where they were laid upon the oaken dresser, ready to be picked up by the users before going up to bed.

When she returned to the kitchen Mary Ann had, as she thought, cleared her mind of 'litter and junk' and was 'looking at the situation in the light of reality, girl'.

'If you go, when you go, they should either recall the servants they dismissed to make way for us, or they will get others. Well, I am sure she will do neither of these things, until I fall flat with my face in the scrubbing bucket. When she heard we were coming she made her plans and she was mighty clever, oh yes, she was clever. She would turn, *bouleverser*, you understand, the situation to her great advantage. She would now have two servants instead of three, she would pay them half the amount she paid the others, she would reduce their food to a minimum quantity and she would have the advantage of knowing we wanted to be here to discover various things for Madame, Mr Hobshaw's daughter, who was anxious about him; *so* she would keep us so busy that we had neither the time nor the will for investigation.'

'So?' Anne-Marie prompted lifelessly.

'So I will see to it that I do fall flat with my face in the scrubbing bucket; it may even happen before I intend it to happen. And if she will not find other servants, the young ladies will be forced to do the housework and the cooking whilst I lie in bed recovering, unless I am turned out. And if I am turned out I will ask Isaak Delph's mother, down the village, to take me in as a lodger and that will turn the mistress sick! Those fearful young ladies, those lazy, utterly useless hags, will be forced to get up and move their limbs about and dirty their hands. They can't all go into a decline . . . it is time they tried activity, otherwise they may soon find they can't move any longer; they'll have, what do you call it? fossilized.'

But still Anne-Marie did not smile, her small worried face,

turned to her mother, took no life from her mother's vigour.

Dear God, Anne-Marie thought, if I do not take care my own dear one herself will go into a decline.

Mary Ann frowned, puzzled. 'Anne-Marie . . . would you like to go back to Brussels?'

She nodded, wordless.

'Well, I have very sad news, which I was keeping to tell you when the sun was shining, perhaps in the morning, a time more suitable for bad news.' And she told her about their lady's Uncle Peter, who was found dead in bed with his book upon his chest, still wearing his spectacles. And the girl wept, but she went on weeping and weeping into her apron, left the kitchen and went upstairs and flung herself upon her bed where she gave way to a veritable calamity of weeping, as though she were weeping for something much more than her dear old man who was so fond of her.

*

'*Heaviness endureth for the night but joy cometh in the morning*': it was not joy which cameth but a certain stability and resolution.

Miss Lavinia would like to borrow Mother's Culpeper, Anne-Marie said as she stood eating a slice of bread spread with dripping.

'What on earth for?'

Anne-Marie had found Miss Lavinia tinkering with a small portable stove in which she burned some kind of inflammable liquid and made herself the equivalent of Mary Ann's tisane at times. Naturally enough, it had not been used for a long time and she had been refurbishing it in the hope of being able to imitate Mary Ann and distribute these curative herb drinks to the family. 'It will not last long,' Anne-Marie observed, 'nothing they may plan to do ever lasts long.' It would appear that the four were quite incapable of sustained effort, and that was that.

'No,' Mary Ann said firmly, 'I cannot or will not, or both, lend or give or allow it in her hands. When have they obliged us?'

'But, Mother,' Anne-Marie argued with much good sense, 'they have the power to make our lives so wretched and Miss Lavinia is the only one, the only one of the four who has made any attempt at decency towards us. I *have* been forbidden to go down to the village of an evening and to meet Isaak Delph, that I have, but they are so indolent that though they are strongly against my going, they have not the physical energy to stop me, which they could. They cannot keep up even hatred.'

Mary Ann was impressed by her daughter's observation but quite unrelenting. 'The Culpeper is hidden,' she said, 'but in a place where it cannot easily be found. Since I act as doctor to the lot of you, I keep it from prying eyes. No doctor would allow his patients to have the use of his book of nostrums and you can tell that to Miss Lavinia straight.'

*

When the mistress and the young ladies were served with breakfast and Anne-Marie was attending to the bedrooms, Mary Ann crossed over to the stable flat where they had prepared their own breakfast and had just finished.

'I am happy you have come, dearest Mary Ann; I have been talking over with Sheffield the proposal I have had and he is happy with it.'

In short, it was just such a suggestion as Mary Ann had had in mind: the large house of a prosperous clothier with two sons, who had a tutor in the local parson, but he knew no French. The hope was that, as they were ten and twelve years of age, Anne-Marie would act as governess-companion and speak French constantly to them. Since the question of time-limit to this arrangement was not important and she would be paid two pounds per month, with one weekend off to return to her mother, it seemed to be a heaven-sent opportunity.

Mary Ann's relief and her thankfulness to the old man were boundless. But there was something else which the old men had clearly discussed and that was the amount of work Mary Ann herself might now be forced to do: the entire housework as well as the cooking, and both made very grave faces on this score.

Finally, Mr Hobshaw behaved exactly as Mary Ann and her father might well have prayed he should; he declared roundly that he would tackle his wife on this subject and they would come to a final arrangement, i.e. that Mary Ann should continue to do the cooking but that one or two women should be added to the staff, as had always been the case. They could either live in or come up from the village every morning at seven. He would insist upon this, he declared firmly and, indeed, for once he did sound as though he were the master of the house.

With how high a heart and with what pleasure Mary Ann now left the old men, she was never to forget for the rest of her life. The happy and carefree life she had upon the whole led for forty years was riven in half shortly after that glad session so that she was never the same Mary Ann again; she lost her absolute faith that there was a God looking after her, from then on.

Two small ragged children stood irresolute in the yard; they had running noses which they had wiped all over their faces and as their faces were dirty they were absurdly smudged. They were barefoot but this did not signify because it was a pleasure to walk without boots on a day like this.

Cowed-looking, they stood between her and the back door and one of them put out a grubby hand with an envelope in it. 'Express delivery from the post coach. . . .' A tip was necessary but as the postmark was Brussels and addressed to her, Mary Ann, with a jerk of the heart, opened it. Forgetting the children she pulled up her skirt and fled up the stone steps, almost flinging herself upon Mr Hobshaw.

It was not yet the worst but it was very bad; Monsieur le Comte had been recalled to Brussels, post-haste, owing to the grave illness of his wife who was said to have contracted a nameless illness. All the servants, as Mary Ann knew from the letter from her lady which she had just received, had been seasonally dismissed and the house was in charge of the English head footman, one time page or foot boy, Nicky West. In what was evidently a cry from the heart, or *cri du coeur*, Monsieur le Comte begged for Mary Ann whom he needed, it seemed, within the hour.

Mr Hobshaw exclaimed 'Cholera!' after distractedly clapping the two sides of his head with both his hands, and immediately started actions right and left. No one remembered to tip the dirty children in the yard.

Mary Ann must go at once; when she would arrive depended upon how soon she could board the boat to Ostend. Anne-Marie must not go with her mother but would be taken at once to the friends with whom Mr Hobshaw had spoken regarding a French governess for their boys; Mr Hobshaw himself would take her in the pony carriage so that her sudden arrival might be explained to his friends.

One of the young ladies, whether she liked it or not, must run to the village for a hackney for Mary Ann to be driven to the nearest coach stage. She should roll up her white apron and throw off her clogs and GO, Mr Hobshaw shouted.

Mary Ann ran to pack her carpet bag and as she did so found Anne-Marie making beds. She caught her by the shoulders and kissed her warmly: 'You are to go with Mr Hobshaw, he will tell you all . . . our dear lady is sick to death, Annie; I must go. Take a hand case, my love, and your small box, there is no time to pack carefully; I will ask Grandpapa to bring over your box in the cart. You will no longer be a half-starved servant, my pretty one, but a keen young governess.'

But the mistress put up a loud and noisy protest; it was also time-consuming and as Mary Ann struggled to keep her temper and refrained from striking her, the young ladies argued it out amongst themselves as to which of them should go for the hackney. Everything in the way of abuse that might be expected poured from the second Mrs Hobshaw's thin lips: was there no consideration for others . . . how did Mary Ann think they could manage without servants . . . if she did think . . . it was impossible to find servants upon the instant, she would have to delay until at least two were found . . . she would never allow Mary Ann back once she had quit her roof . . . as for Anne-Marie! Mary Ann could take her by-blow with her if she did intend, in fact, to go . . . but she could take her countenance away for ever. 'I take it very ill,' she shouted in a final anti-climax.

Mary Ann cried that it was a matter of life and death and she could not stop to listen but she turned back, wringing her hands with despair and begging for information: 'It could be cholera. Do . . . do they ever recover from this?'

Whether or not the mistress knew the answer, it remained unspoken; by now she was roused to a point a long way beyond listening to what anybody else had to say or ask. 'You have us all sadly put about,' she told Mary Ann; 'I shall not put myself about by giving housing room to your belongings; your boxes will have to go before you leave the house.'

So time was to dribble past and could not be swallowed whole; at last Anne-Marie was in the yard in her best outfit in red velvet with a tiny waist and large pleated collar, her pantaloons flapping over her boots, and her bonnet was so large that it was impossible to kiss her face. Mary Ann crushed her daughter's work-worn hands together: 'Keep these out of sight until they have recovered their elegance,' she begged, then pressed them to her mouth, kissing them and letting her warm tears fall upon them. Sheffield picked Anne-Marie up and lifted her into the trap with her carpet bag after and nodded when Mary Ann begged that he should take the box later.

'Do they recover, those who have cholera?' Mary Ann cried as Mr Hobshaw took up the reins.

'Yes, yes, Mary Ann! They do, with the grace of God. . . .'

'Farewell . . . farewell. . . .'

The second Mrs Hobshaw, her hands tucked into her cape, was standing between Mary Ann and the kitchen door and when Mary Ann made to pass her she held her ground. 'Out of the way, you nowt!' Mary Ann screamed and pushed past her.

'What was that your daughter called me, Sheffield?'

'A nowt, Ma'am!' Sheffield repeated pleasurably.

'A nowt.' She turned back into the house thoughtfully, 'A nowt!'

If their baggage were to be cast into outer darkness or carted away to the village tip, everything would have to be packed away and she would ask Sheffield to get someone to help him carry them down and lock them away in his tack room, to which no one was ever allowed entry, until they were required again.

'But shall I ever come back?' Mary Ann asked herself as she folded her uniform dress and clearly sensed the physical well-being and warmth of her kitchen in Brussels and in her mind heard the constant chirp of the cricket behind the stove.

She was ready for the hackney when it came. Two young ladies had gone to summon it and Miss Lavinia had retired with them to start immediate inquiries about servants and, for this reason if not for any other, none of them had returned in the hackney to Underscar but remained in the village. But Sheffield was there, in great state of concern, to see his daughter away.

'Take heart, Mary Ann love, take heart; Miss Harriet is strong and healthy, she never took ill as a child beyond the usual; you'll see her well and strong again, mark my words.

It's a fair pity she cannot come back here for a pick-me-up when she is better but you stay beside her as long as she wants you; you'll be off together to one of those Belgium seaside places you was telling me of, shouldn't wonder and it'll do you both good. No, don't worry so, lass!'

Mary Ann put her arms round her father's neck, thinking that maybe she would never see him again: there was so much to weep for. Then she climbed in beside her bright green patterned carpet bag of which she had been so proud when her lady gave it to her, and lowered the glass. The driver clicked his tongue and flicked his whip.

'Wait, wait . . .' Mary Ann, white as her pocket handkerchief, stared fixedly ahead to the path down to the turnpike. Carriages and carts came up it but foot passengers came up the heather-bordered footpath. And some came very slowly, particularly children. They were the same children who had come earlier, it must have taken them a long time to get back to the post office and to start out once again to their original destination; they must be tired out, poor little things.

Mary Ann could not take her eyes off them and, as they approached, her countenance withered. Sheffield, standing beside the hackney, had the same experience, he guessed for what purpose the children were returned. It was to bring an express letter following the first. He knew what it would have to say. And so did Mary Ann.

'She has died,' Mary Ann said long before the children reached the yard.

NINE

FOR DAYS she was like an automaton; her memory of those first three days left her entirely; she moved about like a sleep-walker, preparing meals, making bread and doing the exact amount of cleaning she had done before so that everything she did was quite automatic. It was as though she had been caught in an exceptionally hard frost and was deep frozen for four days. It would be hard to say which came first, the tears or the thaw. The mistress and the young ladies were awed and even cowed by her and the second Mrs Hobshaw came into the kitchen frequently trying to communicate with her and having no success. When the tears came they poured from her in floods, she sat in the kitchen rocking-chair and threw her apron over her head and after she had cried quietly but extensively for half-an-hour, she was better. She remembered there must be a funeral and went over to see the old men. Her father having gone out to sell a basketful of spoons, Mr Hobshaw was alone, reading *The Times*. By this time he had had a long letter from Monsieur le Comte d'Houdenard which he handed to Mary Ann. He asked where the letter she had received from her Madame was and Mary Ann told him it was in her carpet bag. He feared that Mary Ann's might have the contagion of cholera upon it and Mary Ann said she did not care since she had nothing more to live for. And Mr Hobshaw said that could be said about him but not about Mary Ann who had a great deal to live for. He begged her to burn the long letter but she refused to do so, saying it was the last letter she would ever have and she would never destroy the memory of her wonderful lady.

When she asked about the funeral he said it had taken place the next day, as soon as the family had been able to get back to Brussels for it. She had been buried in the d'Houdenard vault in St Gudule and Monsieur le Comte, unable to bear his own empty home, had returned to Spa leaving the house closed up, as it had been. He had written that Harriet had been taken ill on the evening of her Uncle Peter's funeral and the cholera had taken its well-known course with galloping strides; the footman in charge had called in no less than three well-known doctors but none, from the start, had been able to offer any advice other than the usual. A strong, healthy woman, she had been stricken down as inexorably as a fine tree falls to the ground, struck by lightning.

Then there took place one of those long sad conversations which overtake those bereaved suddenly; there had to be a cause, blame must be attributed; if the dead one had not done this or that, seen this person or that person, made this visit or that . . . all so useless but somehow necessary. They decided that she must have called upon the little dressmaker near the church in the Rue Flamande and found her dying or dead because she had mentioned it in her letter, and they achieved a grain of cold comfort from this.

'Does Monsieur le Comte mention me?' Mary Ann asked at last, looking down at the unread letter in her hands which she both longed to read and could not bear to.

'Indeed yes, Mary Ann, he wants you to go back to Brussels . . .' Her face lighted up for a moment but was instantly cast down again when he went on: 'He wants you to go and sort out all my daughter's possessions. The family jewels have been taken away by him for safe keeping for the boys' wives when they are wed, but he wishes that you should keep for yourself anything or everything personal that belonged to Harriet. But of course, since the house is closed this is not an immediate necessity. Still, I daresay he would like them moved before he goes back to the house, if he ever does. I am greatly grieved for that poor man; he has had enough physical pain for a lifetime and now he has great mental pain from his loss, as well; there seems nothing left for him other than a miracle which would suddenly relieve him of his constant pain.'

'Tell me, please, about Anne-Marie. How did you fare with her when you so kindly whisked her away on that truly awful day?'

'It was a merciful providence, a Godsend, no less. That I should have, the previous day, almost concluded arrangements for Anne-Marie to go to these friends of mine, seeems to me nearly as desirable as the miracle I wish for Monsieur d'Houdenard. Naturally my friends the Shaws were astonished to see me so soon with the young lady we had discussed, Mr Shaw barely having had time to relate his talk with me, to his wife. But they received her with pleasure and when I left Anne-Marie was smiling as I have not seen her for some time. She almost looked happy.'

'Did you tell them . . .?'

'Mary Ann, my love, I have never spoken to anyone other than to my dear Harriet about the relationship between Anne-Marie and myself. If my second wife and the young ladies know, as I believe they do, I have not any idea how they came to know. If you throw back your mind you will see Harriet's house full, at that historic time, constant callers of all nationalities and many, many soldiers' relatives amongst them. Harriet held open house in those Waterloo days. It is not surprising that someone should learn that Harriet's favourite female servant should be *enceinte* by Harriet's soldier brother. It is all ancient history and if people concerned have forgotten everything else, they have not forgotten that Anne-Marie was born on what is absurdly called the "wrong side of the blanket".'

He felt now relaxed enough to fill his pipe and after he had done so he had a few puffs of it and said: 'Is it not a strange thing, Mary Ann, that nobody ever forgets a bastard? I find that strange indeed and can think of no answer. It is such a commonplace happening and it is said now that the age through which we have just passed was a shamefully immoral one, yet now, when many people take their religion much more seriously and the name of God with every other sentence they utter, we have more bastards than ever.'

Mary Ann said nothing, it was too late to make excuses.

'And so,' Mr Hobshaw went on, 'the day I took Anne-Marie to my friends the Shaws I did not say: Here is my lovely granddaughter in whom I am proud. No, I said it was the fatherless daughter of an old friend of the family, and that was that. Nobody is observant enough to see a distinct likeness between Anne-Marie now and my Harriet at her age!'

'But now,' Mary Ann pointed out, 'there is no reason at all for Anne-Marie and myself to be here. Our reasons for coming are . . . are gone with my lady.'

Mr Hobshaw raised his hand in alarm, as though he had been expecting this question. 'There is a motive for your being here at Underscar, my dear Mary Ann, and it is my *reason*,' he tapped his forehead in demonstration of his meaning. 'Good Sheffield and I together have kept the enemy at bay but for how long? The situation over there'—he jerked his head meaning on the other side of the yard—'is past praying for. It cannot continue much longer. It is as though the young ladies are kept prisoners in their parlour and have been for years. To my mind it is a dangerous state for four ageing women (and indeed they are ageing without maturing) to be deliberately isolated whilst their mother follows her obsession, which is to make money. I will grant that she has the ability to do so to an extent which is astonishing in a woman; I have heard her called a genius!'

'But I cannot stay in that house! I could not have done so

after dear Madame has died *with* Anne-Marie and I cannot do so *without* Anne-Marie. I was born and bred a servant but not the kind of servant who is treated as we are treated here. If there is such a kind. If we were lazy, dishonest, dirty, quarrelsome . . . we are not perfect but we do try to please. However, we do not succeed and I do not feel I can stay in that house for another day. I am sorry.'

None of this was a surprise to Mr Hobshaw; he had expected it. But he was immensely grieved for he found the thought of being alone in the flat with Sheffield again, after the pleasure of having Mary Ann close by for a few weeks, totally unbearable.

'But you would abandon your father, Mary Ann?'

It was a cruel stab but when people are badly hurt they try to protect themselves from further injury by these cruel stabs. Mary Ann buried her face in her hands for a long time.

A terrible peahen-like screech came from the yard: 'Mary Ann, Mary Ann, you're wanted.'

Mr Hobshaw strode across to the wide-open door and shouted down into the yard: 'Go away, Lavinia . . . Mary Ann is no longer at your beck and call!'

The woman's face dropped wide open with astonishment: 'Is she dead?'

'No, she is not dead but no longer yours to summon at will.'

*

Mr Hobshaw felt a deal better after that exchange, it had cleared the air.

'Sheffield is a quiet man, Mary Ann, but he is the salt of the earth. He neither sees nor does he hear any evil; he has the qualities needed to make a happy man.'

'I shall never leave Father again,' Mary Ann said soberly.

Mr Hobshaw looked carefully at her, not quite sure as to her meaning.

Mary Ann went on: 'That cottage next the church, now

enclosed with a white paling; there were many Crump children there when I was a child and now just one of them left, Esther, now Delph, with her son Isaak; I had thought I might ask Esther, Mrs Delph, if I could go as a lodger.'

'She was employed here as a cook for a time after your mother died. She came to look after me for some time before . . . before I remarried. She has no need to take lodgers, Mary Ann: I doubt very much if she would.'

'Well, what else do you suggest . . . ?' Mary Ann flashed back with just a trace of temper so that she hurriedly added 'sir?'

'Harriet has not yet been dead a week; one must not make too hurried plans for the future. But I now feel ashamed that I have not made my will long before now; I have talked about it but put off the moment as bringing my death possibly nearer. Foolish, is it not? There is no need to take either you or Anne-Marie with me, I will go by myself to the attorney and do this, the next thing I do. Harriet's death has reminded me that *I* may die at any moment, we should never forget that.'

Mary Ann looked at him, puzzled, she could not understand why he should be saying this now.

'My roots are here,' he said.

'And so are mine, sir. But I can't be bothered about me roots when there's a woman like yon in charge and an unnatural group of women I don't understand all herded together like a blackbird pie!'

'In that case I shall also ignore my roots, but Sheffield is content, he will not want to move. Aside from Sheffield, it might be that Bruno, my grandson, could help. Harriet's Uncle Peter, the friend and employer of Anne-Marie: his house in Brussels has been left to Bruno and Bruno may not need it, it will depend upon what he intends to do. I could live there and as I shall be allowed to spend my money as I like for once, I shall buy a horse and fly and Sheffield will come as groom to me. And you . . . my cook!'

Nothing could make Mary Ann smile now but at least her face cleared. She said nothing but Mr Hobshaw noted her look. He said that he would write to his son-in-law Monsieur le Comte straight-away, he had of course already written his son-in-law two long letters since his daughter's death but now he would write and ask how soon it would be convenient for Mary Ann to come to Brussels to sort out Madame's possessions, as had been suggested. He would also bear in mind that Bruno was continuing to study during his vacation with his Papa in Spa. He would try to discover when the vacation would be over so that Bruno would be back at his Université and Mary Ann would be able to see him and mention Uncle Peter's house to him as a possible dwelling for his grandfather.

'And in the meantime, dear Mary Ann, I beg of you to work so hard, but no harder. Regard her merely as your temporary mistress and if she harasses you in any way, shout at her as is your wont. If I had shouted at her from the start, things would not have gone the way they have.'

*

Dearest Mother,

Are you better? I am very sad and lonely and I wish I was with you to comfort you a little. Do you look more like yourself because I have a picture in my mind of a mother so sad, I have never known your face without a smile. Please tell me.

They are very nice to me here, I eat the same food the family have and I do not sit in the servants' hall but carry my meals up to the school room where they allow me a fire in the evening. I may have the day off on Sundays. There are three ponies and I am allowed to ride.

Avec tous mes sentiments tendres, chère Maman

Anne-Marie.

Bientôt est-ce que nous pouvons retourner à la maison?

Mary Ann was touched by the postscript: can we soon return home? written in French so that it might not be readily understood by anyone reading the matter casually.

Now that the whole reason for her presence was gone Mary Ann rebelled inwardly at having to stay any longer in the house; she made no attempt to approach the mistress amicably or to ingratiate herself with the others. Since her skirtbands seemed inches too big for her she could legitimately have raised a protest against her meagre rations but she did not care enough. She had no appetite; a cook who loses her appetite cannot be trusted to produce mouth-watering savoury meals and the household suffered accordingly.

On the Sunday afternoon Mr Silas Clopton boldly appeared at the kitchen door. Mary Ann had a headache, she was actually sitting by the kitchen table trying to repair a petticoat but telling herself her eyes were failing and that she must get herself spectacles when she heard his step and he stood in the doorway.

'Come, my girl, you are fading away, and there is no one to care, is it not so?'

'It is not so, my father cares very much and Mr Hobshaw and Anne-Marie; so you are talking nonsense, Silas Clopton.'

'And you have all the housework, usually done by three servants, to do yourself!'

'Now that is nonsense if ever there were such a thing, that really is! I'm doing nowt but the cooking, like Mother before me, standing there at the same table. That's all I'm doing and don't ask me what they are going to make of it, I do not care, I shall be leaving for Brussels soon.'

'That's gradely but this is a fine afternoon, come and see my house, it is nearly complete.'

Mary Ann shuddered and Silas Clopton remonstrated. 'What's to do?'

'There's a lot to do.'

'No need to be nasty, Mary Ann, even if you have had as

big a shock as any who lose those they love. I cannot say I have experienced it since I have no folk of my own.'

'I was not being unpleasant to you, Silas Clopton, it is that cuckoo, I shall always shiver when I hear it now, it seems to mock, to make little of one's wounds. An unsympathetic bird.'

'You'll not find me unsympathetic. . . .'

So, without her bonnet but without taking his arm either, Mary Ann strolled out across the moor.

One of the young ladies, happening to be in her bedroom, observed from one of her casements this unnatural occurrence and hurried downstairs to report it to the coven and dark words flew about the room like bats: disgraceful; unnatural; scheming; preposterous; wicked; unforgivable. They took it in turn to keep watch from the casement and report to the rest. But this watch covered what they felt to be an unbelievable length of time. All four in turn watched for half-an-hour, which made the length of absence two hours, and then started again from the first watcher and finally the total amount of time between her starting out (bonnetless) and returning was four hours; the cuckoo was preparing for bed and was silent but the blackbirds and thrushes were in full cadence, taking it in turn to enchant one who had spent a pleasant late afternoon and whose sore heart was soothed.

Silas Clopton was carrying a battered basket crammed with elder flowers, so full was the basket that fragments of flowers fell out at intervals along the track they took. Looking round his as yet unmade garden Mary Ann had been charmed by the amount of haphazard self-planted elder bushes which now flowered profusely. He found an old market basket amongst the new garden tools and together they had snipped off the pale heads and Mary said she would dry them, for they were the first of the herbs to flower. They could be used as a pleasant tea all the year round. And the flowers, if not handled too much, could be infused fresh and drunk either hot or cold, making a delicious muscatel-flavoured summer drink. And as they were picking, Mary Ann declared darkly that if the people for whom she cooked had an iota of decency and pleasantry in them she would make a batter and dipping the fresh flowers in it she would cook some crisp fritters.

Never one to let an opportunity for himself slip, Mr Silas Clopton had begged her to make some for him. So they had gone into the house together and amongst the cooking things found eggs and milk and flour, and Mary Ann cooked their fritters on the new stove as though they were carefree and young.

Silas Clopton had lived for fifteen years, as overseer at the mill, in the factory house and that same week all his own goods and chattels had been carted up to the new house. Furthermore, some of the new furniture had been delivered and laid upon the new carpets, they made a fine show. When they had eaten the fritters, he showed Mary Ann into every room and cupboard, and she could not but exclaim at the good taste and care that had gone into the arrangements of the furniture and pictures, the splendour of the carpets and the curtains chosen to blend with them.

Only in the kitchen did she find disorder and some chaos but she said nothing because it was pitifully obvious that whatever women he had to clean his house, the ones concerned with the kitchen were no housewives. Dirty pans were left about, breadcrumbs, dead cabbage leaves, rusting knives: Mary Ann carefully kept her eyes away from those burning orbs of Silas Clopton who, no doubt whatever, thought himself exceedingly clever. He was aware of the effect the untidy kitchen was having upon Mary Ann and he deliberately said nothing whatever but looked helpless.

The gipsy boy . . . it came suddenly into her head that that was what everyone had called him when he was a ragged, thieving child. She must take care, gipsies have their own methods of beguiling, of achieving what they wished to achieve. Even though he was wearing his beaver hat, his Sunday suit and carrying his silver-topped cane she now realised how much of the gipsy there was about him. Named after the warden, he had said, but no one knew for sure from whence came the name Clopton; Mary Ann told herself that it would not be his mother's name; she would be a dispossessed Lovel, perhaps, or a wayward and wandering Lee. The gipsy code of honour was rigid; had the erring woman been turned out of her family caravan to fend for herself and her babe? These thoughts chased the sad ones temporarily from Mary Ann's mind but she was careful not to raise her eyes and appraise him yet once more.

But as they walked back along the moorland path with the sun setting behind them, Silas Clopton took Mary Ann's arm and she let it stay like that. It was only as they approached the summit of the last hilly bit where they could be seen from Underscar, that he took his arm away but not without giving Mary Ann's arm a slight, only slight, pressure, to show what good friends they now were.

Mary Ann never knew what caused her to say that 'elder was under Venus' but having done so she was embarrassed and hurried on to say that there had used to be elders by the gate at Underscar and she had been shocked on her arrival to find that not only had they been cut down but they had been uprooted and now that she came to think of it it might well be that act of vandalism that had brought them all the bad luck which had been so liberally showered upon them.

'Aye, that's it, without a doubt!' she exclaimed. 'Fancy any countrywoman doing a thing like that and it's not on account of making the garden; they've never done a thing to the garden, so why bother about the elders at the gate?'

And then Mary Ann stopped and looked directly at him, her pale hair suddenly burnished by the almost horizontal rays of the parting sun; her breath was held for a fleeting moment when she thought he was going to lean forward and kiss her.

But he had a lot more sense. He took off his hat, gentleman-wise, and handed her the broken basket of elder flowers with the merest suggestion of a bow. He thanked her with the suave charm learned and adopted by the new business men. They had travelled a long, long way from the slap upon the backside of a mere week ago. It was tactful of him to go no further along the path into the yard; she would much prefer it that no one should see her, more particularly her father and Mr Hobshaw, coming bonnetless down through the sunset with a striking-looking dark-eyed fellow. . . .

The headache with which she had started now quite gone, Mary Ann began to hum, shocked herself and immediately stopped. She took the basket into the kitchen where she tipped the contents lightly on to the table and equally gingerly with one hand dropped them into three piles. One to put into a jam pan and boil with water for a cold summer drink, one to dry so that it could be used all the year round, and the last and smallest she intended for the rough and ready retort still kept in a corner of the larder, on a top shelf and probably unused since her mother's day. Distilled into a small quantity to be kept corked in her little green bottle it, too, could be used all the year round and was excellent for clearing away a headache.

Miss Lavinia, being the only one on any terms with Mary Ann, though they could never be called good terms, ventured boldly into the kitchen, twitching nervously as though she was about to have something thrown at her.

'Well, Mary Ann, we are all waiting for our supper.'

'You can go on waiting,' Mary Ann said vigorously, 'or you can get it for yoursen. I've got to deal with this lot whilst it's fresh.'

'Did you obtain it from Mr Clopton?'

'I did.'

'Fancy!' She stepped closer in the darkening room and peered, stretching out her hand.

'Keep your hands off it,' Mary Ann snapped, 'elder flowers

go black if they're handled.' She was opening and shutting cupboards, looking for a small spirit stove she had noticed. She finally found it, she also found the spirit bottle and filled the heater. Then she brought down the copper jam pan, put the pile of flowers into it, covered them with water and put it on the kitchen range, and all the while Miss Lavinia watched her, evidently trying to make up her mind what to say. Her presence irritated Mary Ann unendurably.

Finally Miss Lavinia said timidly: 'Our mother is very hurt by your behaviour, Mary Ann.'

No reply. She tried again.

'She does not wish to quarrel with you, Mary Ann; she likes you.'

Still no reply.

'She would like to have a quiet talk with you, Mary Ann. About, about future plans: Anne-Marie and so on.'

Mary Ann was determined not to answer and Miss Lavinia was equally determined to make her speak. She said what she had evidently had no intention of saying but which had been one of the many exciting and stimulating subjects of conversation in the parlour for over a fortnight.

'Anne-Marie!' Miss Lavinia said more loudly; giving Mary Ann one last chance to answer. As she did not, Miss Lavinia cast, as it were, her explosive. 'She has missed her courses.' Pause.

There was a pause in Mary Ann's activities too. She stopped doing what she was doing at the table and left her hands over the elder flowers, quite still without looking up, she waited for more information.

'We know . . .' Lavinia changed it to: '*I* know because one day when you had gone out for some exercise I came into the kitchen and found her preparing a tisane. She had a handful of that ugly Bishop's Weed that grows under the trees down in the clough in places. She was infusing it as a drink for herself. When I asked her why she was taking it she said she had a bilious attack and when I said it would not be ready to use because it not yet had white flowers on it she said that she did not know where you had put your book by Culpeper and it would do as it was for the present.'

'Bishop's Weed!' Mary Ann did not raise her eyes, her whole frame sagged and she leaned upon the table supported by her two hands.

'We may not know much about herbs,' Miss Lavinia remarked, backing towards the door. She started to falter, frightened of Mary Ann's latent violence. 'But every country girl will search for a handful to relieve her pains. And . . . I thought her unhappy and tried . . . and tried. . . .'

'Get out!' Mary Ann suddenly screamed. 'Get away, will you?'

*

The idea! Mary Ann thought, the impertinence! And the implication behind it was unforgivable because Bishop's Weed was amongst the many common abortificants and she had no doubt that this was the interpretation that Miss Lavinia had intended her to take from her otherwise uninteresting piece of chatter.

Indignantly Mary Ann moved about between the kitchen and the scullery preparing her remedies.

TEN

LAVINIA was by far the best-looking, indeed, the only tolerable-looking of the four sisters. If she had held herself properly, it would have improved her appearance considerably. But as the youngest of the four, and no doubt the most pecked of them all, she had developed an apologetic shuffle, appearing rejected upon the face of the earth, she was trying to make herself invisible. Her hair was scraped cruelly back from her face and, as though it were severely rationed, she had a skimpy corkscrew ringlet on either side; if anyone cared enough to count the number of hairs in each of these ringlets they could not make the addition more than twenty at most. She was a woman who wished well but she also felt herself to be drastically inadequate and thus she would go to any lengths of spitefulness and ill-will in order to ingratiate herself with her mother and sisters. Her only recognisable ambition was to be an accepted member of the club.

She hastened back to the parlour where they were sitting in the twilight waiting for something to happen.

'I am afraid I may have gone too far, I have made Mary Ann angry. She says we must get our own suppers, she is busy making elder flower wine.'

The sister who had watched the return of Mary Ann through her bedroom window reported that Mr Clopton had been carrying a basket: 'One of those huge baskets the peasants used to carry on their heads; must be fifty years old. She must have been to his house, he has been showing it to her. What does that mean?'

Raised eyebrows all round.

'If Mary Ann was to marry Silas Clopton, Mother would go mad.'

They pondered this portentous remark for some minutes.

'It could not happen.'

'Any . . . anything can happen, do you not know that yet?'

'If Anne-Marie can get up from her scrubbing and change her gown and go off like a fine lady to be a governess and all within a few hours, of course anything can happen.'

The process of Lavinia's thinking was not easy to follow but usually she made irrelevant remarks which, if studied carefully, might have something to do with the matter being discussed. This time her offering was:

'Mr Sheffield always came with us to church, I remember well. He sat at the back with the other lower orders.'

'But Mother has taken the place of God, that is clear,' the eldest sister cried shrilly.

'The devil, you mean,' one of them muttered and the others turned upon her like hissing snakes. There was a pause whilst the effect of this remark died out.

'Mary Ann says she quite likes Mother. . . .'

'Nonsense, she cannot abide any of us!'

'We are a house divided against itself. . . .'

'But so uneven! The women on one side and the two old men on the other!'

'But the men have Mary Ann on their side and she is greatly to be considered. Sometimes I think Mary Ann is more than a match for Mother.'

'Mother is a fine business woman but she . . .' words failed the speaker; as always nobody came to any conclusion when their mother was being discussed. The wonder was that she ever had any children, let alone four, and all of them of unrelieved plainness and lack of charm. But since charm is the desire to please, that could have been remedied with a little thought and goodwill behind it.

One of them poked a bony finger into Lavinia's flat breast: 'Did you happen to mention Bishop's Weed, eh?'

Lavinia nodded.

'Well?'

'She took no notice.'

One of the quieter sisters piped up: 'How could Anne-Marie know about Bishop's Weed? Does it grow in the streets of Brussels?'

'Don't be silly! There is some countryside round the city of Brussels, one supposes.'

'Besides, her mother has a Culpeper, which is at present hidden,' Lavinia remarked, 'or packed in her baggage to take away with her when she was going.'

The eldest nodded wisely as though she had some information which she alone knew, which was not so. 'The bags are not unpacked; Anne-Marie's box is packed ready to be sent off in the cart, taken to her by Sheffield. Mary Ann will be off to Brussels in a day or so, you will see. Being here means nothing to her now that my lady Harriet is dead and she cannot spy for her any longer.'

'Pray God she goes!'

A sound of protest came from the other three mouths. 'Why?'

'For the reason we have been speaking of, the awful possibility of her marrying Silas Clopton. They are of the same age, around. She knew him as a child. She might well wish for a marriage status. . . .'

'. . . as some of us do, but without hope.'

'Everything will go wrong if she marries Silas Clopton. . . .'

'How so?'

'Because Mary Ann will wear the trousers . . . you will see . . . !'

One of them shuddered extensively. 'I hope not!'

'Those trousers are Mother's. . . .'

'If it were not for Mother, the mill would have overspent and be on the way to bankruptcy, or have fallen long ago!'

'Look at her, how she works! Where is she now? Down at the counting house, of course, all alone, adding and subtracting and making quite sure there is not a penny missing. Silas Clopton is one for expansion, and without the means. Look at that absurd house he has built!'

'Oh, but it was out of his savings, Mother made sure of that!'

'Yes, but he would do the same at the mill if he were allowed.'

'Yes, it would finish Mother if Mary Ann were to marry Silas Clopton.'

'Now now, girls, for these past ten years we have been talking about Silas Clopton's marriage intentions and we are no nearer an answer, so let us not get overwrought. It has happened so often before that we suspected it and look . . . he is still a bachelor and getting more grand and the gentleman with every day that passes. There is still hope for one of us.'

And that was how it went on, day after day, week after week, year after year. But with two million surplus women and large families with females predominant, there must have been many such family groups of idle women incarcerated in a parlour talking endless trivialities because it was not the thing for half a million women of the upper class to work. The other million and a half even more unfortunates (or perhaps not) worked their fingers to the bone all their lives then fell down dead because their hearts would beat no longer.

*

It was almost dark when Mother came striding up the bank, her keys jangling loudly, a tocsin, a warning to small furry animals. Her cloak could not have been more tightly clutched around her throat had it been a wild and stormy night. There must have been a time when her body was young and lovely and, remembering perhaps, she was giving nothing away. (Like the miser as he struggled in the river: 'Give me your hand!' a kind passer-by offered and, shaking his head, the miser cried: 'I can give nothing,' and drowned.)

'No supper!' she cried as she entered the gossip chamber.

'We . . . we have to get it ourselves!' It was always left to Lavinia to pass on disagreeable news.

'Who says so?'

'Mary Ann.'

'This is monstrous. The woman is still being paid as a servant; who does she think she is?'

No one could answer this.

'It is only cold corned beef and piccalilli,' Lavinia almost whimpered, 'and small beer, if there is any left.'

'Go and lay it in the hall then, Lavinia, I shall have to have a serious talk with Mary Ann. It is bad enough that she refuses to do any housework but to refuse to do her legitimate work passes all comprehension. She will have to go.'

One of the young ladies gave a bark of laughter which she instantly suppressed: 'She is going anyway, Mother.'

'You know that? Or are you merely guessing?'

'She will be certain to go back to Brussels to collect all the finery her last lady has left her,' another who had been eavesdropping said unpleasantly. 'And there will be nowhere here for her to store it, nor room across the yard either!'

They all exchanged covert glances but did not dare broach the subject that might follow naturally, the marriage they had been discussing.

'Lavinia, see that Mary Ann has no corned beef.' She fumbled with her keys and detached the one for the larder. 'You can bring in the whole piece and I will carve it. She is much too plump; she had better work off some more of that plumpness of hers otherwise she will never be able to squeeze herself into the smart Brussels outfit in which she arrived.'

This was intended as a joke and there were a few polite sniggers but it was clear that their mother was affronted indeed. She hurried away to divest herself of her cloak and to swallow her anger in her office.

*

It was not lack of supper which kept Mary Ann awake, it was Bishop's Weed, also called Cumin-Royal, Herb-William and Bull-Wort. What possible connection did these so dissimilar names have with one another? She had dragged her Culpeper from the depths of her baggage. The Greeks had the words for it and the most important of the list of names seemed to be Aetheopian Cumin-seed. *Ammi majus*. 'It riseth up with a round straight stalk, sometimes as high as a man . . .' Culpeper said and nor was Culpeper too enthusiastic about its abortificant properties. He merely said: 'The fumes thereof taken with raisins cleanseth the mother', but as fashions in abortificants change from district to district and from century to century Bishop's Weed might well have been out of favour for abortion at the time of writing his *Complete Herbal*.

Mary Ann decided not to tear herself to pieces as the result of a spiteful remark. She got up and went out into the dawn, running down to the wood-edge at the top of the clough and shaking off her clogs she walked about in the dew as she had done as a child. The cuckoo was already at it; this morning he seemed to be making fun of her. She had not gone for the conscious purpose of looking at the Bishop's Weed but in passing she noticed a clump of it, well below the height of a man and not yet in flower. But the depressing saying of the eternal Wise Woman, constantly quoted by her mother, repeated itself over and over again with the infuriating monotony of the cuckoo's empty-headed utterances: *As the old cock crows, the young one learns.*

*

'Mary Ann, I understand that you have suffered a great loss in the death of your last mistress but people do die, you know, and the world must go on. You have suddenly become quite, quite intolerable. You are getting ideas sadly above your station. Anne-Marie was whisked away beneath my nose without any discussion whatever with me.'

'It was the master's arrangement, Ma'am.'

'But I am the mistress of his house and you are my servants, both of you. You had no right at all to pack her off without a word. It is very inconvenient indeed for me to engage other servants at present; I have much to do at the mill regarding a new loom, bought at vast expense.'

But Mary Ann was in no mood to dissemble and be mealy-mouthed; she owed this woman nothing, not even civility. She said: 'Anne-Marie was here five weeks and it was never my intention that the girl should be a slave for that length of time. It wasn't right. Anne-Marie has had, by the goodness of my lady, almost a gentle upbringing; she did a little ironing and sewing at the Hôtel d'Houdenard but I have never, in her lifetime, seen her scrubbing and scouring and running up and down stairs carrying in coal and logs in the manner I have had to watch here. I have never before . . .' and suddenly Mary Ann stopped speaking, knocked wordless by a hideous, imaginative thought. Why was Anne-Marie working so wildly and unrestrainedly? Mary Ann shuddered from head to foot because the words which had formed themselves in her mind were so horrifying that they were like the touch of the devil.

Perhaps . . . to bring on her courses?

Oh perish, perish, perish the thought!

The second Mrs Hobshaw was fingering a long black ruler as though she was about to rap Mary Ann with it. 'What is the matter, Mary Ann?'

Who could possibly know at what moment either Mary Ann or her daughter could be desperately in need of a friend?

She rolled her hands up in her apron skirt and holding them against her waistband she gave one of her bob-curtseys.

'Nothing more than concern about our bereavement, I beg your pardon, Ma'am, and Anne-Marie's future.'

'Do you intend to stay here at Underscar, or not?'

'I understand I shall have to go to Brussels but no time for my going has been mentioned. The d'Houdenard house is standing empty, you understand, with no one in it but a footman as caretaker, who has been there years. Monsieur le Comte is an invalid, I cannot see him returning to that great mansion to live there alone without even his children for company, his boys. Monsieur Bruno might, just possibly might, but he is struggling to be an attorney and working very hard. Besides, Monsieur Bruno has been left a house of his own not far away; he might well invite his father to share it with him.'

'So?'

'So it is not easy to guess what may happen. You understand that Monsieur le Comte is unable to get upstairs and of late has been unable to dress and undress himself, he needs constant nursing attendance since he has become totally arthritic, his joints are diseased. For his own well-being it could be as well for him to stay on at Spa. My lady even mentioned Bath as a change; there are doctors there who know about diseases of the joints aplenty.'

'I see. Well, for my convenience, will you stay on now?'

'I cannot say I will and you could perhaps begin to search for other servants. I would like to say that I do not get enough to eat and on the half-rations doled out to me, us, I cannot work as I should.'

'Come come, Mary Ann, you are a fine strapping healthy woman!'

'Even a fine strapping healthy cow needs feeding otherwise its ribs will soon show through.'

'Its ribs!' she repeated in wonderment. 'All my girls have

their ribs showing,' she said in some distaste. 'Since they are not seen naked in public or anywhere else, what is wrong with that?'

'Ay,' Mary Ann had done her best, she had been unusually amiable, she could not keep it up indefinitely, 'that's the trouble!' she shouted, and disappeared before she could see the effect it had on her mistress's face. But she paused and added over her shoulders: 'And I want Isaak back!'

As she returned to her kitchen she felt something like shame, or was it pity or could it have been despair? That she should shout so coarsely at her new mistress, she, Mary Ann, who had become over the years imbued with the speech and manners of a gentlewoman; she who had sat in the window of a Queen and watched the Emperor enter Paris. Could she still be the same woman who could shout 'I want' anything, in gritty Yorkshire tones?

However, upon returning to the kitchen her sense of humour reared an ugly head: so the young ladies all had ribs showing, had they? How did their mother know? And suddenly Mary Ann was laughing till her own ribs ached. Her mistress seemed to have her daughters and cows strangely confused and Mary Ann found this exceedingly funny. It is difficult to continue to dislike someone who can cause a hearty laugh.

*

Mr Sheffield sat in the tack room and waited for Mary Ann to pass, as she was likely to do when she went for a mid-afternoon stroll upon the moor. When he heard her steps across the yard he beckoned her inside.

'Now love, I know you are unhappy and you're not to stay 'ere on my account. We've got Anne-Marie nicely settled now and it will make you more free.'

In her emotional state the kindness made Mary Ann cry a little: 'I don't know what I want, Father love.'

The old man put his arm round his daughter's shoulder and

patted her comfortingly. 'I know, I know. I felt just like you do, when you mother died, like I was cut in half. And you're feeling the same way over Miss Harriet who has been a good friend to you, my word she has!'

'What should I do, Father?'

'I do not like saying this, Mary Ann, because it's grand having you around, it does me good. But over the years I've had to find me own way and I've learned how to live content. It upset me a bit when the master towd me he was coming up to the loft to live alongside me, but we're shaken down and we don't interfere with one another.'

Sheffield was choosing his words carefully; he leaned against the saddle stand, indicating an upturned box for Mary Ann, and took a bit of time getting his pipe lighted.

At last he observed that he had 'shaken down' with the 'new' mistress too, and he spoke as though he had known her a few months rather than ten years. 'She's a queer one that, but I've done some thinking and there's nobbut *wan*' (being the Yorkshire for one) 'thing wrong with her. *Wan* thing . . . she's a miser every inch of her from her yed to the tips of her toes. There's a lot of them about in these 'ere parts. And blow me, lass, it's like having a cancer. *They can't help it!* They make theirselves even more miserable than they make other folks, as I see it.'

He was using immensely more words than he was accustomed to use at one time and there had to be a very long pause whilst he brought up reinforcements.

Finally he came out with: 'Nothing . . . nothing . . . matters to her . . . but money . . . money . . . money and if you can get that into yer yed, yer half way there. Oh ay! it's hard to understand. There's no pleasure in her life beside money.' He raised his twisted and rugged old hands and demonstrated with them as though allowing coins to fall through his fingers. '*That* is her life!' He cleared his throat with an important rumble, pleased with his dissertation and going from strength to strength. 'She'd sell the stars!' He chuckled. 'Afore she's done she'll sell the whole stretch of moor right up to the border, if she can get round the master.' He leaned forward and hissed: 'And that's the true reason why master has moved over the yard; she kept on at him and nobody can last out when they're kept on at, morning, noon and night. She reyther have the town coom up the bank and surround the whole place if she could have the gold coins for it.'

There was another long pause for thought before he said: 'Coom to think on, I like getting the money for me spoons, but what do I do when I gets it? I goes straight to the shop and buys meself some of this fine gentleman's baccy' (tobacco), 'and I'm regular loose with it, the amount I use! And me cider! and me good leather boots! And me grand snuff! And me fine new linen sheets I got meself!'

'Pity,' Mary Ann said, 'all one should feel for her is pity . . . she can't buy comforts for hersen, let alone her daughters!'

'Her daughters, ha!' Sheffield would have spat if Mary Ann had not been present; as it was he refrained and frowned dreadfully. 'You'll not improve anything, Mary Ann, love. You'll work yerself to the bone and yer won't get a farthing more and don't think yer food will improve, she can't do it, it'll be "dirty butter for servants" all the way . . . I can't abide you being there and that's the honest truth.'

Sheffield had spent ten years brooding and assessing the situation and there was no doubt he had summed things up correctly. He was getting great pleasure out of making these profound truths public, if only to his daughter. Upon the whole a silent man, he had a brain which worked.

'She'd not care,' he stated, 'if she was crouched neath a gorse bush on t'open moor with her bag of gold clutched inside her black cloak: no roof over her yed, not much food in her stomach and freezing cold . . . just so long as she had that bag of gold. She jumped at the chance to sack the servants when you came!' He pointed his pipe at her and said he bet she'd not been paid yet, had she?

No, she had not.

Of course not: she was hoping that as Mary Ann was almost a relative of the family she might not have to pay her at all. She'd not offer it but if Mary Ann asked for it she might possibly get it, but it would be a miracle if she did. What she would like Mary Ann to do would be to ask the master for it.

'E . . . e . . . e! I could talk me yed off about misers!'

'So?'

'I'd go, girl. I'd go back to Brussels where you've a lot to do, seems like, sorting out all me lady's things.'

'And then?'

'There'll always be a home for you here!'

'Where?'

'*Here* . . . alongside me, yer father, so long as I live.'

'?'

'And if I don't . . . you'll have to look after the master.'

'?'

'And when he goes . . . he'll leave it so's you've always got a roof over your yed, Mary Ann, the mother of his only English grandchild.' Mary Ann was sobbing again, in her changeable and uncertain state, so she missed the addition Sheffield joined to his remark, as it was said 'under his breath' and it was: 'Well . . . not the *only* one. . . .'

*

So Mary Ann went for her walk on the moor, but not straight along the path, which would take her directly to Overscar, in all its glory, and she was not in the mood for Silas Clopton's vivid and stimulating personality. Silas Clopton was something outside Mary Ann's present area of concentration; there was too much on her mind, which was like an overcrowded governess cart; one more passenger could cause a disaster.

Something about her interview with the mistress must have affected the woman because when she returned Isaak was whistling in the log-shed and, from the shed, logs were being thrown upon the rough cart built for wheeling into the hall. She smiled and went into the kitchen, placing her irons on the stove to heat up for some personal washing she had ready.

'Well I never!' she exclaimed as Isaak limped clumsily through the kitchen with the cart. 'Well, I never did!' But Isaak looked purposeful and unrelaxed, unlike his usual smiling self in Anne-Marie's presence.

'Did they send one of the young ladies down the mill for you?' Mary Ann asked when he returned. She held an iron close to her cheek so that she did not appear to be too interested.

'Aye! I'm on t'new tapestry loom, just got meself put there. . . .'

'Fancy!' Mary Ann said casually, turning away to test the heat of another iron. 'Well I never did!'

'So I'm not so pleased. "Yer wanted up at t'house," foreman said, he weren't too pleased, neether!'

Mary Ann turned to face him, putting her hands flat upon the scrubbed table in her typical manner. She showed herself prepared to listen.

'It's skilled labour, you'll know, and I'm . . . well . . . the way I am,' indicating his monstrous foot, 'it's a big leg up for me,' unsmiling, 'on that new loom. It's an experiment they're trying out: the design is printed on a single frame of pile-yarn, see? and then it's wound on to the loom beam. *Marvellous!* Yer've got yer picture and they call it tapestry! And if it's a success they'll apply for a licence . . .' and the rest came out with a meaningful rush, as though he were nervous of Mary Ann's reaction. '. . . see? And if they gets to making it regular the firm'll make a lot of money, see? and if they do that then there'll be more pay, see? And instead of brushing t'floor I'll be in't charge of a hand loom, *I'll be a weaver!* And I reckon I can get wed, it's time I did 'an all; there's chaps at Hobshaws is wed as is a lot younger nor me!'

With native wisdom he lumbered off to clean the knives, leaving Mary Ann in complete understanding that there was more to come and the nature of what was to come quite evident.

And as she ironed her petticoat she contemplated, contemplated rather than allowed her thoughts to rush about like mad bulls, as they had done in the past week. Why be ambitious, why allow dreams of a fine marriage for Anne-Marie to cross my mind? Why? Who, after all, am I? and *why should* God stand up for bastards? I should be thankful to get Anne-Marie wed to any decent chap with a good cottage and a regular job.

But then, as so often occurred recently, her mind tripped up on a thought laid carelessly across the path. Anne-Marie had sought out Isaak's company and appeared happy in it . . . why? After Bruno, of whom she had been undoubtedly fond . . . why pay the slightest attention to this, certainly good-looking but disfiguringly crippled yokel . . . Isaak?

Here be dragons . . . Mary Ann 'took a hold of herself' and ironed away like one possessed. Do not think, keep sane by not thinking.

Isaak stumped in and out of the kitchen, making much noise as though determined upon constant reminder of his presence. The expression on his face, too, was puzzling.

When Mary Ann had finished her ironing and had piled up the clean things and put the irons where they were kept, down beside the dresser, Isaak finished his work too and came up to her, challengingly almost. ''Ave yer noticed there's neether a cat nor a dog in this 'ere place, neether a cat nor a dog? I'm not comin' 'ere no more, mistress, not to oblige I'm not. I towd Anne-Marie I'd not marry her till I was in a position to, and I am now and coming up here a' working wi' firewood and knives is not a position, and no cat nor dog would stay five minutes in t'place. . . .'

It was not easy to follow his reasoning since it did not in fact exist. But it was clear that Isaak could think of no subtle way of putting across his news and so he wrapped it in cat-and-doggery.

Mary Ann shut her mouth which had been temporarily hanging open from shock. She said that since the mistress was boss of both mill and house, she could force Isaak's presence at the house easy; she'd only to say: no housework . . . no working on the new loom. However this seemed to depress him unduly. She went on to say pleasantly that Brussels, where she had lived for so long, was a famous place for carpets and last year the talk of the town had been the young Scotsman who had brought the new method of printing pile yarns to that city. It had been eagerly adopted for making so-called 'tapestry' carpets because it meant that, for a quarter the cost, carpets that looked like the real thing could be manufactured.

'I'll be off there in a day or two,' Mary Ann went on pleasantly, 'but I'll be back; there are things I have to settle domestically after Miss Harriet's sad death.'

'Oh aye!' Isaak was thoughtful, he was turning something over in his mind and finally it came out. 'I've had a bit of a . . . er . . . well, a bit of a kind of a letter,' he stammered awkwardly, 'from this new job Anne-Marie's in at Shaws.' He writhed with embarrassment and Mary Ann walked to and fro, tidying up in an endeavour to help him to say what he had to say. 'She says to come over and meet her at the North Lodge at t'weekend.'

'How would you get there?'

'On our Tommy, that's the pony . . . Mr Hobshaw had a special saddle made for me with this 'ere big stirrup, he's been very good to me, has master . . . gave me t'pony to replace the one I had as a kid, which died of old age.'

'So you'll be going to see Anne-Marie, well I never!' Mary

Ann said pleasantly. 'Happen you'd tek a note to her from me, just telling her I'm goin' to Brussels and so on. Poor child, she was as fond of Miss Harriet as we all were, she'll have been as upset as any of us!' She could not refrain from adding: 'It's nice she found time to write to you, in her new job and all!'

No conversationalist Isaak, having said what he had to say, he stood scratching his head thoughtfully whilst Mary Ann chattered away: 'You think if you and Anne-Marie married you'd be happy, Isaak?'

'Happy? I dunno. Happy?' He turned the word over in his mind, he had evidently never considered it, never wondered whether he was happy or not since happiness did not concern him. 'Happy!' he exclaimed finally, turning down the sides of his mouth. After a long while he said: 'Yer see, missus, it's time I got married, Mother says so.'

'Oh, I see.'

'I reckon nobody knows but Mother says I'm a bastard and she should know.'

'I see,' Mary Ann said again.

'I towd her as Anne-Marie was ready to wed.'

'What did she say to that?'

'She says: Why not?'

Mary Ann looked affectionately at the youth, seeing, in the mist beyond, a row of handsome grandchildren. She said 'Delph', being the supposed name of Isaak's father, or the name of Isaak's supposed father, which?

Delph was a hilly village on the border of Lancashire and Yorkshire, its bare bones supporting monstrous black clouds. The name would fall easily from the lips of anyone requiring a surname for a child. The liberty to choose might be the only privilege a bastard had. Mary Ann would dearly have liked to have called her child Hobshaw but at the time, because she knew her place, she called her Sheffield. It could have been cleverer to call her Antwerp for instance but at the time Mary Ann gave birth to Anne-Marie she was so happy to have her at all that no question as to her surname arose, she belonged to Mary Ann and therefore she was a Sheffield.

It was too late to worry about that now but it flashed across her mind that the village girl who was Isaak's mother had been 'a lot sharper' than Mary Ann.

She put her hands on Isaak's shoulders and said in her best Yorkshire: 'Tha's a gradely lad, Isaak!'

ELEVEN

AND THUS, a few days later, Mary Ann's gaudy green carpet bag and her smallest box stood on the hand cart in the yard. She had said farewell to the Mistress who had withdrawn even further within herself; wearing an absurdly large bonnet she had been crouched behind her desk and peered at Mary Ann with beady eyes from an abnormal depth within her headgear; it is lonely inside an immense hat.

In temporary silent protest the young ladies, too, had withdrawn into their fastness at least an hour before the expected departure and they might all have died, from the lack of sound coming from the closed door as Mary Ann passed. Mr Hobshaw himself intended taking Mary Ann to the coach terminal on the turnpike and to this end Sheffield was dusting the governess cart which went out seldom.

In her grey alpaca travelling gown and a large plain black straw hat which drooped becomingly round her face, tied over her head with a bow beneath her chin to keep it in place were she to travel on the outside of the coach, Mary Ann looked a picture. With the hat and ribbon she had achieved something as near mourning as possible, far from the shops. She had purchased the hat third-hand from a sempstress in the village and it belonged to the simpler fashions of twenty years ago.

Silas Clopton, too, had taken some care with his appearance. He swung into the yard in his new gig, the fragile spokes of the wheels flashing sparks of light in the sun.

'Nay, Silas Clopton!' Mary Ann cried and as she did so she was strongly aware of how much her speech had deteriorated in how short a time: she was unusually conscious of it because she was wearing her town clothes. Her cry sounded incongruous coming from such an elegant figure, but it delighted Silas Clopton, who sprang down from his seat and took off his beaver with a bow.

Mr. Hobshaw, standing at the top of the stone steps, scowled but looked relieved when he heard her say: 'Nay, I'm not a-comin with thee, lad!'

'Not so long ago you called me a nowt, Mary Ann,' Silas Clopton said angrily.

'Forget it. Happen words escape me, like, I don't mean.'

'Let us hope so.'

'You happen was a nowt once, but you're not one this morning. I'm proud to have you as a friend and that's a fact.'

There was soon to come a time when Mary Ann looked back at this small scene with pleasure, a time when every friend she had counted immeasurably.

After a few more pleasantries Silas unharnessed his mare and tied her up, saying that since his services were not required he would go inside and he and the mistress would get on with some business. 'Farewell, Mary Ann,' he waved his hat briefly and disappeared.

On the way down to the turnpike, followed by Sheffield with the old working horse and cart with the luggage, Mr Hobshaw spoke kind and comforting words to Mary Ann. The previous day Mr Hobshaw had taken Anne-Marie's small box to her and since Mary Ann felt that in this case she should leave matters to him, though she would have liked to accompany him to say farwell to Anne-Marie, she refused and Mr Hobshaw went alone. Though, he had to admit, Anne-Marie had looked tired and her manner was sober, she had, up-to-date, made an excellent impression upon her kind and good employers. They liked her manner and the diligent way in which she spoke not one word of English to her pupils, repeating over and over again her French remark, until they finally grasped her meaning. She would have them at least understanding the language within three months, at this rate.

'You will have quite enough to worry you without thinking day in, day out, whether your child is thriving. Our child I should say, for indeed I love that child, Mary Ann. I will take care to go and see her frequently, since my friends have begged me to do so. You need have no fears at all on her behalf.'

And later as she sat travelling at speed across the flat Flanders fields, 'God has been good to me,' she thought.

A fortnight later, all her fears realised, she was to cry passionately: 'Why has God done this to me?'

*

No sooner had the sound of the horse's hooves died away than there were stirrings in the young ladies' parlour. They could not make too much noise because Mr Silas Clopton was closeted with Mother on business.

They were angry and bewildered that their mother had not yet engaged servants to replace them. She seemed to have made no attempt whatever. And when spoken to on the subject was evasive, no, she had not advertised, no, she had not written to the local journal, no, she had not asked Mr Clopton to help find someone amongst the wives not already in the mill. Well, what was to be done? The second Mrs Hobshaw shrugged gently.

The old men were going to look after themselves, with midsummer still well ahead catering was easier, Sheffield had planted lettuces and was growing some tomatoes in the south-facing window. A village woman was coming up daily with cold chickens, cold legs of lamb, bunches of mint and cold steak and pigeon pies. Though invited to do so by Miss Lavinia, who caught this tame cook coming down the stone steps. she flatly refused to do anything in the big house. She had an invalid husband of her own whom she could not leave for any length of time, though she could cook in her own cottage she could not, or would not, do so in anybody else's house. So the young ladies fell to chattering excitedly about how it would be possible, first to find their whereabouts and second to plead with the servants who had been dismissed six weeks ago. Though it was more than likely these three had found new places, the young ladies were so desperate that they felt they might be able to induce at least one to return.

In time it became quite necessary for one or two of them to go into the kitchen because, frail eaters though they thought they were, they had to eat something. It is not incredible that none, not one single woman amongst them, could cook anything eatable, since they had been brought up as young ladies and young ladies, amongst other things they did not do, did not cook. In the larder they found cooked ham and the remains of a gooseberry pie made with scalded paste, locked up carefully the night before lest Mary Ann should help herself. Eggs were always available though no longer brought up with the milk by Isaak. Thus for three days they managed as they described it, to 'keep body and soul together', but on the fourth day after Mary Ann left, they were, as Miss Lavinia often said, 'quite starving'.

It was their turn to think God had been kind to them when the Shaws' dog-cart drove into the yard and from it stepped Anne-Marie. From it, too, were lifted the box which Mr Hobshaw had taken to her that same week, and her travelling case. There was a driver and footman and this servant ran up the stone steps and delivered a letter addressed to Mr Hobshaw.

Anne-Marie, dressed smartly and wearing her best frilly pantaloons as she had been at her departure, but almost invisible beneath her bonnet, stood watching the equipage which had brought her, leaving the yard, and raised a hand of farewell as they drove away. Then she turned and walked into the kitchen where Miss Lavinia and one of her sisters were topping and tailing gooseberries. She lifted off her monstrous bonnet and put it down on the table in front of her. She pushed her hair back from her face and gave a shuddering sigh.

'So you are back!'

'Did they ill-treat you?'

'Did you not like being there, child?'

'Your mother has gone. . . .'

'Isaak comes no more. . . .'

'We have no one to help us, we are starving.'

'Be sharp, Anne-Marie. . . .'

'Put on your working clothes when you have carried up your box. . . .'

'We need a meal and quickly. . . .'

'Miss Bee has taken to her bed. . . .'

'Please make her a tisane. . . .'

'Where is your mother's Culpeper, surely she has not taken it with her to Brussels for the short stay in an empty house?'

'Tell us why you are back so soon. . . .'

'No, get us food first. . . .'

Be sharp . . . be sharp . . . be sharp. . . .

'Go across the yard, child, and tell your grandfather,' (your two grandfathers), 'you are back, be sharp . . . be sharp!'

But she was not able to do that.

'Go upstairs and change into your working clothes . . . be sharp, be sharp!'

But she was not able to do that, either.

It was endless, it was a kind of torture. Anne-Marie stood quite still beside the table looking down at her own elegant hands recovered from this misuse during her short stay away. She looked round.

'What are you looking for?'

'The cat.'

'You are mad, child, we have no cat.'

'For what reason do you want a cat?'

Anne-Marie looked at them with naked and undisguised hatred: 'To hide my face in!'

They screamed. 'To hide your face in!' They were alarmed, they thought her seriously insane. 'No wonder you were dismissed!' And since she did not contradict, they knew she had been dismissed and were even more shocked, there was disapproval in it as well as surprise.

Miss Lavinia laid hands upon her and shook her: 'What is to do, what is to do?' she cried. 'You shall have a pig's foot hung round your neck, as a naughty girl, I declare!'

Still Anne-Marie looked round, this time with disgust: 'There is not even a cricket in this kitchen, it is too cold!'

For a moment the ugly sisters were silent, exchanging glances, telling one another, in their manner: 'I told you so!'

'Why should she return here?' Miss Lavinia wondered.

'Yes, why?'

'She does not belong here . . . but,' Miss Lavinia held up her hand, 'perhaps she does.' She relaxed her menacing attitude and said in a more reasonable manner: 'Anny, you are putting us sadly about.'

'Oh, for mercy's sake . . .' the other exclaimed.

Mr Silas Clopton was leaving, he had come to the house in his gig and left his cob in the yard, so he had perforce to leave through the kitchen in spite of the second Mrs Hobshaw's wishes. He stood now on the door-sill, a step down into the kitchen and said: 'What is to do?'

The second Mrs Hobshaw stood immediately behind him, hands clutching her cloak at her neck. Thus it was to an audience of four that Anne-Marie, harassed beyond control, screamed: 'I have been dismissed . . . I am in disgrace!'

*

Silas Clopton looked round at the expression of unmitigated horror upon the faces of the assembled women-folk and though the situation was pitiful, he had difficulty in restraining his amusement. So exaggerated was their alarm that they would have no response to match it, were a grave disaster to occur. One and all looked to their mother for guidance; they lived so far removed from the realities of life, so dependent upon trivialities were they, that when faced with a real-life situation they were at a loss. Instinctively they felt that their mother could not allow their snow-white selves to be contaminated and their instinct was right.

'Leave the kitchen, girls,' she ordered, and they meekly did so, rushing to report the event to Bee (Beatrice) who was seedy in bed and Amelia (Amy) who was searching for a button.

The second Mrs Hobshaw stepped foward and peered closely at Anne-Marie: 'This is your mother's business not mine. You must join her. . . .'

'No, no, no, no. . . .'

'She will barely have arrived at her destination,' Silas Clopton said, 'and she intends returning here. She has gone to her old habitation in Brussels for a purpose and she must be left to carry out her plans. Anne-Marie is Mr Hobshaw's responsibility at present, think you not so, Ma'am?'

Still clutching the neck of her cloak as though someone might try to snatch it off her, she nodded. 'Perhaps you are right, Mr Clopton. Still, Anne-Marie is not the first girl to be disgraced; there is no reason why she should not make herself useful in the kitchen. Do you agree?'

'If she can, Ma'am? Do you think you can, Anne-Marie?'

Anne-Marie nodded absently, thinking of something else, she was breathing hard as though she had been running.

'Very well, then. But you must go to Mr Hobshaw for advice.' She raised her eyebrows as though suggesting to Silas Clopton that the matter was now over and he, taking the hint, went out into the yard and prepared to leave. The second Mrs Hobshaw swept out through the kitchen and up the step into the hall, vanishing.

Anne-Marie took to her heels and caught up with Silas Clopton who was going down to the mill and not up the hill across the moor to his new house. He had disappeared over the brow of the path before she caught him up, even more breathless. He reined and looked down at her. 'Yes?'

'Dear Mr Clopton, I cannot, I *cannot* stay there.'

He climbed down and threw the reins over his horse's neck. 'Now listen, you are in no position to say what you can and what you cannot do, you will have to do what is most expedient.'

'But you have no idea, you cannot have any idea of how we are treated in that terrible place. We are not beaten but she would if she dared. We are over-worked cruelly and half-starved, we have different food from the rest and they watch us as though we were thieves. . . .'

'Dear child, you are not in a position to criticise. You are done-for, I mean done-for in that house. But in all fairness, I should tell you that the mistress is going through a very bad period. She has had to spend a great deal of money upon buying a loom which works on a new principle, a tapestry hand loom; it is a daring act, it is one of the first in all England and if it is successful we take a great leap forward as manufacturers, if not, we shall fall back . . . and she has her workers to consider. She is a marvellous woman, Anne-Marie, however much you may hate her. The wonder is she ever had those girls; she has the mind of a man in many ways.'

Anne-Marie stamped her foot impatiently: 'That does not mean we should starve to death . . . people have to live.'

'Not necessarily, not where money is concerned, not to *her*!' But he was doggedly loyal and would say no more than that.

He wanted very much indeed to hear the exact extent of Anne-Marie's disgrace and he waited patiently for her to start to tell him. But she stood wringing her hands and biting nervously at her knuckles and looking so distressed that he perforce said that she could count upon him as a friend and if she wanted help he would do everything to provide it.

'I need help now, now, now!' she cried. 'Where is Isaak? Why did they send him away?'

'Economy!'

'Leaving willing Mother and me to do the rough *rough* work as well as everything else!'

'Isaak has proved himself able to work on the new frame, he is becoming someone of use rather than an odd-job man. We are using him because we have no other weavers willing to help the ones already in charge. You will not be seeing much of him, I fear.'

There was a long pause, he was being patient because he had much to do this morning, with buyers awaiting him in the counting house. He stirred restlessly but still retained the kind expression on his face. She looked at him, a long look as though she sought something in his face. 'Mr Clopton, sir. . . .'

'Yes, Anne-Marie, what is it, child?'

'Would you marry me?'

'No, Anne-Marie,' he said firmly but kindly.

'I could work hard for you in your new house. Mother said you needed someone.'

'I need her, that is whom I need.'

Anne-Marie looked wounded.

'She is old. . . .'

'That she is not!'

'Too old to bear children! I could have children for you, Mr Clopton.'

'If I wanted any children I should want my own,' he snarled, 'not another man's.' It was cruel and he knew it the moment he had spoken; she put her hands across her face as though he had struck her violently. He tried to make amends but when she took her hands away her face looked different, almost ugly.

He said, 'I would be far too old for you, I am older than your mother. I need a grown woman to build me up; you have had her behind you all your life, you should be making a better job of it, Anne-Marie. I have had nobody, the gipsies left me behind as a baby, in a reed basket as a present for the county Palatine. A worker on the turnpike found me and lifted me over the county boundary into Yorkshire; I should soon have died if he had not decided to report his find to the minister. I have been on my own ever since and I am tired of it. Think on, Anne-Marie, what I have told you is why I am devoted to the second Mrs Hobshaw, she has all the business acumen I have learnt and am still learning.' He left her to fetch back his horse which had strayed away with the gig, holding the reins and preparing to mount. Where another middle-aged bachelor might have been ecstatic at Anne-Marie's offer, he was indignant, blowing out his cheeks and muttering: 'Marry her, indeed!'

He made as though to move off but checked his horse and looked down at the stricken figure. 'Your mother is a rod of strength, you need her and soon you will have her back, so hold fast. Six weeks at the most, Anne-Marie!'

TWELVE

TO MR HOBSHAW FROM MARY ANN SHEFFIELD, AN ACCOUNT OF HER VISIT TO BRUSSELS BUT NEVER POSTED

I STEPPED down from the *diligence* in bright sunshine and in spite of the heavy heart I could not but feel a lifting of the spirit for there stood the head footman Nicky to meet me with the light handcart for my baggage. Immensely tall, he was not wearing his livery but he looked smart in one of Monsieur le Comte's cast-off suits. Monsieur le Comte had informed him, from letters from home, of my imminent arrival and he had met every transcontinental *diligence* arriving for the past three days. It seemed an absurdly long time since we had parted and of course I fell upon his chest and wept.

His wife Nina in the lodge had a meal prepared for me and we sat over it a long time trying to talk ourselves back into the olden days of barely two months ago but knowing nothing would ever be the same again.

He told me every turn and twist of my lady's last three days upon this earth and how Nina, who was not part of the household, had come into the house and had ministered to my lady as best she could in the few hours of her mortal illness. 'Just after she died, her face was lovely . . .' Nina told me.

I said it was always lovely but Nina said this was something special as though she were a small child again. After we had all wept away any tears there were left, I had to start work.

Nicky told me that Monsieur le Comte had had an offer from the English Consul to rent the house for a period of five years and he had almost decided to let him have it. The elder boys were with their regiments and did not have to be considered but Bruno was not yet settled as to habitat or to what he now intended to do in the light of his mother's death. None of us could see Bruno as an idle young man of fashion. Though Monsieur le Comte was rich it had never been intended that Bruno should be a young man about town. The two elder brothers would have to share the running of the Houdenard estate in the country near Bruges when they left the Army but it had always been understood that Bruno would be an attorney. I asked Nicky if he was working hard at it and surprisingly he shook his head. Bruno, in Nicky's opinion, was not turning out the studious young man everybody expected. Nicky wore such a sly look as he told me this that I could not but infer that Bruno enjoyed a good time, probably, in fact certainly, in the company of the fair sex.

And shortly after I had set to work to unpack and put away my things, I heard Bruno himself in the hall, shouting for me, and I went down to greet him. He was cast down, yes, of course, he was cast down but when we were not talking about his mother it seemed he had a sprightliness and bounce which exceeded his previous youthfulness. But he had lost none of the delightful charm of manner and a striving to please.

I asked whether he would avail himself of the little house left to him by his Great-Uncle Peter and he said indeed yes. He was relying upon me to supervise the turning-out of all the personal household clutter just as soon as I had finished here. He intended selling all the out-dated and crumbling furniture and starting again with smart new furnishings from an *atelier* with which the family had long been connected. He could not abide heavy oak carvings and chests big enough to take a man. He wanted light walls and yellow curtains and decorative French furniture of the most elegant.

He caused me to promise to spend the following afternoon with him at the house and regarding the disposal of the things.

I was too excited, nay overwrought and tired from the journey to absorb all of the talk and it is only now, two weeks later when I am writing it down for dear Mr Hobshaw, that I realise he did not once mention the name of Anne-Marie.

Such, I am learning fast, is life.

*

Nay, I am at a loss to comprehend how it comes about that Bruno has not mentioned his friend and companion of but two months ago. At first I guessed he had forgot her already and I remained of that opinion, but after ten days during which I have seen him at least every day and he has still not mentioned her I am convinced that he deliberately fails to speak of her.

God forbid that I, a woman of the lower orders, should cast scheming eyes upon a young man of quality but I always understood that the friendship between Bruno and Anne-Marie was tolerated because of their relationship. That Anne-Marie was the illegitimate cousin of the d'Houdenard boys had never been mentioned in my hearing. But since my lover Giles Hobshaw, that hero of Waterloo, had been blown to pieces in battle, our liaison achieved the status of romance and not mere sordid backstairs fumblings. It would seem that there was nothing left of their beloved Giles save the baby Anne-Marie and their affections were extended to her in a manner that would never have happened otherwise.

My dear lady's bedroom and boudoir were a distressing sight; everything was always kept in perfect order but upon entering for the first time after my return I was startled and upset by the disorder caused by the City Authorities' attempts to disinfect the suite of rooms: the casements sealed and all drawers pulled out and left upon the floor, bedclothes hung about the room and the wardrobes emptied with the clothes strewn upon the furniture.

The sickness that destroyeth in the noonday I have heard it called and as I unhappily sorted out the beautiful garments, the winter cloaks, the pretty bonnets, I remembered April 14, after our arrival at Underscar, the two old men setting out for church (not chapel) after the young ladies had left, saying that this day they must go because it had been 'appointed for a National Thanksgiving to Almighty God for the cessation of cholera. So I shall thank God for that prolonged black frost in March, which is the only remedy for stopping cholera,' I remember Mr Hobshaw saying.

Nicky waited upon me with the utmost attention and I found myself on excellent terms with this servant who, though top male servant, had been my inferior in order. He was head footman and would have been below the steward in the usual manner but over all the years I had been in the d'Houdenard household we seemed never to have had a satisfactory steward. Either they stole bottles from the wine cellar to re-sell or they drank the wine to excess and it would be a surprising result were I to add up the number of stewards who had been dismissed for having been found dead drunk. There had been certainly two who had raged through the house with Delirium Tremens. Nicky had never wished to be elevated to steward; he would have had to give up the lodge and sleep in the pantry when the family were at home, and also he much enjoyed his work waiting upon the glass coach and the briscka. Thus when Monsieur le Comte was away Nicky was given the keys of the wine cellar finally and though I was head servant, with my own room downstairs, he was appointed head male servant and tried to keep a watch on the stewards which came and went. Nevertheless, there had always been a big gap between myself and Nicky and it now gave me much pleasure that we were friends and equals and, since all the personal possessions had fallen to me, I was able to give a great many things to Nicky's wife.

Indeed, I do not know what I should have done otherwise; there was so much. Nicky sought out all the boxes and trunks he could find and these I filled. Everything else I gave away, over and above Nicky's wife, to acquaintances and friends. I felt it exceeding strange that I should have so many possessions but I looked forward to the sorting out and altering of many of the clothes for Anne-Marie.

For a long time I pondered over dear Madame's beautiful dressing case with the silver-topped brushes and bottles. This would suit the future Mrs Silas Clopton, I thought and could not help smiling. It would suit Mr Silas Clopton exceeding well that his wife should possess such a luxury! Perhaps I should take it away with me and not try to sell it in Brussels, and perhaps, if I liked her enough, I would give it to that future wife, whoever she might be, for a wedding present.

Monsieur le Comte, had, of course, taken all my lady's jewels to a safe deposit for his future daughters-in-law but he had left everything else in the way of trinkets for me. I was lucky in being able to sell them well, putting the proceeds away carefully with other savings for the small cottage I had in mind for my old age. Within a week the rooms were quite bare of everything personal of my lady's and thoroughly cleaned out for the reception of the consul's wife, if it be she who will take possession.

I turned my attentions to my lady's Uncle Peter's house and in this task my constant companion was Bruno. He retained all the books but everything else was carted away to an auction room; his shabby old clothes were sent to the poor and also the cooking implements from the kitchen, so well worn and old-fashioned. Dusty old baskets were used to pack everything in and the kitchen was cleared down to its bare bones.

'And now, Mary Ann, Father would like to see you. He wants you to go to Spa for a few days and talk about Mother. Will you have time to stay longer or are you needed at Underscar?'

As I had said not a word about ourselves, Anne-Marie and I, our position or anything else, I paused for thought before answering. I thought at that time that Monsieur Bruno did not want to know. I did not like the idea of tiring him by telling him what he did not want to know. I saw Monsieur Bruno with a busy and full life of his own. Once or twice I had seen him in the company of two very pretty giggling young ladies and once, though we were all in the deepest mourning, he had mentioned that he was off to a whist rout.

'Will Grandfather Hobshaw be missing you unbearably?' he asked as I had not answered.

Until then he had asked me nothing about Grandfather Hobshaw; I chided myself that I was hovering upon the edge of being hurt and even annoyed but I was equally determined to be as superficial as he.

On that last day, when Uncle Peter's shabby four-poster bed was taken to pieces and carried down to the loaded wagons with the faded and torn curtains on top of the pile, Bruno had no bed to sleep on and returned to the family home until the new furniture he had chosen could be delivered. I had been in Brussels nearly a fortnight and had completed my tasks; I decided that, though I had no longing to do so, it was my duty to go to Spa to see Monsieur le Comte as he desired. I felt, in addition, that my dear lady would wish me to do so and I was packing my travelling bag to that effect when the express letter arrived from Mr Hobshaw.

Even in an emergency, in an express letter, he had to refer soberly to *the second* Mrs Hobshaw as though to demonstrate that he never for a second forgot the first Mrs Hobshaw.

> The second Mrs Hobshaw has died suddenly
> your presence is urgently needed here.
> H. Hobshaw.

I am not shocked but I am astonished. It is something not to be expected of the second Mrs Hobshaw. It seems only to be the salt of the earth, those whom we cannot do without, who die before their term is run.

In the corridor my boxes and baggage were piled; though I had discarded almost wildly I seem still to have acquired a large amount of goods, nine pieces in all and I have left it to Nicky to make arrangements for them to be stored until such time as our future is decided upon.

So I am on my way back to Underscar and an immense weight is fallen from me, I now wonder how I could even have contemplated returning to that house *with that mistress*, who has now conveniently died.

I showed my express letter to Bruno and asked him to communicate with his father. I am feeling some relief that I have not to go to Monsieur le Comte, I cannot feel at ease with foreign noblemen however pleasant they may be. I prefer to admire them from afar.

It was not possible to catch the next boat from Antwerp but I reckoned upon taking one the following day which sailed from Ostend. So Bruno went with Nicky and me to the *diligence* and before I climbed in and took my place, which Nicky was keeping for me, we turned to one another and I saw at last that dear familiar Flemish boy whom I had known since his birth; so English, as my dear lady and I had agreed. He was sober and at last himself and not the over-cheerful young spark he had been during the labour we had done together.

He took both my hands in his and said: 'Dear Mary Ann; I must say this, I feel my mother would like me to do so. You were my mother's life-line; she was never the European and in her more sentimental moments she told me she was always the Yorkshire lass and that she was proud of me in that I was "every inch a Hobshaw". She loved my father dearly but she was always detached, seeing him as a charming Flemish nobleman to whom she was proudly married: "... but oh, Bruno, how different he and the boys are from us!" I remember that I have often heard her remark in exasperation: "I shall never be a good Flemish housewife, however hard I try." '

Bruno looked round to make sure we were not overheard. Then he continued: 'So I have always *tried* . . . I mean, I have always remembered my English side and spoken English when the others spoke Flemish and French: Mary Ann, I hope to become an attorney but, don't laugh, I hope then to go to England and read Law in the English Law Courts. And Grandfather Hobshaw has a friend at the Inner Temple to whom he has written and with whom I am exchanging letters: in two years or so, it is possible that I shall be in London, that is, if I pass my examinations here. I am bi-lingual, you see, so I have an opportunity that, in a way, others as ambitious as I might not succeed. I have, or I shall have, knowledge of Continental law, and that could be of use, so my grandfather's friend says . . . Oh, Mary Ann, you have to go, the *diligence* is about to leave, Nicky is waving!'

I could have fainted when he stooped and planted a big kiss on my right cheek. He should then have said: Give my love to Anne-Marie, but he did not do so. He thanked me for coming and wished me farewell. Nicky kissed me too upon the cheek and I was packed inside. But much to the annoyance of my fellow passengers I stood up, blocking the glass-half of the door and cried: 'But Monsieur Bruno, would you leave your new house, newly furnished with the elegant furniture?'

'That is an investment, Mary Ann; I could let it, our Uncle Peter has discussed this with me often. . . .'

'But Monsieur Bruno. . . .'

But the official blew a pip-pip on his absurd little horn and we were off, with only my handkerchief (or rather one of my dear lady's lace ones) blowing in the breeze.

So now I am sitting in the sun on the quay at Ostend, my hand baggage beside me and, owing to a delay in departure from the early morning fog, I have written all this upon the little writing pad I had with me, the last page of which is now reached.

Since I shall see Mr Hobshaw, for whom it is written, before the post with the letter could reach him, I am taking it back with me so that he cannot complain that I did not write, even to tell him I had arrived. 'As you will understand,' I shall say, 'I was too busy.'

THIRTEEN

Anne-Marie was in what had long been called the dairy, though it was many years since butter had been made in it; any grass that had been suitable for the nourishment of even a single cow had long disappeared beneath the acid bracken. She knew how to use the retort for a distillation but she was trying to guess for what her mother had been using the retort whilst she had been away. There was a large jug of elder flower 'wine' upon the slate shelf and after sniffing thoughtfully at the contents of the small green bottle she decided it was a simple distillation of the elder flowers and drank the contents. Distillations, she understood from her mother, were always more potent than mere syrups. It was bitterly harsh that she should have arrived back at Underscar under this terrible cloud, only to find her mother had already left for Brussels.

Though many a girl may have needed her mother as badly as Anne-Marie now needed hers, no girl had ever needed her mother *more*, and Anne-Marie held her head in despair as she tried to remember, tried to remember the talk she had occasionally heard amongst the rough young Flemish servant-girls at the Hôtel d'Houdenard about the herbs to bring on their courses. She remembered the names of the favourite herbs but she did not know the English for them, and even if she had, the precious Culpeper was not to be found.

She was entirely bereft of hope and time was passing more quickly than time had ever passed. She could work till she could barely stand, without success, and now she was vomiting before meals so that as she tried to prepare their meal for the family she was constantly rushing to the sink under the critical eye of Miss Lavinia, who crept about the kitchen in a kind of hopeless endeavour to 'help'. Miss Lavinia knew it all but she was a dark one. She had probably not told her mother of Anne-Marie's condition but had she told her sisters?

It was only a matter of time and Anne-Marie was sure she would be flung out, as she had been thrown from the house where she was governess; dismissed with all the haste and abandon that might be required if someone had developed cholera.

After a particularly unpleasant bout of vomiting Anne-Marie, hoping she had been unobserved, was wiping her sweaty brow when Miss Lavinia slipped up to her confidentially: 'Where is your mother's herbal?' she asked her in a low voice. Anne-Marie could not answer but shook her head to show she did not know.

'You should have it,' Miss Lavinia said, 'because it is my guess you are taking things to bring on your courses that are poisoning you.'

'I care not if I am poisoned . . .' Anne-Marie turned away despairingly.

Three hours had passed since the note from the Shaws had been delivered to Mr Hobshaw before Sheffield was sent across the yard for Anne-Marie; as he crept into the kitchen Anne-Marie was startled by the expression upon his countenance, so sad was it. She must go across the yard and see Mr Hobshaw at once and her grandfather put an arm round her shoulders and walked across the cobbles, almost supporting her.

So there she was, standing between her two grandfathers and the scene would have made a wonderfully poignant engraving entitled: DISHONOURED.

Mr Hobshaw quietly handed her the note he had received from his friends. It said that it was with very great regret that they had had to return Miss Sheffield to him because it was so evident that she was in the early stages of pregnancy and, dear Mr Hobshaw, much as they would have liked to retain the services of his protégée they were sure he would fully understand that they were unable to do so. They were his most sincerely. . . .

Mr Hobshaw wasted no time at all but came straight to the point: 'Is it young Isaak?' he asked gently.

His kindness made Anne-Marie's eyes fill with tears. She shook her head. Had Anne-Marie been in a condition to think at all, let alone rationally, she would have wondered at the immense relief that came so evidently over the old man; a relief, it would seem, out of all proportion to the denial. And Sheffield's face, too, lightened considerably; the old men nodded at one another conspiratorially, as though reassuring each other. Sheffield even nodded as though he had known it all along: he patted his pockets, half hoping his pipe was handy.

'Who is it, then, Anne-Marie? I have a right to know,' Sheffield said.

Anne-Marie shook her head: 'It is no man here.'

'Here? What do you mean by *here*?' Mr Hobshaw asked.

Anne-Marie ran her tongue nervously over her dry lips. 'At home,' she croaked, 'I mean in Brussels. . . .'

'Then you are far "gone", child!' Sheffield exclaimed.

Anne-Marie shook her head. 'Not far gone, two months and a little more perhaps.'

She was shaking now and Mr Hobshaw made her sit down. He fetched a chair and poured her a glass of wine from a decanter standing in a silver coaster upon a rough wooden table at his elbow. 'Drink this. You can talk to us, tell us everything, child. We only want to help you; the world is still hostile to a girl in your position, and becoming more so as we become more, as they say, advanced. Do you not think so, Sheffield? As our pockets become broader to hold the money with which they are filling, our minds are becoming narrower. As I told Sheffield and his wife years ago at the time of their own trouble, with Mary Ann pregnant in Brussels, there was nothing to be ashamed of that their daughter had no husband. I believe your father, Giles Hobshaw, would have married your mother, Anne-Marie. He intended leaving the Army to be an artist but after knowing Mary Ann for some time his ambition changed to settling down at Underscar as the squire; he said in a letter from him that I still have, that he was greatly "in love with" Mary Ann Sheffield and he hoped it would not be too great a shock to hear that he proposed marrying her and bringing her home as mistress of Underscar. Our Giles had suffered a bad jilting from a young London lady of noble parentage; he wanted security.'

Gradually he had talked her into a kind of tranquillity.

Sipping her wine, Anne-Marie never took her steady gaze from his face and after a time she felt the warm comfort of the wine and the warm friendliness of Mr Hobshaw and she realised that her grandfathers were both her friends and wished her well and loved her.

'Does my mother know about this, this letter you speak of from my father?'

Mr Hobshaw said that he had not only told Mary Ann's parents, he had gone to Brussels expressly to tell Mary Ann herself, how her dead lover had regarded her. 'It gave her much comfort,' he said. 'And indeed upon receiving the news of Giles's death it comforted me that my son should have left behind him a child, even if not yet born. I prayed for your successful birth, Anne-Marie.'

Then Anne-Marie, weeping now, told them how much she loved her mother and how much she wished to keep her from knowing about her condition. She told how her mother had warned Anne-Marie, saying lightly that 'her virginity was a woman's best friend' and how she had told her never to repeat that and how most people would be profoundly shocked but that it was the best advice she could give Anne-Marie, even though she herself had not taken it. She had told Anne-Marie that loose behaviour with men was wrong and, they said, always led to unhappiness but that in her particular case it had led to great, very great happiness, in that she had given birth to Anne-Marie, a child of whom no mother could be more proud or delighted.

'So what is she to think of me?' Anne-Marie asked, raising her pretty, drenched eyes in despair. 'I would die rather than hurt her.'

'If you died it would hurt her most of all,' Mr Hobshaw put in sensibly.

Sheffield was still standing, miserably wishing he had his pipe upon him, for if ever a situation demanded thinking over with the help of a pipe, it was this one. He remembered his own feelings, before Waterloo, when Mary Ann, the daughter of whom they were so proud, had written to tell them of her condition. Both he and his wife were still proud of her and his wife had even whispered, during the night after the news was received, when they lay in the dark side by side, unable to sleep: 'To think she will be bearing *a Hobshaw*!' and both knew the other was smiling though neither of them could see it in the dark.

This time he had not that consolation but he felt himself quite unable to feel the necessary anguish, disgust, anger or any other feeling but a guilty pride in the fact that he would soon, with luck, be a great-grandfather. He badly wanted to say this to Mr Hobshaw and if he had his pipe in his hand he would find it easier to keep it behind the barrier of such teeth as he had left.

'Light your pipe, Sheffield,' Mr Hobshaw barked.

*

So no conclusion was arrived at, because what conclusion satisfactory to all could there be? The second Mrs Hobshaw would instantly turn Anne-Marie out of the house (for fear the young ladies might be contaminated?), she might not actually use one but here was the horse-whip mentality. Where could Anne-Marie go? There was nothing left to offer in the flat, it would only be a truckle bed in the tack-room, which was absurd.

Since the situation was intractable with no answer to it, or no easy answer, everything that could possibly be regarded as an escape from the worst effects had to be dragged out. And since she was clearly amongst friends as well as close relations, Anne-Marie was sensible enough to creep out of the reserve inside which she had been locked ever since she arrived at Underscar.

'I have worked harder than I ever thought I could,' she told them, 'far, far harder than I should, in order that I might . . . I might be rid of . . . you know. But it has not worked. I have taken various herbs and simples two or three times a day . . . until now I am desperate because I cannot find new ones in Mother's herbal. The Culpeper has gone, Mother must have taken it with her. There are only two things left . . . either I shall have to jump into the mill pond, which would hurt my mother more than anything, or . . . and this is the last wish I have left, except that of not hurting Mother, I shall have to marry Isaak Delph.'

Mr Hobshaw stood up suddenly, he picked up the decanter and poured into an enamel mug standing upon the table a good helping of the red stuff; he also charged Anne-Marie's glass. He slumped down into his chair and stared across at Sheffield who, content now with his pipe, was supporting himself against the edge of the table. Sheffield remained unmoved.

There was a long pregnant silence whilst Mr Hobshaw swallowed the contents of the enamel mug.

'The million to one chance . . .' he snarled bitterly, 'has happened!'

'Nay . . .' from Sheffield.

'What do you mean *nay*, Sheffield, you sound like a demented donkey. *It has happened!*' And with his mouth screwed up bitterly he stared down at his feet on the shabby hearthrug. 'Coincidence, indeed! It is the hand of a revengeful god!'

All this being above Anne-Marie's head she said that Isaak was a young man she had a liking for and he was not without ambition; he did not intend to sweep the factory floors all his life. He had often said how Mr Clopton had him in mind for working on a loom, and Mr Clopton would not forget him when there was promotion going. And as for his club foot, she said with unconscious humour, when they were wed she would get used to it, she would never notice it after a time, sitting at the table or in bed she wouldn't be able to see it anyway. 'And look how handsome he is!' She was almost talking to herself; clearly all this had been churning round in her head for a long time.

'Be quiet, Anne-Marie, be quiet,' Mr Hobshaw held his head. 'I must think; I'm an old man, too old for this kind of situation, I have forgot how I should behave . . . my mind is rusty . . . I cannot abide shocks and . . . How I wish my first wife was here still; it was she who did the thinking!'

'You can't marry Isaak Delph, lass, so that's that!' Sheffield barked.

With a pliant young girl that would have been enough, but Anne-Marie, for all her pretty broken-French accent, was stubborn Yorkshire to the bone-marrow.

'Why not? He wants to wed, and it's only that he's not thinking of getting wed this week. I could easy make him, easy.'

There was some heavy breathing from Sheffield whilst Anne-Marie continued: 'It is the only thing to do. The only one. He knows Parson well, it was he baptised Isaak! He lives next the church and I can go and live there, there's plenty of room in that cottage of his mother's. Whatever you say, Grandad,' she turned to Sheffield, 'it's the only way out. I'll make him a good wife,' and she ended with an expression she had caught from everyone around her: '. . . that I will!'

Goaded beyond endurance, Sheffield behaved as he would never otherwise have done in the presence of his master. He cast down his pipe and standing up he shouted: 'I'll not have incest; there's a limit to what the young folk can go to but I'll not have incest, and that's a fact.' And he banged his fist down upon the table, taking no notice of the hurt, and glared across the hearth at his grand-daughter. Anne-Marie, having no idea what the word incest meant, stared at him in surprise. It was a word strange to her, and strange, she would have thought, to Sheffield.

It was too much for Sheffield. He retrieved his pipe with a grunt or two, stumped down the stone steps and retreated into the tack-room, where he slammed the door and went into retreat.

'He means . . .' Mr Hobshaw could not get it out. He subsided into silence until he proceeded: 'He's a better man than I am. More courage. I'll tell you what incest means, Anne-Marie, even if it has to quench your innocent youth. It means having a relationship of the flesh with . . . with your own flesh and blood. In this case it means . . . having carnal knowledge of your half-brother! That's what it means.'

Anne-Marie looked down at her hands with interest, as though she had never seen them before.

'Isaak Delph is the son of my son Giles (your father) and a pretty village girl. Quite an ordinary situation. *Droit de Seigneur* is the polite name for it, the right of the squire, or squire's son, in this case. The girl was fortunate in that she managed to marry the man Delph in good time and whether he knew or not does not signify. Most of the village knew, I daresay. It was a commonplace event and there were those, no doubt, would say the girl was fortunate, since she was well endowed, by me. When the child was born she thought the club foot was a punishment of the Lord, so she told me. But it has been an advantage because everyone wants to help a cripple.'

Was Anne-Marie never going to speak again?

'They say a coincidence is without apparent causal effect but there are those who would truly believe of a coincidence like this one, that it was a finger of the Lord. I do not know what I think *except* . . . I do not want your mother to know. Giles's amatory adventures have apparently never been revealed to her and I am thankful. But I have no doubt the second Mrs Hobshaw knows, since she knows everything and under certain circumstances, if she wished . . . she could tell your mother. But you agree, do you not, Anne-Marie, that your mother should not, at least, be told by us? Maybe Giles told her himself, but I think not, if he had she could never have allowed your closeness with Isaak to flourish!'

Anne-Marie nodded, and stood up. Mr Hobshaw noticed her stiffness of movement and roundness of shoulders. He put a hand upon her arm. 'Has it not helped you, this unhappy talk we have had, we three? Is it not better, Anne-Marie, that everything should be known by us three, your two grandfathers and you? We love you dearly and we wish you well and we will help you all we can. This is not the awful disaster you envisage; it happens all the time in every family.'

'Perhaps . . .' Anne-Marie said drearily. 'But not every girl had a mother like mine, one she loves so much and must not wound. One who would take it more than hardly, since what she had always prayed would not happen to her daughter . . . has happened. So I am better dead!'

'How wicked, how wrong! Better dead!' Mr Hobshaw took her by the shoulders and shook her. 'There!' He apologised. 'I'm sorry, Anne-Marie, but you deserve that. You must not take this so hardly. I have been sick with it for hours since that note came, because I thought it was the fault of Isaak, but now we know it is not . . . I feel the problem can be overcome, *and will be*. . . .'

But long after Anne-Marie had crept away down the stone steps and Sheffield had emerged from his retreat and was whittling away at a piece of bone, Mr Hobshaw stood in front of him and said: 'What shall we do? Shall we send her after her mother to Brussels?'

'It would be best, Master.'

'Monsieur le Comte would be only too glad to have Mary Ann back as houskeeper. I shall talk to Anne-Marie about it tomorrow, the poor child has had enough for today. And on second thoughts, Sheffield, I should take her myself. I could perhaps bring some comfort to my son-in-law, Monsieur le Comte—but best of all, I can see my grandsons.'

That an idea and a reasonable one should have come to them seemed marvellous. They were almost happy, relaxed.

'But I tell you what, Master,' Sheffield said, 'begging yer pardon, sir, but this 'ere bastardy as they call it, does seem to run in your family like wooden legs.'

'And yours, Sheffield . . . and yours!'

FOURTEEN

THE DAY that she was dismissed as governess seemed endless; in the early morning Anne-Marie had been summoned to her employer and told she would have to go. Her employer had been kind but by no means understanding; she was simply bewildered, not being able to understand how a person who had Mr Hobshaw as her patron could be discovered to be in such a condition. She had no curiosity on the subject; she gave her a small amount of money due to her for barely two weeks and arranged for her transit back to Underscar, writing the note to Mr Hobshaw whilst the girl packed.

Thus Anne-Marie was back at 11.30 and the long day wore on. It was past dinner time when she returned from the flat but the wine had 'settled her stomach', as she called it, and she started to reduce the pile of washing-up left in the scullery from the young ladies' dinner.

She was in no mood for the wandering Lavinia but it seemed Lavinia could not leave her alone. To be in Anne-Marie's presence seemed to be irresistible to the pathetic woman, as though being near the 'fallen' girl gave her some of the warmth of humanity. She had an unconscious envy of Anne-Marie, who swam in a stream of life such as never touched Miss Lavinia.

Of the four sisters Miss Lavinia seemed to be the nearest to a human being, the others appeared mere cardboard cut-outs in whom every natural thought or wish or physical sensation or emotion had been ground out by circumstance. Lavinia carried round, within her, an almost overpowering feeling for Silas Clopton, being the only man, apart from her father, in whose presence she had ever been alone for any longer than a minute. What she felt for Silas Clopton was without words but over the years had come to her the absolute conviction that Silas Clopton entertained within his lonely heart an equal passion for her. She was convinced that her mother knew this but bent all her energies in preventing anything to pass between them. Of the four sisters she was the only one possessing a scrap of imagination and in some this quality can become a burden, as it had in her case. This image-making faculty had at least coloured her life somewhat since her mother's re-marriage, it had been both an intolerable burden and an ecstasy; it had been at least something to think about, whereas her sisters had nothing more important than a painful corn, perhaps, to occupy their minds.

It was Anne-Marie's aura which attracted her; Anne-Marie had 'been with a man', she had become warm and exciting and mysterious and different; she was everything Miss Lavinia wished and longed and hopelessly hoped to be and for which she would never give up longing. So now Miss Lavinia followed Anne-Marie about the kitchen premises.

'Mother has had no dinner,' she announced, ' 'tis her liver, as it was last time when we gave her the potion made by your mother, Anne-Marie. Cannot you remember what it was?' She held up the small green bottle.

'Wormwood, probably,' Anne-Marie said shortly. 'A terrible taste.' She bent over the tap in the stove, holding a large earthenware jug into which was pouring hot water with which she intended to wash the personal garments she had brought back from her situation.

Her mother, she told Lavinia, would never bother to make a distillation of wormwood at this time of the year; with all the tisanes she made through the summer months she crushed the herb and poured hot water over it from the tap in the range. 'She uses that small green bottle only to make an essence, which is much stronger than an infusion: she probably made elder flower essence before she left intending to take it with her,' Anne-Marie would guess, 'for use on the journey if she felt sick on the ship. But *I* feel sick, I have drunk it. Put the bottle back where it was, pray, Miss Lavinia, when Mother returns she will be searching for it.'

'How do you use the glass machine and the little lamp?' Miss Lavinia queried.

'If you make a distillation,' Anne-Marie said amiably because, though she did not like her, she pitied Miss Lavinia, 'you can use it diluted with water.' She carried the heavy bucket to the scullery sink and then, in the dairy, she showed Miss Lavinia how to make a distillation with the retort. She picked up the little green ribbed bottle with the cork in it, holding it up and saying that there would be no more than would half fill it. But that she could keep it for use another time, diluted in water. 'You will find wormwood aplenty down in the clough; it is flowering now. But certainly give your mother a long hot drink, a tisane, of fresh wormwood if she can take it.'

Off went Miss Lavinia, knife in hand, to harvest the herb and Anne-Marie did her washing.

She was hanging up the clothes in the yard when Mr Hobshaw called her up the stone steps.

'Anne-Marie, your grandfather and I, your other grandfather and I, I should say, have decided upon an action which would be the best for you and relieve you of some of your trouble. You must see . . . this cannot remain concealed from your mother!'

He told her the proposal: that he should prepare at once to take the journey to Brussels with her, returning her to the care of her mother in a place where they had both been happy. Monsieur le Comte would be only too delighted to have her mother back as housekeeper and in the large city Anne-Marie's personal trouble would be of little account to anyone. She could have her baby in the knowledge that no one would have to know she was un-wed.

Faltering a little as he watched the unhappy changes in her expression, he went on that, with any luck and according to the sailings, they would be able to start within three days and be in Brussels by the end of the week. He would despatch an express letter warning everyone concerned of their arrival.

No! No! No! Tight-lipped and as white as a camelia Anne-Marie said that could not possibly happen. That plan, she said, was quite impossible. Her face wore a determined closed-up expression and her eyes became quite blank. She refused to give him the slightest hint as to why she was taking up this attitude and the old man, in desperation, called Sheffield to his assistance. In vain they pleaded with her that it would be the best thing for her; the second Mrs Hobshaw would undoubtedly turn out of the house both Mary Ann and Anne-Marie. Even though the house belonged to Mr Hobshaw and he would forbid any such behaviour, she would get round it by making their lives intolerable. He knew his second wife only too well. He warned Anne-Marie that her life simply would not be worth living were she not to take their advice.

'But why, why?' Anne-Marie cried at last. 'Why is she so wicked?'

'It would take too long to tell you,' Mr Hobshaw said curtly.

Mr Sheffield shook his head at her as though begging her to desist.

'There are reasons,' Mr Hobshaw said, 'believe me. Life has dealt very hardly with that woman and her temperament is such that she has not been able to withstand the blows of fate. Everybody is made differently, Anne-Marie, the reactions of one person to an event can be the exact opposite from those of another person.' He thought for a few moments, then: 'As, for instance, your reactions to our scheme for your comfort. Look at you, Anne-Marie, declaring you will not fall in with our plans! I would call you stupid if I knew you were not. I will accept that you may have a strong reason or reasons for not agreeing but what are they? You must, if only for simple civility, tell me why you will not come with me to Brussels to be delivered to the mother you profess to love so much. *Why, child, why?*' he finally shouted.

'I cannot tell you, sir. I cannot tell you,' and Anne-Marie left the two bewildered old men and fled down the stairs.

Mr Hobshaw opened his separated hands, showing the emptiness thereof to Sheffield who observed:

'Stubborn, like her mother and her grandmother before her.'

'But stubborn can mean stupid and she is not stupid, Sheffield. Stubborn is to go on resisting without a reason but I am convinced she has a reason and if you continue to resist with a reason, it might be termed steadfast, eh, old man?'

*

Mr Silas Clopton, very late that same evening, sat at his brand new oaken desk with a fine tooled leather top. Holding a perfectly ordinary quill pen which he had sharpened with care, he was writing upon a card, in his best copper-plate handwriting, rules for the employees in the newly enlarged counting house.

NOTICE TO EMPLOYEES

(1) Godliness, cleanliness and punctuality are the necessities of a good business.
(2) This firm has reduced the hours of work and the clerical staff will now only have to be present between the hours of 7 a.m. and 6 p.m. on weekdays.
(3) Daily prayers will be held each morning in the main office. The clerical staff will be present.

(4) Clothing must be of a sober nature. The clerical staff will not disport themselves in raiment of bright colours, nor will they wear hose unless in good repair.
(5) Overshoes and topcoats may not be worn in the office, but neck scarves and headwear may be worn in inclement weather.
(6) A stove is provided for the benefit of the clerical staff. It is recommended that each member of the clerical staff bring in 4 pounds of coal each day during the inclement weather.
(7) No member of the clerical staff may leave the room without permission. The calls of nature are permitted and the clerical staff may use the garden below the second gate. This area must be kept in good order.
(8) No talking is allowed during business hours.
(9) The craving for tobacco, wines and spirits is a human weakness and as such is forbidden to all members of the clerical staff.
(10) Now that the hours of business have been so drastically reduced, the partaking of food is only allowed between the hours of 11.30 a.m. and noon but work will not *on any account* cease.

He was energetically underlining *on any account*, his pen spluttering in protest, when he received the fright of his life. A wild peahen-like cry came to him through the quiet darkness from some way off. He ran to the front door and flung it open, listening. It was a dark night, no moon or black clouds scudding across the sky. Dark and slightly foggy so that the damp evening fog had caused the two side curls worn by Miss Lavinia to straighten themselves into two pencils on either side of her livid face.

'Mr Clopton . . . Mother . . . she is lifeless, lifeless like death. She is surely dead.'

Mr Silas Clopton seized her by the arms (the first time a

man's hands had ever touched her, though afterwards she had no memory of it), 'Miss Lavinia, what are you saying?'

He drew her inside where she became hysterical and threw herself upon the brand new horsehair sofa in the hall, screaming and kicking like a mad thing. Mr Silas Clopton went for his third-class brandy and forcing a finger and thumb into her mouth he poured a liberal amount down her throat. Some of it went in her eyes, a little into her ears and quite a lot down her neck.

He was obliged to slap her face but not too hard. Finally she sat up, hiccupping, and assured him that her mother was dead. She had not felt well during the evening with pains in her stomach such as she had had before upon several occasions. A foul-tasting tisane of hot water and wormwood had been made for her once by Mary Ann and had been beneficial; after drinking the bitter brew she had soon fallen into a peaceful slumber. But this time, she had been sipping it and had partaken of almost the whole glass when she stood up and shouted out loud with anguish and fell . . . fell . . . and there she was, still lying on her office floor. One of the girls had rushed across the yard for assistance from Mr Hobshaw and Sheffield, both of them were abed, and she, Lavinia, had started across the moor. It had taken a half-hour of careful running in the dark.

Mr Silas Clopton squatted down beside the sofa and took Miss Lavinia's lumpy wrist in his hand. 'What are you doing, Mr Clopton?'

'I am feeling your pulse, Miss Lavinia, it is going much too fast. You shall ride back behind me. I must go and saddle Duke whilst you lie here and recover.'

It was her finest hour.

Too dark to take the horse across the moorland path, they went along the turnpike with Miss Lavinia sitting sideways but with her arms tightly round Mr Silas Clopton's waist, as he had instructed.

The three young ladies, Mr Hobshaw and Sheffield were all in the hall, sitting round the big table; the precious tea caddy had been brought out from Mother's sanctum, the key found, the caddy unlocked and all were partaking of tea at the midnight hour.

Mr Hobshaw had pronounced the second Mrs Hobshaw quite dead and she had been reverently covered with a tapestry carpet-like tablecloth from her own new loom. They would leave it till the morrow to send for the doctor from the town.

In the meantime there is no doubt that they were enjoying their tea, brewed in the big gipsies' teapot with two handles that Mr Hobshaw regarded thoughtfully, since it had never been used since his first wife died. Nor did they ever partake publicly of tea other than on Sunday evening. Mr Silas Clopton could not but remark, albeit to himself alone, that there was a loosening of the rules within a remarkably short time of the death of the mistress of the house.

Not having yet heard anything regarding the sudden (and disgraceful) return to the house of Anne-Marie, Silas Clopton made no remark as to her absence from the party and it was only after the initial discussion of the disaster had taken place and Silas Clopton himself had been given some now cool tea, that Miss Lavinia, in one of the moments of silence, said, loud and clear: 'Anne-Marie has not yet been told. She is in bed, asleep!' The idea of anyone sleeping through the noise and commotion was absurd. Silas Clopton wanted to know how it came about that Anne-Marie was there at all and Mr Hobshaw filled the awkward pause by saying that he would tell him in a few moments if he would come over to the stable flat.

But Anne-Marie was not asleep in her bedroom, she had left the house just before the event, she went to seek Isaak, her half-brother. She had gone to tell him that he was her half-brother and she woke him by throwing a handful of gravel at his window in order that she might do so.

Isaak awoke and came down to sit with her on the pig

bench under the apple tree but, awakened from his first sleep, his senses were deadened to the drama of Anne-Marie's news; he held her hand limply and was a disappointment. Since more was expected of him, he made an effort and in a short speech expressed his pleasure in having a sister, if only a half-sister. He was disappointed that he and Anne-Marie could not now be wed but it was clear that for the present his interest in his work superseded that of his marriage.

Anne-Marie wrung her hands; would she gain anything by telling him of her condition? Would he be able to suggest another man who wanted a wife? But she needed desperately simply to talk about her trouble to someone of her own age, sympathetic to her, and that she could not do. He would be affronted that her wish to marry him had simply been to do so as a convenience, giving a name to her child. She longed to say that since they were both, Isaak and herself, bastards, unwished-for children, why should it be unthinkable that her condition should be made a matter of public rejoicing? Beneath all the guilt and anxiety to keep secret that which could not be kept secret much longer, she was enchanted with her condition. But since her talk yesterday with the old men, she had another worry. That word incest; she yearned to know whether she had, in fact, committed incest, something which, until yesterday, she had known nothing whatever about. Yesterday, she had yearned to ask her grandfathers: But if you commit incest do you give birth to a monster?

Alas, alas, that her happy, carefree life had crumbled to dust in her fingers and was no longer worth living, for the baby she carried, though it gave her great secret glory, enchanted nobody else.

She gave bewildered Isaak a sisterly peck upon the cheek and ran back up the hill all the way, in one more desperate physical effort to exhaust herself. She was surprised at the activity that appeared to be going on inside the house, candle-lit windows and everybody up and about. But her personal distress was so great that she sought her own bed and pulled the bedclothes over her head to deaden any sounds there might be.

*

Promising that he would see to the doctor being summoned from the town, Mr Silas Clopton quitted the house about 3.30, riding back through the fish-coloured dawn. He had left his own house unlocked and the candle by the light of which he had been writing his new NOTICE TO EMPLOYEES had long since spluttered out. He went across to his desk and stared down at his work. He picked it up and threw it across the room, snarling that he was done for. He flung himself into a chair and started to bite his nails, as he had done as a child.

He had no liking for the dead woman but he had a great admiration for her. She had been the only child of an exceedingly wealthy cotton manufacturer of the town of Manchester in Lancashire. She had married a man of good family of the name of Hester. Unfortunately Robert Hester had been a quite spectacular blackguard and a drunkard of the very first order. At his father-in-law's death he had insisted upon a sale of the business and since the husband's word was, literally, law, his wife had had to comply. Then he had set to work to drink his way through the capital which had seemed so large that a reservoir of spirits might be drawn off without any appreciable reduction. Most men would have died from alcoholic poisoning but Rober Hester had a majestic constitution, he not only lived to see his four plain daughters come of age unmarried but he developed Delirium Tremens which for most drunkards is the end of the road. A madman, he smashed the furniture, tore his bedclothes to shreds and chased his young daughters around the house with lascivious sexual intent. Many times they were gathered screaming into their mother's arms and taken away in an omnibus until the danger seemed over but always they had to return because Mrs Hester must, perforce, try to keep some sort of control of her fortune over which, again perforce, her husband had, by law, complete dominion. And even in the end he did not die abed from the sickness from which he should have died long before, but was killed in a fall from a horse, not a spectacular fall either, he simply was too drunk to stay in the saddle and rolled off on to his head, breaking his neck quite completely.

For the only time in her life Mrs Hester went down upon her bony knees and thanked the Lord for His mercy.

Silas Clopton's carpet slipper business had expanded magically but Silas had not the capital necessary to become BIG; he allowed himself to be absorbed into the Hobshaw mill and though he became Under Manager he found in himself an insecurity which badly needed to be dug out by the roots, so he set to work to educate himself and did so up to the point of being able to simulate a gentleman; he could read and write and speak less broadly when he wished, he could dress like a gentleman and had good manners, he knew what the house of a gentleman should look like and he wore his hat with some style. All this took time and the pursuit of his aim did not leave him opportunity to look for a wife fit for a gentleman.

In the meantime Mr Hobshaw, retiring from the Diplomatic Service to devote himself to the thriving mill affairs, lost his dearly loved life's partner and, in the ensuing bewilderment and lack of judgement which can follow such a bereavement, he married disastrously a second time, the Hester widow with four unmarried daughters.

He encountered the widowed Mrs Hester at the funeral in Manchester of a mutual relative; though the iron had long since entered her soul she still remembered to behave with decorum and showed an interest in this Yorkshire squire whose business was growing, in the Yorkshire Dales. As the daughter of a successful business man (albeit cotton rather than wool, which is a very different substance), she conversed with an impressive knowledge of business affairs and Mr Hobshaw, who constantly felt tired and sick at the mere sight of a ledger, pursued her with lively persistence, quite failing to remember the necessity of going to bed with a wife. He needed her as he would need an excellent cook. Though relatives and friends waved flags of warning, expatiating upon the horrors of the four spinster daughters he would be taking on, he pressed his suit regardless. A wife to him meant one person, precious beyond rubies and now lost to him for ever. What he must have, at all costs, was a business manager and he was perfectly willing to swear before God that he would, etc. etc. 'until death us do part' in order to secure her services. For a few anxious seconds he had, in fact, fallen upon his knees before her, as she had boasted.

That she brought a great fortune with her counted not in the least, that she also brought the four grey-clad sad-looking spectres of bridesmaids to the altar behind her was nothing more than a nuisance.

So it was in fact the inexorable millstone of LIFE that ground the second Mrs Hobshaw from a reasonable, fairly warm-hearted but anxious woman, to a soulless miser, bereft of any human feeling, who would, as a matter of course, provide dirty butter for the servants. And it was this same relentless millstone to which were added their mother's constant warnings, that caused the four young ladies to believe that, beneath a calm exterior, a man was a ravenous animal to be avoided at all costs.

Secure in their parlour, the minds of the four young ladies shrank and shrank; their bodies suffered too since they took exercise mainly upon a Sunday to church and back; there was nothing they wished to read or to see beyond one another, nothing they knew about eating, other than the wretched diet provided, so they aged beyond their years and they all required spectacles and false teeth.

What will become of them now? Silas Clopton asked himself, not caring because they were not his business but mildly interested because they were heiresses in their own right and now at the mercy of their stepfather, Mr Hobshaw. As no one cared less for money than Mr Hobshaw they would leave his house well endowed, '. . . and good luck to them,' Silas Clopton thought, though it was clear that it was a hopeless wish since they had never had any luck. Nor had they even possessed a cat, let alone a dog; it was unlikely that the fortunes would end up benefiting either of those in any endowment of a home for lost quadrupeds. Not for one instant did the thought enter his head that he might marry, at least, one of them.

Silas Clopton, stiff in the cold dawn, pulled himself out of his reverie and went to get himself a long drink of rough cider, which he drew in great gulps from the jug, wiping his mouth upon the back of his hand as he would never do in company, and saying out loud that he was on his own now, and longing for Mary Ann. 'I'll show her,' he declared, 'I'll show her what I can do on me own.' A resolve which is the spur to fame and fortune.

He had not unsaddled his horse but left him tied to the post against the mounting block at the drive edge; with the bridle stretched as far as it would go, Duke was now standing with one foot on the doorstep, looking expectant. Silas Clopton fetched a bucket of water and watched him drink, then he climbed into the saddle and made for the turnpike.

'But from what has she died?' the doctor, still in his red nightcap, wanted to know.

'That I know not but from the talk I hear she was a-drinking a tisane as they call it, a warm drink of some medical property to cure a discomfort she suffered. These folk often have aches and pains and the cook, who has recently absented herself, brought a lot of new foreign ideas into the house. She is abroad at present but her daughter is in the kitchen and I understand it was this daughter from Belgium who concocted the potion and it was as Mrs Hobshaw drank it, she gave a groan and fell to the floor.'

'You're sure she is dead?'

'As sure as a layman can be, I could feel no pulse and her eyes are wide open. Yet she could be in a coma.'

'That is bad, if the eyes are open. I will come at once.'

*

'But I was not in,' Anne-Marie said.

'Anne-Marie, you made the potion!' Miss Lavinia screamed.

'I made *a* potion. . . .'

'For whom?' the doctor asked.

'For myself, sir.'

'For yourself!' the doctor repeated, surprised.

'It was a herb of which I know not the name but I have seen my mother use it.'

'Is there any of this left?'

'No, sir, I drank it all. The dregs I threw out of the window, the scalded and mashed leaves will be there on the ground outside the scullery window.'

'Why did you make a tisane, as you call it? For yourself, Miss?'

'I needed some drink, I came back here yesterday morning, starting early, no food was offered me, or drink. I did not want much food but I found some stale bread and cheese. I drank some of last year's cider in the morning but the barrel was empty after dinner. I prepared myself a tisane which I went down the clough to gather. I went out after that in the evening, as it became dark.'

'Where to?' Did it matter?

'I went out to see a friend who lives in the village.'

Anne-Marie looked round at the doubting faces; the four young ladies scowled accusingly and Silas Clopton raised his eyebrows. 'Why are you here at all, Anne-Marie?' he asked genuinely puzzled.

'I left the position Mr Hobshaw found for me.'

'I see. . . .' Of course he did not see. He had come without his hat or his stick and he did not know what to do with his hands, he had lost his jaunty saunter and had the uncertain feeling that there was something he ought to know but did not.

The doctor too looked and felt uncomfortable. 'Forgive me if I ask a number of questions,' he said, as though to everybody. 'But it is my duty to report upon every death and in the case of a sudden death it is essential that I come to the correct conclusion. We have only recently given thanks to the Almighty for the deliverance from cholera, that dread disease that kills within hours. I am not saying that this is cholera but it might be an allied condition, showing itself in an unusual form. With cholera there is vomiting and other familiar manifestations but in this case, you say, all of you, that there was no vomiting or undue recourse to the calls of nature, previously? You, Miss Lavinia, you actually witnessed this? I understand you took the glass from the . . . er . . . this young lady here' (he had been about to say young lady, changed it in his mind to 'servant' but could not bring himself to use the appellation and finally decided for 'young lady', but from the faces of the young ladies in his audience, he had chosen wrongly) 'and took it into your mother's study and handed it to her. Tell me what happened then, Miss Lavinia.'

'I have told you, Doctor. She drank it and fell.'

'Very, very unusual,' the doctor shook his head, thoughtful and unhappy. 'She had no kind of minor fit?'

'No.'

'Nor foaming at the mouth?'

'No.'

'Nor cry of pain?'

'No.'

'Wonders never cease. Well, well! I shall order the body to be removed from here. It is still very early in the day and we should have the body in the hospital mortuary before dinner-time. An examination, *post mortem*, I regret to have to tell you, must be performed. You will be informed of the result.'

Busily he stuffed the tools of his trade into his black bag. 'And I must tell you that if we are not satisfied with the result of the examination, I shall be forced to send up here for an examination of the sanitation arrangements; there is no residence in the land, high or lowly, that can be regarded as immune from the dread danger of Cholera Morbus.'

He left a circle of pale anxious faces and when Mr Hobshaw and Sheffield, who had returned to their beds for a few hours' sleep, were informed of the result of the doctor's visit Mr Hobshaw said: 'We must try not to send for Mary Ann.' By which he meant that despite Anne-Marie's stubborn refusal, he intended to carry out his plan to take her to her mother.

*

Mr Hobshaw was shocked and deeply distressed but if he were to have analysed his feelings (which he afterwards did H.H.) he would have discovered that he was afflicted by the extreme failure of his second marriage; now that it was over and he was relieved of it, he blamed himself for the breaking-down thereof. He sadly perceived within himself the germs of great sloth; at school and taking his examination for the Diplomatic Service he had the utmost difficulty in bringing himself to hard work. He possessed great qualities for the enjoyment of his life but none for the betterment of the community. The chance of a seat in Parliament had been offered him but he had declined it without any consideration whatever; he would not take the trouble. And even his attendance upon the Bench was meagre. Upon his second marriage he had been only too ready to let the whole burden of running the mill fall upon his wife, who seemed pleased to be able to do it. But it had brought out and encouraged all the bad qualities in her and turned her into someone with whom he found it impossible to live.

But the bad qualities, he realised, had been brought out in himself also. He had become a peace-loving, yes, but lazy and selfish old man, concerned only with his own immediate comfort and his own interests.

So his second wife had had all the strain and anxiety of struggling with the industrial problems and it had tired her out; her heart had proved unequal to the exertion. He was deeply sorry.

But when the doctor reappeared and told him, the following day, that he was not happy about the cause of death of the second Mrs Hobshaw, he felt an angry impatience. He had been planning a fine funeral to take place in Manchester, in the heart of that rapidly expanding town, his second wife's home-town, in the grave in which her first husband lay in the old churchyard. She had had no friends but all the relatives and connections of the Hesters would be asked to a grand funeral breakfast at the new Duke of Wellington hostelry. It would be similar to the funeral at which they had first met.

This way his conscience would be ameliorated but with the fussy doctor riding into the yard and tying up his mare and scrambling up the stone steps breathing heavily and announcing that he *was not satisfied*. . . .

'What do you mean . . . you're not satisfied?'

'I mean that there are no signs *post mortem* that Mrs Hobshaw was not a perfectly healthy woman. Certain organs have been sent to a laboratory and it will take some little time to cultivate and grow the microbes which might have killed her but I have seen several cadavers of victims of cholera and there is not the slightest sign of it, none at all.'

'What is to be done?'

'In view of the fact that I have retained these organs and that the examination will continue, permission will be given for interment and the funeral arrangements can go forward.'

And then, as he was leaving, he became less stiff and sympathised with the bereaved husband. 'I have been turning over in my mind the testimony regarding the herbal remedies she seems to have been taking from time-to-time. These are very old-fashioned, you know, Mr Hobshaw; some of us in the medical profession find this continuing witch-doctoring the bane of our lives. It is perfectly sure that many herbs are excellent medicinally and will always be used for classic conditions, ergot, for instance, to mention but one. But with the march of progress we cannot have the old village dames handing out potions right, left and centre . . . it's not right, you know. There are folk whose reaction to this and that medicine is different from others; one man's meat, you know, is another man's poison, eh? Do you not agree?'

He agreed, yes.

'Well, we found a good glassful . . .' he held up his thumb and middle finger to show the size of the glass he had in mind, 'of that filthy herb wormwood. Now, I have never heard of anyone dying of a draught of wormwood or *artemisia absynthium* and it claims curing any number of conditions but I'd say the "cure" just about equals what a good cup of tea would do the patient. I would stop it, if I was you, Mr Hobshaw. You have a houseful of women and they have possibly taken up herb-culture as a change from their embroidery; there is no telling what they gave Mrs Hobshaw, hoping, of course, to cure whatever it was she was complaining of, but who knows what common poison they may have picked up? I could mention as many common poisons as I have fingers on my two hands but I haven't time now. Good day to you, sir. I will communicate with you again if they discover anything helpful.'

*

'I took the glass from Anne-Marie . . . it was hot, I took it to my mother with a cloth round it, and she held it and sipped a little, till it was cooler. Then she drank it up, making a distasteful face,' Miss Lavinia testified.

Anne-Marie cried: 'She is lying! I made myself a potion from something I gathered in the clough which I know but not by name. I drank it myself before going out. I went out later when it was going dark. I do not know what time I returned.' She had gathered up, from beneath the scullery window out of which she had thrown it, the sodden little bunch of scalded, dead leaves.

All this was said to the ugly sisters, to Sheffield, to any neighbours who called in sympathy, to Isaak, to Isaak's mother, and, more than once, to Mr Hobshaw. Then suddenly it was a commonplace: 'Anne-Marie poisoned Mother.' Mr Hobshaw felt sick with horror when he first heard it said by someone but the arrangements for the funeral went ahead.

'Now is the time,' he said to Sheffield, 'when your Mary Ann must be recalled from Brussels to this mad house; take this express letter to the post, for me. And I do not know how you will behave to all your village friends if you stop to talk to them. The news is all over the West Riding. I do not know how it comes about that news travels so much faster than a human can.'

'I'll not talk to nobody,' Sheffield said soberly. 'And I'll tak no spoons to market, neether. They'll not see Sheffield till they've given over telling lies about our Anne-Marie.'

FIFTEEN

STARTING in the early morning the funeral party drove in hired four-horse coaches over the bare, bleak moors, foggy at first even in May, into the County Palatine of Lancashire and there, with all pomp and ceremony, the second Mrs Hobshaw was laid beside her first husband; there were many present who had known the Hester couple and who made some virulently sharp, and even witty, remarks.

But over the funeral baked meats and wine, benevolence set in; three of the young ladies sat starkly wretched but Miss Lavinia, ignoring her mother's relatives, carefully chose a place next to Silas Clopton, who had ridden over the moors. She seemed to be almost enjoying herself, though Silas Clopton was not by any means putting himself out to be anything more than civil. He remarked upon her manner, verging upon, but not quite, gay.

His second wife's brother-in-law deliberately sat next to Mr Hobshaw and offended that gentleman by saying that they must have a 'confab' about what was to be done 'with the girls, eh?' Mr Hobshaw regretted Lancashire manners but he positively deplored his wealthy brother-in-law, uncle of the young ladies. He said stiffly that there would be time enough for that.

'I bet you want to get clear of them,' his first wife's brother-in-law shouted, 'and I've a proposition to put to you.'

Mr Hobshaw declined to discuss it but his second wife's

brother-in-law nudged him familiarly in the ribs and said Mr Hobshaw wouldn't half be surprised at the plan he had. He'd drop over next week and 'spill the beans'.

Sheffield was having the time of his life, sitting with the hired coachmen and others at the bottom end of the room, reserved for the lower orders. It was a long time since he had been to a social gathering of any kind and after a mug of small beer (there was no discrimination under Mr Hobshaw's jurisdiction but they preferred it to wine), he became aware of the full glory of the merciful release at Underscar. For ten, as he called it, 'long' years this great black cloud had hung over the house, making everybody within the domain miserable. He had spent his whole life in the service of the Hobshaws, but the last ten years had been the unhappy ones. The drink went to his nose, colouring it brilliantly, and he began drinking the health of all his new friends. He had 'never enjoyed a funeral more', he told Isaak Delph, who was sitting up beside him in the gig on the way back home.

*

It was evening when Mary Ann climbed down, in the village, from the stage coach and looked round for the porter with the cart to carry up her baggage. Finding one waiting for the coach, she engaged him and set off up the moorland path in a leisurely manner, looking round her with pleasure because, in spite of her love of Brussels, she was home, the place where, until the last two months, she had always been happy. It must not in cold blood be said that she was extra happy because the new mistress was dead but in truth she was. The second Mrs Hobshaw was as out of place in that happy house, she put it, 'as a bull in a china shop'.

In the distance she saw the Scotch pines and soon she perceived her beloved child, head lowered, mooching about upon the edge of the clough. She called, she waved, she stopped and waited as Anne-Marie ran across to her. But not smiling:

anxious and ill-looking. Mary Ann clasped her to her heart: 'You're not looking well, lovey,' and the almost forgotten worries came rushing back to envelope her. 'Why are you not at your employment?'

'They have dismissed me,' Anne-Marie said clearly and distinctly, without any shamed mumbling. There was no secret to be kept any longer regarding the future. This new person who had been accidentally formed within her would have to be acknowledged sooner or later and it was now later rather than sooner; Anne-Marie, whilst still mooning amongst the herbs, knew that it would come to pass.

Mary Ann and Anne-Marie exchanged the stylised words that a mother and daughter, since the world began, have exchanged on this subject, mainly concerning: 'Who is the father?'

'A married man,' Anne-Marie lied, 'and I shall tell you no more, Mother. *Je ne savais pas . . .*' and Anne-Marie resorted to French. What she said, in effect, was that she had no idea how it happened; why had her mother not warned her in detail of the mechanics of sex? And Mary Ann could not answer that question in any language. Getting no reply Anne-Marie went on to say she had used every remedy she could remember having heard of but in the absence of the Culpeper she had not been successful and thus added to Mary Ann's guilt since she had taken the herbal with her.

Mary Ann said if she had tried all the usual abortificants and none of them had succeeded then it was a good sign, a sign that she would have a strong healthy child, and Anne-Marie stared in amazement at her mother's calm affirmation, but Mary Ann had experienced it all before, the anxiety and the final acceptance and in the long, long run she had had so much delight.

'It brings ill luck to work yourself into a frenzy,' she said practically, 'and now that the mistress has gone you will be able to have better food.' As she climbed on up the hill she took Anne-Marie's arm and pressed it to her side. 'What has she died of?'

Anne-Marie, after all the anguish she had gone through alone, felt a resentment at her mother's attitude; she intended to dismay her by snapping in reply: 'They say I have poisoned her.'

'Deliberately?'

Anne-Marie shrugged, at her most French.

'And did you?'

'No. Why should I?'

'Because she made our lives wretched, that is why.'

'Well, I did not, Mother. Miss Lavinia made her some tisane of wormwood; you gave the mistress one not long ago, you recall? Miss Lavinia might accidentally have added something else . . . we had not the Herbal, you must remember. The doctors have examined her body and they are not satisfied and it is all over the village, probably over the whole West Riding, that I have poisoned the mistress and for the reason you have just mentioned. And Isaak tells me a girl was hung for that crime, the poison of arsenic. . . .'

'Be quiet, Anne-Marie . . . this is no laughing matter.'

'I was not laughing, Mother.'

When they arrived in the yard they found the funeral party returned and the hired coaches leaving by the path down to the turnpike.

An astonishing sight met their eyes: the two old men, Mr Hobshaw and Sheffield, were directing an operation in which the four young ladies were struggling down the stone steps in their new mourning dresses and enormous black bonnets, with Mr Hobshaw's tall desk at which he always stood to work. They were making the most of their physical efforts, gasping and jostling as though undergoing a hard contest.

Mary Ann saw, at once, that the countenances of the two old men bore witness to gravely damaged feelings.

The reunion was sober in the extreme, the young ladies

taking the opportunity to stand aside from their task momentarily, and adjust their clothing which was only slightly in need of it.

Having wasted no time in re-establishing the long lost *status quo*, Mr Hobshaw said that as soon as his desk was back in its old place in *his* library he intended interviewing Mary Ann after supper and tomorrow morning *all* the young ladies, starting with the eldest, so that he might hear the version of each of them regarding their poor mother's sad end. If, in the meantime, the girls would be good enough to prepare a meal for them all, they would partake of it.

He went up to Anne-Marie and, with his hands on both her shoulders, he kissed her gently on her cheek.

'Get on with it,' he cried to the young ladies, 'and, Sheffield, you will eat with us and see to it that they do not damage the panelling with that piece of furniture.'

A new leaf had, without a doubt, been turned. Mr Hobshaw had clearly made certain resolutions regarding his unfortunate stepdaughters and lost no time in putting them to good effect. They must be kept busy, he told Mary Ann, they must have plenty of exercise and discipline. They were a miserably unhealthy lot and that was all owing to lack of exercise. As Mary Ann went to her room to take off her cloak and bonnet she could not help but smile; the years had fallen from Mr Hobshaw and he was, once again, the master of the house.

*

He could never remember their names, nor t'other from which. But he started with the eldest, Amelia or Amy, having refreshed his memory regarding their names, from Lavinia. She was thirty-eight and looked every day of fifty-eight; her skin was fawn-coloured and wrinkled and the backs of her hands had brown freckles which had certainly not been caused by the sun, grave-marks he had heard them called. He made her sit down whilst he leaned, folded arms upon his desk.

'Now, Amy, I want you to tell me your version of the night of your mother's death. Now don't cry, it is absurd to cry every time your mother is mentioned, pull yourself together, woman.'

'I am unnerved, sir. I cannot recall what occurred. . . .' A heavy sigh and then: 'Mother was cross with us.'

'What about?'

'I cannot recall, sir . . . she was often cross with us.'

'Surely you must know *why*. . . .'

'We are so . . . so. . . .'

'Yes?'

'She loved us so much, she was . . . she was afraid of losing us. She wanted to keep us by her always,' she was deeply agitated.

'Amy,' Mr Hobshaw said kindly, 'why cannot you tell me clearly, what I have asked?'

She pressed her handkerchief to her lips and simply shook her head.

'Do you know what they are saying . . . about Anne-Marie? What do you think, do you think it possible that she deliberately gave your mother something from which she died?'

'Nobody liked poor Mother; servants have always left, as you well know, sir. *We* understood her, we knew she loved us and wanted to keep us with her always.'

Mr Hobshaw was exasperated and felt himself reddening with annoyance. 'Go away, Amelia, fetch your next-in-age sister.'

She stood up sniffing, dropped her handkerchief and stooped to pick it up, bumped her knee against the chair she had been sitting in and scuttled away.

If he had had any hopes of Beatrice or Bee, they were quickly dissipated.

'Now you're not to be cross with me and look at me like that,' she squeaked excitedly, 'because I know nothing about anything; I . . . I've very bad eyesight, you see. As Mother always said, it takes me all my time to get about, let alone do any thinking.'

'Get about!' Mr Hobshaw exclaimed. 'That's the trouble with all of you, you do not "get about"; you stay in your parlour and bless me if I know what you all do all day.'

'There's our work, well, I can't do any because of my eyesight but I watch the others, and sometimes do the pressing. And I play the piano. And I have a little reed pipe I play; haven't you heard me?'

Yes, Mr Hobshaw had heard her, it would go on for hours when he lived in the house, like a stark north wind piercingly whining through a gap in the casement.

'Did you love your mother?'

'Well, I did often wish she would let us have a cat.'

'Why did she not?'

Miss Beatrice pursed her lips. 'Well . . . another mouth to feed, you know. But I must say I would have loved a kitty, I often told Mother so.'

'And what did she say?'

'No!' she answered simply, but wrinkled up her nose and looked to see if Mr Hobshaw had any idea of the fearful deprivation she felt. 'So now I am going to have one, I shall buy one with my pocket money; we all have pocket money, you know.'

'But how do you spend it?'

'Oh, we spend it admirably, we sometimes go down to the village, as you know, you have seen us. And then there is church collection, you know.'

'But what do you buy in the village?'

'Well, cotton thread and sweeties and *eau de cologne* and sometimes Amy buys *The English Woman's Domestic Magazine*, and once or twice . . .' she nodded naughtily, 'she has bought . . .' she brought it out in a whisper . . . 'penny dreadfuls!'

'Is that all?'

Beatrice looked exaggeratedly thoughtful: 'Let me see. Oh

yes, there's Euphemia's tonic water. She buys that herself if she goes to the village; she gets it from the old man who brings the potatoes. It makes her so happy and gay; she has a great deal of it. Sometimes we all have some, when Mother is down in the counting house, but we have to eat bull's eyes after because it smells, rather,' she raised her shoulders up to her ears and hissed with laughter: 'Oh dear, I shouldn't, should I?' Meaning laugh, he supposed. Or did she mean . . . tell him?

'Tonic water,' he repeated thoughtfully.

'And if it is bad weather, Isaak used to bring it up, he doesn't now, of course, with this new appointment on the loom.'

'Did your mother share the . . . tonic water?'

'Oh no . . . o!' Never! She was once very cross when she knew Phemie had had some, so we never dared let her know. Oh, I'm afraid we're very naughty, you know, and we all feel so full of remorse now . . .' but she was nowhere near tears, it was said almost defiantly.

'When did you last have some of this treat of Euphemia's?'

'Oh, Mr Hobshaw, that's the trouble. I hardly like to tell you but it was such a cold, cold evening, we had no fire in our parlour, and Mother came home so cross from the mill; poor Mother, she was not feeling well. She came straight into the parlour and said she did not want any supper. So Lavinia asked her if she would like a hot tisane and she said she would, so Lavinia went off to get it and . . . Mother came in here with the account book she carried . . . and, well, we had all had some tonic water so we became very very silly, like we do sometimes, very silly!' She spoke in a manner which made it appear she was scolding herself. 'I went up to bed, upon my word! It is nothing to be gained by asking me what occurred. The others woke me to tell me Lavinia had gone to fetch Mr Silas Clopton because Mother was in a faint. And that is all I can tell you.'

'Miss Bee,' Mr Hobshaw said persuasively, 'shall you miss your mother?'

'Oh yes!' She paused, 'Well, no. I know she loved us very dearly but, but, please do not tell my sisters, *I do not want to be loved so much.*'

'Why not, Miss Bee?'

'It means we are kept safely because we are so precious, kept in our little parlour-prison so that no harm shall come to us.' She said earnestly and nodded amply, 'I must confess, I should like some harm to come to me, I would indeed. When we lived in Manchester our father used to chase me round the house sometimes when he had partaken.'

And now Mr Hobshaw was revolted by the expression on her countenance: 'Sometimes I really wished he would catch me but he was inebriated, you see, so Mother never let him capture me. I said once to Mother, I said: "What is '*harm*', Mother?" and she stared at me so, I was quite afraid. She would not answer so I shouted after her I would let it happen and see for myself, if she could not explain. She came back and whipped me with her keys!'

Mr Hobshaw tried unobtrusively to wipe his brow with his bandana handkerchief. His immediate concern was to stop her.

'Perhaps some harm will come to me now,' she said complacently, 'now Mother is gone. Oh dear, how wicked I am being but I really am tired of being taken care of, Mr Hobshaw. I remember, when Mother married again, she told us: "Mr Hobshaw will take care of you" . . .' she tapped her fingers on the undersides of the chair in which she was sitting as though she were demanding a demonstration of being taken care of.

'I want to travel,' Bee almost shouted, 'I do not want to sit here for the rest of my life so that no harm shall come to me, I want. . . .'

'Good God!' Mr Hobshaw shouted. 'Fetch your sister in and save my reason!'

But when Euphemia came in Mr Hobshaw advanced from behind his desk and deliberately leaned over her as though concerned for her comfort in the chair in which she was sitting.

Just as he thought, gin, at twopence a pint! The smell was penetrating. He retired behind his desk and stared at Miss Euphemia in something like admiration. Nonentities? Then the word nonentity needed re-defining.

'Phemie,' he started confidentially, then stopped. He felt, suddenly, a brute. All these years these four women had lived in his house and he had taken no notice of them whatever. They were four ruined surplus women, part of the extraordinary upsurge of feminine cells of the nineteenth century. They were children mentally, they were also potential mothers; they were totally useless. Mr Hobshaw had never been a victim of the groundless veneration for females which bedevilled his era, but he was seized with a tiresome pity for these undeveloped and pitiful human beings, it annoyed him because it took his mind off the object of his inquiry.

'Phemie,' he said again and in the last hour he seemed to have become someone he barely recognised as himself. 'Tell me . . . are you sorry your mother has died?'

'What a strange question, Mr Hobshaw!'

'Yes, is it not?' he murmured and waited.

'The answer is yes and no, Mr Hobshaw.'

'Indeed!'

'I am dreadfully sorry if she suffered. . . .'

'Yes?'

'But I must be honest.'

'Please do.'

'We are getting no younger, Mr Hobshaw, in fact we are becoming antiques, yet we are kept as though we were precious pieces of marvellous china, in a cabinet. But we are four ordinary ugly women, Mr Hobshaw. Our mother loved us, nay, adored us is the better word; she wanted to keep us safe, safe from harm.'

Mr Hobshaw had heard enough about *harm* for one day: 'You see, my dear, it is being said, I know not how or why, that Anne-Marie has poisoned your mother and I am anxious to discover all I can regarding your mother's last moments. Do you know that Anne-Marie is my grandchild, my only grand-daughter?'

Euphemia hung her head and acknowledged that she knew that much *harm* had come to Mary Ann Sheffield at the time of Waterloo . . . she also knew that a great deal of *harm* had recently come to Anne-Marie herself, one way and another, but having led, with her sisters, a very sheltered life, she did not feel herself capable . . . etc., etc., etc.

'To hell with *harm*,' Mr Sheffield shouted. 'Do you think—in your opinion, did Anne-Marie administer to your mother something which caused her death?'

'I cannot say, Mr Hobshaw, much as I would like to help, I cannot.'

'Were you in bed, Miss Euphemia?'

'Yes and no!'

Mr Hobshaw clawed at the fringe of beard which grew around his countenance. 'Say that again and I'll. . . .'

'Yes and no,' Miss Euphemia answered obediently.

Mr Hobshaw leaned heavily upon his desk and stared at Miss Euphemia who became confused and embarrassed. 'I do not know why you take so much interest in us at present,' she cried. 'Though you did look at us when we were your bridesmaids!'

'Bridesmaids?' Mr Hobshaw looked puzzled.

'At your marriage to our mother. We were wearing grey *mousseline*, we were there! Do you not remember? I saw you looking at us.'

Mr Hobshaw began to feel he was losing touch.

'It may have been the last time you looked at us, Stepfather,' Miss Euphemia said sternly, 'you have taken no account of us since.'

'Was I wrong in that?'

'Well, Mother said she was obtaining a new father for us, to see we should come to no *harm*. . . .'

Mr Hobshaw held his head in his two hands. 'I took no account of you because I found you had empty heads and vitiated blood.'

'What is vitiated blood?'

'Lifeless, owing to inanition.'

'Oh dear, Mr Hobshaw, I cannot help you if you will continue to use such difficult words.'

There was a very long pause, then: 'Miss Euphemia, do you know what is the exact Greek meaning of your name?'

'Of course not.'

'It means . . . it is a word which is used for a less distasteful word: *tonic water* for *gin*, for instance, is a euphemism.' The silence was so long that Mr Hobshaw began to hate himself. What is the point? he asked himself angrily. Am I trying to make this woman tell me something vital or am I merely goading her?

Oh, valiant Euphemia! she did not protest or scream or become hysterical; she said very simply: 'You mean, regarding the gin?'

Mr Hobshaw nodded.

'I have, I had to have, some release, Mr Hobshaw, some hopes, some dreams; we are, were prisoners, dearly-loved prisoners, but prisoners none the less. I had to manufacture some escape for myself, and perhaps for my sisters. She loved us, so much, you see, my mother. She adored us.'

'I see.'

'So I am glad she died,' Euphemia murmured, looking dreamily out of the casement, 'because now the door of the cage is open and we can go out into the world and start to live, except that we are now too old and too . . . ugly . . . and too . . . childish . . . and too, much too stupid!'

'Did you poison your mother, Phemie?'

'No, Mr Hobshaw! I was not brave enough, even with my tonic water! But Lavinia did.'

Mr Hobshaw held his breath which caused his face to become

abnormally red. He waited so long for further information, afraid that he would break the spell of intimacy that was upon them, that he was obliged to let his breath go and it came out as a great sigh.

'But it was kindness in her to do it; we could see no future for Mother. Her marriage to you was not . . .' he thought she was going to say 'not a happy one', but instead she said, 'has not agreed with her. She had a terrible life with Father and when it was over we all thought how wonderful for Mother! But then she wed you and took over the responsibility of making the mill prosper, as she called it. It was like an illness: it ate her up. And though she loved us so much, she had no time for us, no time to make friends in the district, no time to simply sit with us and talk. Yes, it was an illness, Mr Hobshaw, and if you had a cat which you dearly loved and the cat could never sit still by the fire but was a rangy, restless, roaming cat, you would put it out of its misery, would you not?'

Euphemia looked up at him, her countenance was blotchy and her eyes bloodshot. 'I like you, Mr Hobshaw, the girls do not, they think you selfish, but I admire you and that is why I am trying to help you. Do not worry yourself, you are an old man and it is best for you to lead a quiet, unworried life. Now I have told you the truth you need worry no more. I shall not tell the other girls I have told you.'

Mr Hobshaw felt that he was trying to walk across a path of eggs without breaking the shell of one of them, were he to press too heavily he would be ankle-deep in smashed eggs. As delicately as he was able, he pointed out that the doctor suspected that her mother's death was unnatural and, as Anne-Marie was apparently the one who had at least knowledge of other tisanes made for Mrs Hobshaw, it was natural that she should be suspected of . . . tampering, let him say.

Miss Euphemia accidentally hiccupped slightly, gave a small giggle of apology and waved a vague hand in the air: 'Never mind, never mind, leave well alone, it will blow over.'

Well alone. 'But things are not well,' Mr Hobshaw pointed out, 'far from it. The penalty for deliberate poisoning is hanging . . . and not only hanging but drawing and quartering, even for a woman!'

Miss Euphemia hiccupped again and said it sounded terrible but, if you were dead by hanging, the drawing and quartering was neither here nor there . . . was it? 'Dead is dead,' she quoth soberly, 'I am sure you will agree.'

Mr Hobshaw leaned his whole weight upon his desk because he had need to do so, he felt weak at the knees.

'Now please, sir,' Miss Euphemia begged, 'let this be only between us. You may share one of the secrets that my sisters and I have betwixt ourselves . . . amongst us only and it would be unkind for you to repeat anything I have told you. So may I rely upon you, and hope that what I have had to say will be of assistance to you? No, of course, *no* blame must attach to poor Anne-Marie but as there is no proof available, none at all, the whole matter will . . . will die out.' She looked hopefully at him, expecting a hand-upon-heart declaration of complete silence.

'You must trust me, Euphemia, to do as I think best.'

She pressed her lips together and the knuckles of the hands she had folded upon her knee whitened.

'I can promise nothing,' Mr Hobshaw continued, 'because I do not know how matters are going to turn out. But I will promise to repeat no details of our talk, Euphemia, you must be content with that, my dear. I have the welfare of the four of you *and my Anne-Marie* at heart, you may rest assured.'

*

The preceding conversation might have made a man of sixty-eight feel a great deal older, disastrously shocked, defeated; Mr Hobshaw was shocked to a great extent, he was also stimulated. The four depressing corpses with which his house had been burdened for nearly ten years had suddenly turned out not to be corpses at all. They might be even greater burdens than corpses but they were at least alive and in that condition promoted active feelings and with a variety of active feelings one is far from moribund. Mr Hobshaw could be said to be feeling much younger and his head was seething with the speeches he would make to his fellow justices upon the Bench. How in the privacy of the Chamber he would plead for the life of his step-daughter Lavinia Hester in rousing terms. He would point out the iniquity of publicly hanging, recently at the market cross in the town, the young woman of twenty-eight who poisoned her husband.

'Cowards we!' he would cry. 'We fail to keep law and order so we resort to taking life as a revenge, fie upon us . . . ;' long before his time, he wished the whole abominable panoply of public hanging to be abolished. Miss Mary Blandy in Henley-on-Thames, eighty years before, had administered arsenic to her father and that at the instigation of her lover who had actually sent her the arsenic to give him; she had been publicly hanged in Oxford but there were those to this day who believed her innocent.

But, after a time, he realised that Miss Euphemia Hester, in her cups, had spoken astonishingly competently; nothing could be done to anyone without proof. If Miss Lavinia had, in fact, deliberately poisoned her mother it was deplorable. But proof would have to be found before anyone could be charged, even in these harsh times when there was no police force beyond the village constable who was simply 'one of us' sworn in by the magistrates.

It was now his duty to talk to Miss Lavinia but Mr Hobshaw told himself he must postpone it until he had had time to assimilate what he had just heard.

*

Hearing no sounds, Mary Ann entered anxiously. 'You are tired out by the young ladies, sir.'

Though he looked it, Mr Hobshaw denied it vigorously. 'Far from it, I have never been so astonished in my life. Mary Ann, you would never credit how those women occupy themselves; they are a small kingdom unto themselves, and far from being dead, they are alive, if like children. They have never grown up and they believe themselves to be infinitely precious and loved; they believe that is why they are virtually prisoners. Is it not marvellous! How many of us can coolly regard ourselves, ask: "Am I adored?" and receive full assurance that we are, indeed, affectionately treasured. Capital, Mary Ann, capital!'

He assured Mary Ann he could tell her no more now, but regarding the present troubles he said that he was convinced Anne-Marie was innocent of the preposterous charge that was abroad concerning her. But no warrant could be issued or official charge made, he declared, unless there was proof that she did this ghastly deed. What they must now do, he declared, was to seek proof and if no proof was found, no charge. He almost echoed Euphemia's own phrase—'It will die out'—but refrained (from superstition). 'So please take me into the kitchen and dairy and show me the utensils you have used for your tisanes, infusions, syrups, distillations, potions and all. Then bring out your Culpeper and let me study it from cover to cover. And, Mary Ann, I have an idea. Socrates, that wise man who went too far, died by drinking, from his own hand, a cup of hemlock.' He waved an arm: 'Hemlock grows everywhere . . . down in the clough. Could an infusion of this have been made and given to the second Mrs Hobshaw *accidentally*?'

'Sir,' Mary Ann reproved, 'it is an excellent remedy for external use, for inflammations and swellings anywhere on the surface of the body, but deadly poison to drink. But, as everybody should know, it does not begin to flower until August!'

SIXTEEN

MR SILAS CLOPTON came down the moorland path in a thoughtful mood; in the past ten years he had sometimes ridden over to Underscar along the turnpike, clattering into the yard and tying up his horse; other times he had walked, as he did this day. In a stroke, the habit of this past decade had been vastly changed and he realised how much he had relied upon this Lancashire business woman whose services to the business were now terminated with shocking suddenness. That last venture, for instance, the purchase of the new tapestry loom; he would never have had the courage to invest so much money in something so uncertain unless he had had the assurance of the second Mrs Hobshaw behind him.

He felt now that he must not fail to give the impression that he was absolutely certain of himself so that he would inspire confidence down at the mill. If only he had Mary Ann as his wife, established in his grand new empty house! A woman of the world, he considered her, someone who had seen life in addition to having a vast resource of common sense, she would give him great boldness.

But this morning he had heard what 'they' were saying; it was his opinion that the poor little half-foreigner, Anne-Marie, was mentally abnormal, he had never thought much of her. Her mode of speech was suspicious, her manner, her clothes, everything about her was alien and, therefore, suspect. He did not understand her and felt uncertain of himself in her company. However, with Mary Ann in such a desperate state of anxiety regarding her young daughter, there was no chance of getting her into the mood of even considering union between them.

He had now no clear reason for going to Underscar but he thought of the excuse of taking away with him the file of immediate business which he needed to consult, and as he crossed the yard Mr Hobshaw came out of the kitchen door where Mary Ann stood, one hand on the door jamb, thanking him for something. Silas Clopton bowed, he had taken much care to get his bow right and he raised his hat as he did so.

'Good-day, sir,' to Mr Hobshaw, 'Mrs Sheffield, you are back under sad circumstances, I fear, but how good to see you!'

'Well, sir, I must get on.' Mr Hobshaw was carrying Mary Ann's Culpeper and he said that before reading it he intended to write to Monsieur le Comte, he had left his quill pens in the flat, he would return to his desk. He hurried up the stone steps with a gait exceptionally brisk.

Mary Ann smiled; 'The master is once again his own man.'

'So I see . . . now tell me, Mary Ann, tell me everything.'

And she gave him a rough outline of events, ending with the condition in which she now found Anne-Marie. 'She has been so persistent in her attempts to bring on a termination to her trouble that she has made herself ill, I am keeping her a-bed today, the child is reed-thin and will damage her baby if I do not take care. Can you imagine the misery she has been in since our first arrival here? It was barely a week after we arrived she suspected her condition and that accounts for the frantic energy she put into rough work which she should never have been asked to do; it also accounts for her abnormal behaviour with Isaak Delph whom she hoped to marry before things went too far, you understand.'

She could not repeat all that Mr Hobshaw had told her last

night on his return from the funeral, when she had sat with him in the study and heard the story of the relationship to Isaak Delph, and many other things besides. The master had thought she would be unduly distressed to hear of her lover Giles's 'philandering' in his youth, but no, she said steadily that Giles had told her he had had many 'affairs'. And she looked past him and out over the moors and did not wish to discuss the matter further.

She looked past Silas Clopton too, and said it was possible that whoever had caused Anne-Marie's condition might be discovered and that Anne-Marie's greatest concern had firstly been that her mother should not know of her condition and secondly, she should not know who was responsible for it.

'And, Silas, my mind has become suspicious of everyone in the d'Houdenard household; there were fourteen servants and eight of them men, two tall good-looking footmen; Nicky, for instance, I have even thought of him! The stewards which passed through that house were legion, we had a terrible bad lot and the last one was as bad as any; I attached too much importance to the knowledge that my child shared my room in Brussels, and was therefore safe. I lost touch with the fact that, if you will excuse the vulgarity of it, Silas, sex does not only happen at night amongst foreigners. I was stupid. Do not smile, I blame myself entirely. She was supposed to be with the old Professor all day and every day and it never occurred to me for a second that she was not. I shall never forgive myself, never. I was enjoying my life, I had many friends in the city and no problems to worry me; I was selfish and careless and entirely at fault. No, do not try to comfort me, I deserve all I am now suffering, all of it! Stupidity is as unforgivable as vice, every bit.'

And after she had repeated Anne-Marie's account of the day she returned from her engagement as governess with the master's friends, in disgrace, the day, in fact, during the late evening of which the second Mrs Hobshaw died, she said she could not, however hard she tried, believe that Anne-Marie would occupy her mind upon that particular day (or any other day) with the poisoning of the second Mrs Hobshaw. Her first concern had been to find Isaak Delph and suggest their marrying at once, which she did, after he had returned from work and was indeed a-bed in the late evening.

'Why did he not instantly agree? I understood he wanted to marry her.'

Mary Ann was evasive, that was another family secret never to be divulged.

'The things I use for my brewing and distilling, the jugs for the elder flower "wine" I made before leaving for Brussels . . . they are kept in the corner of the old dairy and nobody ever touched them, not because I forbade it, not at all, but because nobody but myself was interested in them. Everything, I saw at once, had been used and Anne-Marie is vague about what she did; perhaps deliberately, I know not; but she says she drank the contents of the small green bottle I use for distillations; I had left it full of elder flower essence which is an excellent tonic and which I had intended to take for myself on my sea voyage; Anne-Marie says she knew it was elder flower essence and drank it . . . why? She says she knew it was a tonic and she drank it because she felt wretched. She drank it absently, as it were, not thinking. Well, I can get no more out of her than these vague replies; when I asked if she had given anything to drink to the mistress she said: "Perhaps I did, I could have done anything," and in the mood she was in, I understand she cannot be precise. She had a great shock, being dismissed immediately when her employer Mrs Shaw discovered her early morning sickness. And then Mrs Hobshaw's demise. . . . After a great shock, the doctor tells me, one can have loss of memory . . . the word he used was trauma which is what can happen to the body after an accident . . . a morbid condition he called it; he says that can happen to the mind as well. He told me that loss of memory as to the exact events could very well be the case . . . an excuse for Anne-Marie's behaviour . . . but he nevertheless believes the deed to have been performed by Anne-Marie.'

Never was there a more unsuitable moment to mention the matter of his own marriage but Silas Clopton was nearly driven to it when Mary Ann said that the best possible action would be to gather up their boxes, already packed anyway, and return post-haste to Belgium; she could find a room with friends, without a doubt; she could also find employment within hours. Mr Hobshaw himself had had this idea before the death of the mistress, she thought he now would prefer them to stay: but his mind was at present too occupied for her to ask him. She would not throw herself upon the mercy of Monsieur le Comte, far from it, she would not even let him know of her presence. But if, in due course, he needed her, she would go as housekeeper, she might even return to the Hôtel d'Houdenard to act as housekeeper to the British Consul who, it would seem, intended taking the house furnished for a term.,

He wanted to put his hand upon her and beg her, nay, on his very knees, not to go. His face was twisted with the pain he felt at the thought of losing her.

But Mary Ann placed her hand upon his arm. 'Do not grieve, dear Silas Clopton, this is much the best plan. I am branded, I know full well, but I am fortunate; my "mis-fortune", which I do not consider to be a misfortune at all, happened at the time of Waterloo and with one of our brave heroes; and furthermore, in those days folk were more tolerant, easy and open-minded. Now our minds have shrunk and are still shrinking, as Mr Hobshaw says, changes are upon us so fast and money is now distributed far farther afield than twenty years ago, as people gain in money they seem to lose in . . . tolerance. I notice it strongly in my own village, a pursing of the lips, a hardening of the eyes and the gossip behind the scenes. . . . Alas for the Good Old Days, Silas!' And she added that she would miss the two old men exceedingly.

He raised his hands despairingly; dropping his silver-topped stick he stooped to retrieve it.

She said nothing about missing Silas Clopton but went on, 'So now Anne-Marie, the bastard, is turning out as everyone might have expected; the grand-daughter of Sheffield who is greatly respected and pitied is nobbut a . . . well, you know the word I have in mind! And "clobbering" with foreigners, too! No, in Brussels it will all go unnoticed; they are incurably sentimental regarding birth, even wrong ones; they like babies, even bastards. Besides, I might fabricate a story that my child was married and her husband was . . . what . . . killed from a fall from his horse? Nay, anyone who knows how long we were away, not three months, will not believe that. You are very silent this morning, Silas Clopton!'

'You are doing all the talking, Mary Ann Sheffield.'

Mary Ann sniffed, 'Makes a change!' She added after a moment, 'So, God willing, we shall go.'

'But if they come with a warrant for Anne-Marie's arrest, eh?'

'Mr Hobshaw says they cannot do that without proof. I am convinced they will never find proof, it does not exist, because Anne-Marie did not, *could not*, have committed the terrible crime.'

'An unhinged mind, Mary Ann? Unhinged with anxiety?'

'Dear God, you sound as though you wanted her found with proof on her!'

And as he walked down to the mill with the week's file under his arm he decided that, unworthy though it was, when he said it, he actually did want it because it would keep Mary Ann here. Kept here and living in his house as his wife, he would be able to console her amply.

*

Presently there was a great cloppering of hoofs and standing at his desk, pen in hand, Mr Hobshaw looked up and was dismayed to see the vulgarian from Manchester alighting from his coach with the coachman holding the door open for him. Instantly Mr Hobshaw snatched up his cloak which he had worn the previous evening, when the air turned chill, and threw it over the muniment box, a spectacularly mediaeval device which had probably not been moved from where it stood, below the casement in the room his second wife had called the office, since the house was built. Though he was but merely acquainted with him through meetings at weddings and funerals, Mr Hobshaw knew this Mancunian through and through.

He waited for Mary Ann to announce him but the wise woman had shown him into the hall and left him waiting upon the master's pleasure.

'Shall you see him?' she asked Mr Hobshaw.

He nodded and went out into the hall.

This brother-in-law of the second Mrs Hobshaw would seem wildly improbable to those who did not know the type; he was, in fact, the absolute replica of the north manufacturing countryman, thrown up by the first industrial society: loud, brash, mannerless and single-minded. He made no attempt to dissemble, he had not come as a courtesy call, he had come to find out about 't'brass'. As the second Mrs Hobshaw's nearest living relative it was his responsibility to inquire into the exact situation.

Though an inch or two shorter than he had then been and stooping slightly, Mr Hobshaw showed only too clearly what a fine figure he made when he was His Majesty's Envoy to the Sublime Porte. His stiff bow, his pleasant expression, his deep voice: everything about him subdued the Mancunian. At the funeral Mr Hobshaw had not been 'his own man' but now, re-established in his own home, he was much more impressive. He called Mary Ann and asked her for two glasses and the second-best Madeira decanter but he did not invite his caller to sit down. Standing by the great refectory table that ran the length of the hall and had been built into the room so that it could not be removed, he poured out wine for them both, and sipped his own in an absolutely quelling silence. His guest swallowed his drink in one mouthful, throwing his head back and smacking his lips appreciatively. Mr Hobshaw, immensely dignified, refilled his glass and continued to sip gracefully at his own until it was empty; this took about five minutes of deathly silence.

Then he asked if the visitor would like to see the 'young ladies'.

'Nay, it's you I've coom to see.'

Mr Hobshaw then gently explained that regarding his late second wife's estate, his attorney, his late second wife and himself had, long ago, upon their marriage in fact, made full and complete arrangements regarding his late second wife's money.

'But what about . . .' the visitor jerked his head in the direction he guessed the young ladies to be, probably cowering behind the parlour door, in a huddle, trying to hear what was being discussed.

'A trust was formed for them, they have been receiving the proceeds from this, as far as I know, and their future is ensured. There will be more than enough to purchase an establishment for them wherever they would like to go.'

'You're not 'aving them 'ere, then?'

Mr Hobshaw said that it was as yet far too soon to discuss the matter with the young ladies. He, personally, considered it desirable for them to move to somewhere less isolated where they might make friends. Harrogate, for instance, was becoming a delightful town . . . Buxton? It was for them to choose.

'And now that you are reassured . . .' Mr Hobshaw moved towards the front door, only too glad to see that the horses had not been unharnessed and taken round into the yard for water. The coachman was waiting; Mr Hobshaw opened the great door in a leisurely manner and the vulgarian had no alternative to leaving.

Mr Hobshaw made no false valedictory statements about it having been kind of him to drive all this way so courteously; bowing again, he raised a hand in farewell and shut the door.

In view of how grateful he was shortly to be to this individual, Mr Hobshaw often deplored his own cool restrained behaviour upon this occasion.

*

He went back into the study and pulled his cloak away from the muniment box. He stared down at it as though he had never seen it before, when it had been a favourite perch of his as a child. At the age of three he had claimed it as 'his boat' albeit tied up alongside the quay, as it were. Four men could barely lift it. Until ten years ago it had contained ancient receipts, tithe statements and other documents concerned with vestry business. After his marriage he had cleared it out, since its contents were nothing which should be kept. The second Mrs Hobshaw had marvelled at the strength of it, finding even raising the lid an unexpectedly severe physical effort. Mr Hobshaw had kindly oiled the hinges and the lock and told her she could use it for her housekeeping money and/or valuables and he took the key from where it hung and gave it to her, saying that it would be too heavy for her key chain. She disregarded this last advice, however.

She seemed to have no personal valuables, he realised now and only now, at the moment in fact when the coach had driven up, that there must be something of value in the chest and this sudden thought had caused him to cover it with his cloak.

And another thing, and one which he intended to keep secret because it was more than enough to make a person's blood run cold, was that when he was called by Lavinia's screams to come and see . . . their mother had fallen dead and he had later been left alone with the body, he had knelt down and drawn aside the tapestry tablecloth and then her cloak which hid one hand, to find that in that dead hand was clutched, apart from the numerous keys, that one great key of the muniment box. He hurriedly covered it again with the cloak but, much later in the night, he drew it back once more and found that the clutching hand had mortified so severely that he was unable to release the key from the clutch of the long skinny fingers. The physical effort he had to make to attain the key caused him to have an acute attack of an icy ague. Finally, he not only detached the key from her fingers but from the chain as well. He was so cold and shuddering so violently that he hurried across the yard in the coming dawn light and gave himself a stiff brandy; he had thrown the key down somewhere in the flat and it would still be there.

He went back to his desk to finish his letter to Monsieur le Comte, his son-in-law, and to carry it down to the post.

*

There was a day or two of calm in the house, everyone slowly recovering their equanimity and restoring their normality. So that when the village constable, a man well known to them, who in childhood had held one end of the skipping rope over which Mary Ann had scored the all-time record of two hundred and fourteen jumps, trudged soberly into the yard with two assistants, it caused no sensation.

Nor did anyone have hysterics when he apologetically presented to Anne-Marie Sheffield a warrant for her arrest on the charge of causing the death of her employer by the administering of poison. A vehicle, he told them, was waiting, or would be waiting presently, down at the turnpike, to convey her to the town gaol to await the magistrate's pleasure. It was signed by two of the magistrates who had happened to be available. Mr Hobshaw knew them both, of course, and castigated himself severely for not having suspected that this might happen suddenly, before the next meeting of the Bench.

Mary Ann's first concern was for herself; she could barely stand and waves of blackness enveloped her. It was absolutely essential that she keep calm and upright and it was sheer will-power that caused her to smile at Anne-Marie and tell her it was all a mistake and Mr Hobshaw would have everything cleared up within hours.

Miss Lavinia who somehow was always, unnoticed, around, mounted the staircase with Anne-Marie to help her to pack a few essentials. 'Never worry,' she murmured as she pulled Anne-Marie's shawl across her shoulders, 'they never hang a pregnant woman.'

'How did you know?' Anne-Marie murmured back.

'I know everything, Anne-Marie, I make it my business. . . .'

'Then in that case you will know I did not do it and not frighten me talking about hanging. I am not afraid . . . they cannot hang you for something you did not do!'

Lavinia made no reply.

And downstairs and out in the yard again she said the same thing to Mary Ann.

And Mary Ann made no reply either.

To Mr Hobshaw she said she needed a book, or even two.

The young ladies were now upon the scene, one of them dashed away and returned with several copies of *The English Woman's Domestic Magazine* containing excellent stories, advertisements and a coloured fashion plate; these had never appeared for public viewing in the lifetime of their mother. It was Miss Amy, and before handing the magazines to Anne-Marie she astonishingly opened the top one and pointed to the story she recommended, 'This is capital; they address you throughout as "Mademoiselle the Reader", is not that quaint?'

Mary Ann was forced to turn away and walk unsteadily into the house, where she collapsed, half-lying upon the kitchen table. It was Sheffield who upheld the family sturdiness by coming forward and putting his arms round his granddaughter, 'Never you mind, love; they're in a mistake and the master will soon put things right, I'll come along down to t'turnpike with you.' And as the procession left the yard he was asking her if she would like to try her hand at 'chipping' which was his own expression for his craft. He would visit the prison tomorrow with a sharp knife and some horn and she could make a start at it; they would allow visitors, so in the meantime she would not have to worry.

Mr Hobshaw saddled his horse himself and overtook them as the grim party walked down the brow of the hill to the turnpike; he was on his way to see his friend the Chief Magistrate.

*

Amongst the things the doctor had officiously removed from the house had been the empty small green bottle in which Mary Ann had poured the precious drops from the retort, of elder flower essence which she later intended to take with her on her journey and which Anne-Marie had, later still, poured into her mouth. Empty though it was, this had now been tested by the experts and traces of the contents proved it as having contained a deadly and instantaneous poison. Certain insects kept for experiments in the laboratory had died immediately upon a minute application and a few drops of a dilution of what remained in the bottle had killed a full-grown rat.

When Mr Hobshaw told the young ladies and Mary Ann this on his return, one of them said: 'But the bottle was empty!' Her hands flew to her mouth as though to prevent the words, which had already emerged, from coming out.

Nobody noticed. Often people did not notice Lavinia.

'There is enough proof for an arrest, Mary Ann, but there will not be enough proof when the evidence is in the hands of one of the country's best barristers.'

Mr Hobshaw said he would be much occupied in the next few days; he would have to go to London, when he would obtain the advice and services of a barrister, if it came to it. 'I can afford whatever barrister my attorney recommends, Mary Ann. There is no longer any point whatever in concealing the fact that Anne-Marie is my grand-daughter; in our madly unequal society this fact will . . . will help.'

'But do they not know what the poison is?' Mary Ann cried.

'They cannot at present put a name to it but it is one which affects the nervous system upon the instant, organic they think . . . there cannot be many such. They say they will presently know the substance used. I am told it differs from the sleepy poisons, such as opium, and it has the property of causing no inflammation in the parts against which it comes in contact. This is why nothing showed at the physical examination.' Mr Hobshaw looked vaguely round: 'Mary Ann, it must be some poison around us, easily available. It *must* be something my second wife herself took accidentally: the contents of her bed-chamber have been carefully examined and there is an almost total absence of medicaments of any kind. With all your knowledge of herbs, think hard. I have read carefully through your Culpeper, it has taken me three nights from dark till early dawn to read through and I am not yet finished since I am studying carefully WORMWOOD. It is in alphabetical order and I am within a few items of the end, which is the letter Z, and at a glance I see there is no entry under that letter or the letter X, at all.'

'Sir, a herbal similar to the Culpeper but more simple belonged to my mother and I read it when required since I first learned to read so I knew it almost by heart; it finally fell to pieces. I know of no poisonous herb or plant which kills upon the instant. Certain berries are poisonous and one has always to warn children not to eat them, such as yew, for instance, and of course, certain toadstools, which, in fact, do not grow around here. But in any case there are no toadstools at all hereabouts in May.'

'And now, Lavinia,' Mr Hobshaw said, 'come into my study; I wish to talk to you more than I do to the others because you were the last to see your mother; perhaps it was for this reason I left it till now . . . come!'

So Mr Hobshaw set himself to have the kind of heart-to-heart talk he had had so successfully with her three sisters but she annoyed him in that she was too matter-of-fact and unemotional. She had seen Mary Ann making the tisane: she brewed, or infused the wormwood by crushing it and pouring boiling water upon it. Everybody found the taste detestable but the soothing properties were so excellent that it was suffered. When asked, she replied that she loved her mother, of course she loved her mother, though she did sometimes wish that her mother did not love them quite so fully; it meant that she was so possessive that they were kept almost prisoners in their stuffy parlour. It also meant that they had no friends and the companionship only of one another.

The atmosphere between them was more than faintly hostile so that Mr Hobshaw could not find it in himself to mention the precious tonic water and by now he was too worried and too full of plans for helping his grand-daughter out of her troubles that he could barely keep his mind on the limp female who stood before him. She seemed merely to be repeating hearsay; he could barely listen, in his present state.

SEVENTEEN

SILAS CLOPTON was not displeased with the manner in which he had conducted himself in the mill since the disaster. Nor was he pleased. He felt there was much room for improvement and this could be done with help, and the help would come from the source which so thoroughly occupied his mind.

What can I do, he thought desperately, what can I do to make her even remember I exist? Now that nothing whatever mattered to her but the release and proved innocence of Anne-Marie, he was further than ever from the realisation of his dearest wish. He felt that if he were to find some proof that Anne-Marie was not guilty, he could bribe Mary Ann. There were seeds of wickedness within him of which he was constantly aware; as he grew older he learned how to keep them sterile and inert. He was well acquainted with the difference between Good and Bad and he wished and endeavoured to keep clear of the Bad and on the side, always, of the Good because to do so made life so much easier. And, upon the whole, he had also learned, on his way along life's roughish road, to do so was infinitely more productive of success.

So the idea of presenting Mary Ann with proof and saying: 'I shall produce it before the justices *if you will marry me, Mary Ann:* if not . . . not!' was certainly not good but positively evil.

Nevertheless, he felt that to find absolute proof was easy

since he, with his knowledge of the mistress, and it was considerable since he had seen her four days out of every week for ten years, he felt certain that she had taken the poison *by accident.*

But why did he feel so certain?

Because she was the most unhappy wretch with whom he had ever come in contact and because, miserable though she was, she did not want to die. In fact, the thought of dying filled her with terror; she could barely be persuaded to go round the mills when the looms were working lest she have an accident. She would not go near the dye vats lest she accidentally slip on the stone flags and fall in. She would not even step upon the observation stage near the biggest carpet loom lest a piece of the loom should detach itself and hit her. She never wished to watch the raking-over of the raw wool because the floor was too greasy with lanoline and she would not go anywhere near the washing troughs in case she were hit by the rakes.

So it was an accidental death and he would stake his life upon it if required. But how could he prove it?

*

And as he pondered these things there was a tap at the front door and opening it he found Miss Lavinia upon the doorstep with the humble mien of a favourite dog who has been astray far too long, yet upon returning is sure of a warm welcome. She skipped inside, talking happily in a warmer way than he had ever experienced in her. Freed from the bonds her mother tied around her, she was in a totally uncalled-for mood of surrender, living in an imaginary situation and putting the onus entirely upon Mr Silas Clopton.

She made him strangely uneasy, scouring his mind for any action on his part that might have encouraged this mood in her. She had always been the one he met, if he met anyone, the mornings he came to discuss business with her mother and he had always greeted her civilly, to be sure.

Her manner was slightly flirtatious but so unnatural and ill-fitting that it repelled him and he could find in himself no response to her. She chattered and shrugged and cast him chilling sidelong glances and he understood quite what the position was. She had imagined herself in love with him and it was a condition which occurred frequently with women desperately anxious to marry but not having the least experience of life and no knowledge of how to set about it. He could not but feel sorry for her and anxious for himself.

He asked her to tell him again in detail what had happened on the night her mother had died, and she prattled away as she had done before, as though she had the whole thing off by heart.

'Then you think Anne-Marie poisoned your mother?'

'Of course.' She was shocked that he could consider otherwise. 'Of course she did, there was no doubt whatever, poor girl.' But this was no time to discuss unpleasantries, Miss Lavinia came closer and closer along the sofa and Silas Clopton shrank away as far as he dared, but now, if ever, was the time to probe into her mind. 'But you did not love your mother, you naughty one!'

'Oh, yes, I did! Oh, no, I did not, I did not. But she loved us much, so much.'

'Indeed? Then why did she keep you virtually captive so long?'

'She thought some harm might come to us.' There was a long pause and then she said: 'She was frightened that some man might want to marry us for our money and if that happened she would have had to use some . . . money, I mean. In fact, she thought the West Riding full of men waiting, ready to snatch some of us and marry us as heiresses. Mother knew how much money she had . . . nobody else did and I do not think one solitary man has ever thought of marrying us, except you.'

Silas Clopton picked up her clammy, limp hand. Though

she did no housework they were strangely red, he might well have been holding a dead trout.

'Can you cook?'

'Oh yes, I could, but I never have to do so.'

'You will have to do so, will you not, now you have no servants?'

'But we have Mary Ann. . . .'

'Do not astonish yourself if she leaves . . . you surely do not think she would stay with you under the circumstances?'

'She must!' Alarm sounded in Miss Lavinia's voice.

'But she will stay where her daughter is; if they were to hang Anne-Marie. . . .'

'Hang her!'

'Of course, for murder.'

'Murder!'

'By poisoning . . . poisoning of her mistress . . . your mother, Miss Lavinia. Have you not a full realization of what has occurred? You have told the doctor, I understand more than once, that Anne-Marie made the tisane and handed it to you to give to your mother, you have said all that and that is why Anne-Marie has, for the present, been detained. You will be forced to tell the justices everything you told the doctor, in court.'

'In court!'

'Of course, in front of the Bench.'

'Mr Hobshaw will be there. . . .'

'Not he! He will refuse to sit, since we now all know the girl is his grand-daughter, on the wrong side of the blanket, as they say.'

He was sitting so close to her that he could feel Miss Lavinia shuddering. Instinctively if unwisely he put an arm across her bowed shoulders.

'But why shall *I* have to go to court?'

'Because yours is the only evidence.'

'What is evidence?'

'The details, the . . . the whole story, which could hang her.'

After a long pause Miss Lavinia said she would not go to court.

Mr Silas Clopton had a good idea; he had a half-bottle of that unpleasant ardent spirit distilled from grain and flavoured with juniper, a half-bottle of which had been left behind by the builders; one particular plasterer needed a swig of it frequently, he had told Silas Clopton: '. . . in order to get my corners straight.'

He went into the wash-house and took the dingy-looking earthenware bottle into the kitchen. When he poured some of the contents into a glass he found it quite as clear as clean water, he sniffed it. It was Dutch Genever all right. He filled the tumbler half full and took it back to the drawing-room. He handed it to Miss Lavinia, now nibbling anxiously at the sides of her fingernails. She took it and sniffed. Her face lighted up: 'Tonic water!' she cried with pleasure. 'The only thing that makes our wretched lives worth living,' she amazingly exclaimed.

'I shall keep you company,' Silas Clopton said and going back into the kitchen he gave the brand-new iron handle of the well one turn and returned to the drawing-room carrying a similar glass containing similar-looking fluid. He held it up in cheerful greeting and drank it off; Miss Lavinia did likewise.

And now Silas Clopton longed to have a man there with whom he might make a bet that, in one form or another, he would get the truth, be it a grain or the whole story, in a few minutes.

*

Much later he saddled his horse and getting astride he pulled up behind him an almost, but not quite, inert young lady who moaned with the pleasure of being man-handled. He rode along the turnpike and turned up the rough drive to Underscar; nothing mattered now; Underscar had no mistress craning her neck to see who approached. He cared nothing for the other three young ladies so he tied up his horse at one of the Scotch pines immediately in front of one of the windows. He did not look to see if they were watching, he knew they were. Very gently and tenderly he lifted down his burden: 'How do you do, Miss Lavinia?' he asked. She grunted blissfully and kicked up her foot from which he saw she had lost a slipper, she was wearing only a knitted winter stocking. He took her foot in his hand and stared at the stocking; here and there were sharp green pin-like spikes. The slipper had dropped off somewhere along the turnpike.

He propped her up gently against the wall and remounted without a look back; it was, at least, not raining, he would leave her to her sisters to deal with her.

Slowly he rode down the hill back to the turnpike, his eyes fixed upon the ground. At walking pace he rode back the way he had come, turning up through his own gate and up his newly-gravelled driveway. Upon the fine wooden gate was a painted sign: OVERSCAR. He never passed now between those new gateposts without a feeling of pride. He had begun to despair of finding the other slipper when he saw it, lying just beside the entrance, at the top of the three steps down which he had carried the young lady. He dismounted and retrieved it, and into his flat palm ready to receive them there fell out of the slipper half a dozen or more spiky 'leaves' of the yew tree.

So now he had the visible proof he needed.

He also knew where, within a radius of five miles, two yew trees grew and that was on either side of the seat on the path up to the church, in the churchyard. He knew, too, whose cottage overlooked that part of the graveyard: the mother of Isaak Delph.

Straightway he rode down to the village and called upon Esther Crump-that-was. Leading from the exchange of pleasantries of a social call to a good gossip about the fearful 'goings-on' up at the Squire's, he was able casually to ask if she ever saw any of the young ladies.

Oh yes, Esther Delph saw them from time to time in the village, never in a group . . . in twos perhaps and sometimes alone. It was a pity they had not a dog for company, those poor women.

Dogs having nothing to do with what Silas Clopton wanted to know, he pressed on with an even more apparently irrelevant subject; had she ever seen any of them strolling in the churchyard?

Once or twice quite recently, oddly enough, she had seen Miss Lavinia. It had struck her as strange since the graveyard was a bleak and cheerless enough place. She had wondered if Miss Lavinia was going into a melancholy.

He refrained with difficulty from leaping on to his horse and with a cry of delight rushing to Mary Ann with the complete 'evidence'. He succeeded, however, in not doing so and Mistress Delph was so unsuspecting as to give him a glass of sloe wine before he left.

He cantered back along the turnpike with his hat at a more jaunty angle than ever. If he now in his pleasure and excitement still remembered his thoughts about 'bribing' Mary Ann with 'Proof' it all went by the board when, as he approached Underscar, he saw her standing, or rather leaning, against the wall hard by the front of the house, talking to a young man dressed in town clothes and holding his hat in his hand. Upon closer examination Silas Clopton did not know this young man but Mary Ann raised her arm and beckoned to him. Dismounting, he approached.

'Look, Mr Clopton, who has come at the fastest possible speed upon receiving Mr Hobshaw's letter to his father with *all* of our news . . . Monsieur Bruno d'Houdenard, the youngest son of Mr Hobshaw's daughter, Madame d'Houdenard, my late lady.'

'Pleased to meet you,' Silas Clopton said, holding his hat and bowing and not yet knowing how pleased, in fact, he soon would be. 'He will have come to see his grandfather,' he remarked, wondering where Mr Hobshaw was. But it was no time for social dalliance; Silas Clopton wished urgently to speak to Mary Ann.

'Mr Hobshaw has gone to visit the Chief Magistrate and is waiting upon some of the other justices, he will be some time. The long letter Monsieur Bruno's father received from Monsieur Bruno's grandfather has caused him to make his way here post-haste.'

Silas Clopton again raising his hat in the attempt to appear at his most gentlemanly, humbly asked if he might see Mary Ann alone for a few minutes, it was a matter of urgency.

*

So, when it came to the point, Silas Clopton put no price upon the information he had to offer, he was amply rewarded by the pleasure he received from Mary Ann's very evident relief. She examined the slipper.

'Yews!' she exclaimed. 'And Miss Lavinia was the only one who spent any time in the kitchen; I often left my Culpeper on the dresser; she has read in it, probably many times, she has seen me using the retort for distilling, too. A quiet little thing, in and out of the kitchen like a shadow, saying nothing but observing everything.'

Yew was such a simple shrub; farmers could become extremely agitated when their cattle were anywhere near it; but they made sure it was never allowed to grow on their farms. Mary Ann said she had always understood that the danger to cattle was the sharp-pointed spike-like leaves which, it was believed, perforated the stomach lining and thus caused death. Children were warned by parents not to touch or lick the soft pretty pink berries which it bore in autumn; they were considered deadly poison but Mary Ann had herself experimentally eaten one or two as a small child, without any effect whatever.

She ran for her Culpeper and read out extracts from the entry under the heading YEW:

'This tree, though it has no place among medicinal plants, yet it does not deserve (at least in our climate) so bad a character as the ancients give it, viz. a most poisonous vegetable the berries of which threaten present death to man or beast that eat them; many have eaten them in this country and survived . . .' (me for one, Mary Ann put in). 'However that may be, it has very powerful poisonous qualities, that rise by distillation. In this form it is the most active vegetable poison known in the whole world, for in a small dose it instantly induces death without any previous disorder; and its deleterious power seems to act upon the nervous system without exciting the least inflammation in the part to which it more immediately enters.'

Distillation was no mystery; in English country villages there could always be found one or two who kept their equipment hidden from prying eyes, yet who distilled spirits out of grain or anything else they might try, for private consumption or for sale to close friends. Gin was so cheap that it might hardly seem worthwhile to manufacture it at home, but to consume it free was better than having to pay twopence a pint for it. When a man received ten shillings and sixpence a week pay, every half-penny counted.

'And to think,' Mary Ann exclaimed when all the more important thinking was done, '. . . to think the master read through this old book of mine as far as W . . . E . . . Eh by gum! There's nobbut four entries come after, and this about Yew is one of them!' And after they had exclaimed over this ceasing to study the Culpeper on the very edge of discovery, Mary Ann said more soberly, 'Miss Lavinia has been looking all over the house for her lost slipper, asking us if we had seen it; it annoyed me, as if it could matter what had happened to her slipper at such a time!'

Silas Clopton took the footwear containing the damning evidence and replaced it carefully in his pocket. 'The doctor and the Chief Magistrate have been dealing with all this together. Mr Hobshaw being in consultation with the Magistrate I will take this now to that busybody of a doctor —but he's quite right—and tell him my findings. Do not expect Anne-Marie to be returned to you at once, Mary Ann, it will take a few days: Miss Lavinia will have to be questioned officially, of course.'

*

And so for Mary Ann, for Sheffield, for Mr Hobshaw and most of all for Anne-Marie herself, there took place that which happens upon occasions in life: the awakening, the discovery that it has all been a nightmare; still sweaty with fear, dizzy with dismay, hopeless with despair, they looked round and all at once . . . it was over.

Two days later, a solemn procession once again approached Underscar: the village constable, the magistrate's officer and a bystander to give a hand in case of trouble. Miss Lavinia was not sitting with her sisters but, thoroughly unnerved by events, she was doing what she had never done before and humbly helping Mary Ann to scrape the first new potatoes of the year, because whatever disasters occur there are people left for whom meals must be prepared and life, such as it is, must go on.

The deputation almost apologetically presented the new warrant and arrested Miss Lavinia, and Mary Ann ran for her cloak and some few necessities in a valise belonging to her dead mother, for Miss Lavinia, never having been anywhere, had no valise. Mary Ann wished there was time to warm up the tongs and re-create the two thin, thin ringlets that fell down either side of the girl's pathetic countenance, the sight of which caused Mary Ann almost to weep; *almost*, because inside she was so relieved on her own account that she was happy.

But in the end, as the small procession took the pathway down to the turnpike, Mary Ann did weep because she found it sad: Miss Lavinia *did* give her mother a cup of hot poison, which was wicked, but she gave it in self-defence because she wanted to live the life that her mother had given her and not to finally slip out of it, a mere rotten vegetable.

*

In the meanwhile, Mr Hobshaw, in spite of the awfulness of his task, felt he had been listened-to sympathetically both with the Chief Magistrate and subsequently, at a private meeting in the vestry, with the rest of the Bench.

In fine rolling prose he had voiced his noble sentiments; the first Reform Bill was two years old, the Whigs had entered the best phase of their history; for a decade, liberal attitudes swayed the country. He prayed his fellow Justices to consider the case of Anne-Marie Sheffield with compassion; in a descriptive matter which surprised nobody more than Mr Hobshaw himself he set forth in words the manner in which the second Mrs Hobshaw had brought up and treated her girls. He attributed no spite or blame but the impression he left with them was that she was a grim gaoler. Anne-Marie, if indeed she were guilty, had built up against the second Mrs Hobshaw a great fear out of all proportion to her mistress's actual intent. She and her mother, as servants, had been half-starved and grossly underpaid and Anne-Marie had had to work in a manner she had never experienced.

'Dear sirs,' he ended with humility and a touching honesty: 'she is my only grand-daughter, conceived at a highly emotional time in our history and born to the sound of the guns of Waterloo. As some of you may know, I, in my early days, was a selfish fornicator and I must admit that my beloved son Giles inherited some of his wicked desire to deflower a young girl, but in his case I do believe he intended to marry the girl.

'History has repeated itself, alas, and the unhappy victim, in terror lest her mother should know, *may have acted* as she *may have done*, from a mind that was become unhinged. Bear this in mind, my good sirs and friends, I beg you, when you come to consider both your verdict and the penalty. . . .'

The five Whigs who bore him company upon the Bench banged their feet and cried: 'Hear! hear! the penalty!' whilst the Tories looked down their noses and later, amongst themselves, deplored the freedom from reserve; these chapel folk really did overdo it; his little impromptu speech was sadly tainted with the red-hot-gospel manner of the chapel-goer. But though one might deplore him it was impossible not to like Mr Hobshaw, and when it came to the final verdict of Guilty at the full-scale trial by jury in York the fact that the Justices had requested that the prisoner, though she turned out not to be the same girl for whom Mr Hobshaw had pleaded, be recommended to mercy, bore weight.

*

When Mr Hobshaw had taken to the post his last urgent letter to Monsieur le Comte regarding the condition of Anne-Marie, he had greatly hoped for an immediate response. He had felt it expedient to acquaint Monsieur le Comte with the whole calendar of events at Underscar. He was proud to discover that he had judged that nobleman correctly; Monsieur le Comte had at once summoned Bruno and asked him point-blank if he was responsible for Anne-Marie's condition. And when Bruno had willingly admitted it, his father, not without one of his shrugs, had commanded Bruno to make haste and repair the damage, marrying her at the earliest possible moment in whatever impossible circumstances he might find at Underscar. In spite of the total disregard of the parental advice that had been given Bruno, Monsieur le Comte said liberally, it could turn out to be a happy state of affairs, Bruno was, after all, only his youngest son.

Thus, in less than a week from the posting of his letter, Mr

Hobshaw was able to welcome his grandson at Underscar and, during the delay that had to be endured before Anne-Marie was safely back in the fold, he took his grandson round the mills and for long walks across the moors to demonstrate the extent of the Hobshaw domain.

And Bruno, on his side, whilst walking across the moor, told his grandfather that his mother, seeing how close the two young things were becoming in Brussels, had had a serious talk with him. Bruno had said he wished to marry Anne-Marie and his mother had replied that she would not be averse to this provided Bruno waited till he was of age and, in the meantime, had some experience of other girls. She said that experience should crowd upon a young man like Bruno, living a gay life in a large city; he would not have to wait so long, but *wait*: that was her message.

His father, on the other hand, had been dubious; they had some talk on the mechanics of sex and his father advised him to restrict his sexual activities to experienced women and that when Bruno had had some observation of events he might consider Anne-Marie in quite another light. Propinquity, and Monsieur le Comte had been quite familiar with this unusual English word, which he used proudly amidst his French, was a wicked propagator of '*mesalliances*'; 'You are apt to marry the girl you are accustomed to,' was the translation of something else he said, in his wisdom. And, as a final shot, he had reminded Bruno that hasty behaviour on the part of his, Bruno's, English soldier uncle, had been responsible for Anne-Marie's existence, so the girl was his first cousin. The marriage of first cousins, his father told him, is by no means undesirable but there were certain hereditary hazards, such as the inheritance of one undesirable element in the parents' character being inherited by both offspring. But . . . and Mr Hobshaw could see the Count's exceedingly foreign shrug, both hands outspread: '*Vraiment ça ne fait rien . . .*' it depended upon how much one believed in heredity.

And after they had tramped another half mile or so and Mr Hobshaw had thought over the parental advice with which he wholly agreed, he said: 'And yet, Bruno, after all this excellent opinion given to you . . . it is you, and not one of the house servants or the drunken steward, who is responsible for Anne-Marie's condition.'

Bruno clawed his hair in exasperation at his grandfather's words.

'Of course, it is not one of the house servants, Grandpapa: Anne-Marie was not one of them.'

'No, but . . . how did the little newcomer-to-be get where it is, then?'

'I loved Anne-Marie and I love her now and I am still certain that she is all I need in the way of a wife . . . sweet beyond words, clever above average . . . gentle and loving. . . .'

'But?'

'Well, sir . . . I was saying our last farewell, sir; I beg you to use your imagination. We . . . we went . . . too far, that is all.'

'All!' Mr Hobshaw snorted.

'I have told you everything, Grandpapa, everything. I told Anne-Marie all that my mother had said and what my father had had to say about us two and we agreed, upon our solemn honour, crossing our hearts, that we would not see one another or write for three years. And in order to make it easier for both of us when Mary Ann's time came to return to Brussels she would not come back with her mother but remain in Yorkshire and find a position as a governess somewhere near here, near you. And that, I believe, is exactly what she did but they threw her out when they knew she was *enceinte*!' he added bitterly.

'That is only human nature,' Mr Hobshaw told him. 'They could not keep Anne-Marie in her condition with young people around her. They are kind, understanding folk, I have waited upon them and they have spoken highly of Anne-Marie's abilities. To them this . . . this pregnancy is a disaster.'

'So fate has taken a hand,' Bruno said happily. 'Now I must marry her and with great willingness. She is the most steadfast creature alive; what other girl would have withstood the necessity of getting in touch with me and telling me I must marry her at once? She would have seen herself hanged first.'

'But I would not!' his grandfather shouted.

Mr Hobshaw gave Bruno a great enthusiastic clap upon the shoulders and said a problem now arose as to who would marry them as they were both Catholics and Catholics in England, in spite of the constant splendid castigations of the Reverend Sydney Smith, were not favourite people. He would find an answer.

*

Mary Ann received notice that her daughter would be returned from the gaol and the exact time of her arrival was notified. She was coming home at the country's expense, since she had been wrongly detained.

She arranged to be absent, not very far away, when the arrival was expected and she left Bruno, on his own, to welcome her home.

When she returned from her walk on the moors, the couple were watching for her to come down the moorland path to the yard; Bruno's arm was round his girl's shoulders and Mary Ann, opening her arms wide, pressed them both to her.

*

Later, when they had talked it all over, Mr Hobshaw said: 'Their happiness-ever-after will not be total, Mary Ann, it never is, but I feel sure that those young people have as much happiness ahead as they deserve.'

He moved totally back into the big house and Mr Sheffield de-contained himself in that he spread himself back over his three rooms and had pleasure in leaving his carvings exactly where he put them down and not having to tidy up; he chuckled with pleasure at the happy ending, as he hoped, to their disastrous predicament.

Mr Silas Clopton bided his time.

Mary Ann willingly took over the cooking but Mr Hobshaw insisted upon two young girls from the village coming daily to do the housework. Bruno and Anne-Marie were married by a private chaplain at the nearby house of Catholic friends of Mr Hobshaw. Six coaches-and-four drove the wedding party over for the ceremony and back to Underscar for the wedding breakfast and later Bruno and his bride drove away, back to Brussels amid a shower of flower petals some of their guests had gathered from the syringa bushes. The young ladies, three of them now, had not thought it seemly to attend the wedding but they stood wistfully at their windows and waved as the happy couple left.

What will become of us? they asked one another gloomily.

*

It cannot be said that, during Bruno's prolonged stay and the preparations for the wedding, Miss Lavinia was forgotten. This would have been impossible for Anne-Marie was the chief witness both at the Court of Summary Jurisdiction and at the Trial by Jury itself. It was all quite simple and clear; Miss Lavinia had prepared a distillation of yew leaves in the period when the house contained only the four young ladies, no servants; Anne-Marie in her employment as governess and Mary Ann in Brussels after the death of her lady.

The small green bottle with the elder flower essence had been in the dairy along with everything else concerned and Miss Lavinia had prepared her essence in a small cream jug; she had had to use the retort several times before she could obtain what she considered to be enough, and she had carried the dregs, that is the wet and pounded finished-with yew leaves, out to the compost heap where all other vegetable matter was thrown. It was found by the village constable after removing the top layer of waste material. It was one of the exhibits.

When Anne-Marie had returned in great distress from her dismissal from the Shaws, she had drunk the contents of the small green glass bottle because she knew it would contain a tonic made by her mother, it was always used for such. She replaced it where she found it. Miss Lavinia had decided to use this same now empty little green bottle for her essence rather than leave it, where it could be found, in the small jug. She had been able to carry this bottle about in her pocket until the right moment for its use, and as she carried the hot infusion of wormwood from the kitchen into her mother's sanctum, she had taken out the cork and poured the yew fluid into the glass. She did not taste it because she did not wish to poison herself, but she knew from shuddering with distaste at the wormwood infusions she had drunk, that any taste it had would be wholly disguised by the wormwood.

Mary Ann's evidence was mainly technical details as to how the distillations were done, and she told the court what a small amount of fluid came from distilling, and how it might have to be done several times owing to the dry quality of the yew 'leaves' (as the book called them). She had described her astonishment that this plant should have been used and she also described the strong blanketing flavour of wormwood.

It was a strange affair that not once during the Summary Jurisdiction and later at the Trial by Jury, not once was Miss Lavinia asked why she did this foul deed. The attorney retained by her mother's family spared no expense in having sent down from London the best barrister that could be obtained. He had a majestic presence but it would seem he had hardly read his brief. He was, however, quite satisfied with himself since he relied heavily upon the Magistrates' recommendation to mercy. After the verdict of Guilty he rose to the occasion and gave an excellent oration upon the subject of 'attenuating' circumstances (nobody on the jury knew to what he was referring) and begged His Lordship to be guided by compassion and reduce the penalty to one of deportation.

One can only guess what went on in the mind of His Lordship (and that is always plentiful but imponderable). He gathered his robes about him and left the Court to commune with himself, returning an hour-and-a-half later with the answer required: deportation. Miss Lavinia fainted, but that mattered not.

*

Nobody cared what the young ladies at Underscar were up to because that could scarcely have amounted to anything; their immediate worry, other than that of distress for their sister, was how to dispose of all the empty bottles which had increased so alarmingly in number. Their walks, two at a time, became almost daily and became greater in length, to far further than they had ever walked, across the heather and the ling.

But yes, rescue was coming.

Mr Hobshaw looked up from his desk, where he was standing with his quill pen, scratching away very fast, to see no less than a coach-and-four pass the house and drive into the yard, for there was no room in front of the house for such an immense equipage.

It was the vulgarian from Manchester who, having been unsuccessful last time, deemed it expedient to be drawn from Manchester across the turnpike over Blackstone Edge by four horses this time, complete with extra coachman and two footmen.

'How d'ee do, Mr Hobshaw, how are you keeping?'

It was a form of greeting Mr Hobshaw detested, he always wanted to answer that he was not keeping but going steadily bad, like an overhung grouse. Later he was to deplore this in himself since the relative from Lancashire brought glad tidings amounting to salvation.

Self-important as this cotton manufacturer was, he had no need of any newspaper publicity to boost it, but he was pleased and flattered by it all the same, referring to Miss Lavinia as 'my niece, poor thing' and accepting graciously all the sympathy poured upon him by the sycophants of the town of Manchester. He enjoyed benevolence, he felt it suited him and no doubt behind all his absurdities there beat a kind enough heart and a genuine wish to Do Good.

Here was unexpected and capital news; he had a married daughter in Australia, married three years to a rising young sheep farmer and right down in the convicts' country of Tasmania which had begun development at a fine pace.

The Commissioner in charge of the reception of the convicts at Botany Bay was a man of sensibility, so he had heard, the newly-arrived offenders were sorted out, graded from murderers down to simple sheep-stealers and those in the lower scale were found positions with the local inhabitants, such as they were, and many of them made good.

The deportation ships were deplorable but in the case of women, though there were not many, special arrangements could be made, with money paid by relatives, and they could be sent in twos and threes in cargo ships, herded together but separate from any ordinary passengers.

These newly-arrived women offenders were much sought after by the families of settlers in New South Wales and, provided their crime had not been too violent and grave, they settled down and in due course many of them married, in an almost womanless newly-developing country.

'And this is where we come in, Mr Hobshaw, sir. My Maggie has two kids already, a boy of two and a baby and she is desperate for help. I have written her but it will be a long time afore I get a reply. She will jump at one of my nieces, but what I'm aiming at,' he rubbed the side of his nose and grinned with immense pleasure at his own acuity, 'what I'm aiming at is getting the lot of them out of the way, eh? Does not that suit you down to the ground? I mean to say, what else can we do with them, eh?'

Mr Hobshaw had been so happy at the way his own family affairs had gone that he had not given much thought to the young ladies. Now his release broke over him like a great light and he shouted for the *best* Madeira decanter to be brought.

'But your daughter will not wish to be burdened with three ageing gentlewomen!' he exclaimed after a moment's thought.

'Governesses! She has half-a-dozen or so friends, they all have growing children . . . they will be grabbed as soon as they land. Niece Lavinia will have female company on her voyage out and her sisters will be seeing the world; you will have no trouble persuading them; they will pack their belongings and I will return for them and keep them with me till the sailing dates from Liverpool. And we must remember . . .' he leaned forward and hissed, 'the shortage of women over there is acute, acute it is! The eldest may look it, but I happen to know, she is not yet forty! Now . . . I'll take a bet, Mr Hobshaw. . . .'

*

When the old house was empty and Mary Ann threw wide all the casements and with her two assistants and herself gave their rooms a 'good red-up', Mary Ann found the bottles of which they had not succeeded in disposing. Or perhaps they had deliberately left them, as a message. . . .

*

Mr Silas Clopton had been very busy since the mistress died; as Managing Director with a 'sleeping Chairman', as Mr Hobshaw described himself, he had all the decisions to make and he found himself able to do so. He appointed a man to do the job for which he had yearned himself, that of commercial traveller to the United States of America, and he had high hopes of his success.

But he had also kept away from Mary Ann deliberately.

Until after the wedding she too had had more than enough to do; he chose his moment carefully.

'Mary Ann, I have not seen you for a long time; have you missed me?'

'You saw me at the wedding.'

'But not to talk to.'

'I'd not time to talk.'

'But you have now.'

'What about?'

'About marrying me.'

'No, Silas Clopton.'

'Why not?'

'I do not know why not.'

'You're daft, girl! You'll not marry me because you don't know why not. Do not turn your face away, Mary Ann, I know you're smiling. And I know I'm only a nowt (remember?), a nowt you called me. But when the old gentleman dies and your old man dies, and let's hope it'll be a long time afore they do, there'll still be a long spell of years for a big strong lass like you to be alone.'

'You should marry somebody younger.'

'Why?'

'Because you need to have a family.'

'You and I'll have a family all right!'

'I'm nearly forty.'

'I'm older than that. . . .'

'I do not think you are a nowt, Silas Clopton, and I am sorry I said it. I do like you; I won't say as I love you but I could do, I reckon I could do! In time, that is.'

'Then marry me, love?'

'I tell you what, I'll have a talk with Mr Hobshaw. He'll know if I should or if I shouldn't marry the gipsy lad.'

'The rising industrialist. . . .'

*

'Mary Ann,' Mr Hobshaw called a few days later, 'please come here.' He held open the door of his study until she arrived from the kitchen in her white-bibbed apron, her hands covered with flour. 'I ask you to look at this!'

He had forgotten, in the hustle of the past few weeks, the muniment chest, one foot high, with its great iron bands and huge hasp which, over the centuries, had caught the dust irrevocably. Now he had found the great key hanging upon a large nail in the stable flat where he had thrown it down and he applied it to the lock. No oil was needed and no pressure; it opened as smoothly as though it had been used every day, and when the monstrous lid was opened back against the wall he stared within, in astonishment. Sugar bags in thick blue paper lolled over or stood with sovereigns falling out of them in abundance. The bottom of the chest was crowded so that not another bag would fit. It was only half-full but the chest, even half-full, held an immense amount. A double row had been started and it was these out of which the gold spilled.

'The miser's treasure,' Mary Ann commented.

They stared down in amazed silence for a time.

'She spent almost nothing all these ten years since I gave her the key of the empty chest. I paid all the household expenses to her, she surely put most of it away in there, she must have saved and saved. . . .'

'Aye! She did that!'

'And the transactions she did in private regarding wool and dye and other portable requirements! She dealt with the actual cash herself, Silas Copton studied the books with her but he was paid on a salary; as he did all the practical working of the mill, she gave him a pretty big one. In effect, Mary Ann, this is now mine.'

'Yes, sir,' Mary Ann agreed.

'But what did she intend to do with it?' he asked himself.

Mary Ann made no reply, what she wanted to say was . . . nothing; the mistress just wished to have it and to hold it and to increase it. Maybe, sometimes, simply to let it run through her fingers.

Mr Hobshaw kneeled down and started to pour the spilled sovereigns back into the sugar bags. He filled one to the brim and handed it to Mary Ann: 'Your wedding present, with my regards!'

'No, thank you, sir, you have already given me that lovely mare for a wedding present and I am deeply grateful.' She shook her head: 'I would rather not have this.'

'Take it, Mary Ann . . . for your future children.'

'No thank you, sir, it might bring me bad luck.'

Yet still she lingered with her hands tucked into her apron bib. 'I could tell you what to do with it, sir, if you do not want it yourself for any project.'

'Please do, Mary Ann.'

'You could sink it in a fund for six or more very old people of the village; I declare, there would be plenty over to build at least half-a-dozen almshouses in that spare ground on the far side of the church; there would even be enough to pay a Warden to look after them all. . . .'

Mr Hobshaw slapped his thigh: 'By Gad, Mary Ann! That is a first-class idea, capital, capital! I shall start straightaway to make enquiries as to the architect we shall engage. And we shall call it "The Second Mrs Hobshaw Memorial Fund" . . . eh, Mary Ann? Why are you laughing?'

'You cannot call it "The Second Mrs Hobshaw Memorial Fund", you cannot, sir.'

'Well then, let me see . . .' he clicked his fingers, he tapped his forehead: aghast, he turned to Mary Ann: 'Do you know, poor soul! I cannot even remember her christian name!'